Portia Da Costa is one of the most internationally renowned authors of erotica.

She is the author of *Continuum*, *Entertaining Mr Stone*, *Gemini Heat*, *Gothic Blue*, *Gothic Heat*, *Hotbed*, *In too Deep*, *Kiss it Better*, *Shadowplay*, *Suite Seventeen*, *The Devil Inside*, *The Stranger* and *The Tutor*; as well as being a contributing author to a number of Black Lace short-story collections.

D0270529

Also by Portia Da Costa

The Stranger

Black Lace Classics

Portia Da Costa

BLACK
LACE

9 10 8

First published in 1997 by Black Lace
This edition published in 2012 by Black Lace, an imprint of Ebury
Publishing
A Random House Group Company

The Random House Group Limited Reg. No. 954009

Addresses for companies within the Random House Group can be
found at: www.randomhouse.co.uk

A CIP catalogue record for this book is
available from the British Library

The Random House Group Limited supports The Forest Stewardship
Council® (FSC®), the leading international forest-certification
organisation. Our books carrying the FSC label are printed on
FSC®-certified paper. FSC is the only forest-certification scheme
supported by the leading environmental organisations, including
Greenpeace. Our paper procurement policy can be found at
www.randomhouse.co.uk/environment

Printed and bound by CPI Group (UK) Ltd, Croydon, CR0 4YY

ISBN 9780352346759

To buy books by your favourite authors and register for offers visit:
www.randomhouse.co.uk

Chapter One

The Man in the River

There was a storm coming.

Claudia Marwood looked up at the sky, and seeing only its high, blue canopy pasted with a thin scattering of hazy gauze-like cloud, she wondered why she found the lovely sight portentous. It was a perfect summer's day – a classic – yet something inside her sensed the distant threat of thunder. She couldn't hear or see it, yet she knew it was on its way.

Idiot!

She paused in the scullery, eyeing her umbrella and the light cotton jacket she sometimes wore in the garden on cooler days. Don't be a wimp! she told herself firmly, taking only a broad straw sun hat with a yellow ribbon before stepping out on to the terrazzo tiled patio at the back of her house. If it does rain, you'll get wet. So what? It won't kill you!

As she crossed the lawn, adjusting the angle of her hat as she went, she analysed her burst of small-scale bravado. She felt wild, sort of, and slightly daring. It suddenly dawned on her that she was actually very happy.

What a relief! At last! Striding out faster, almost skipping, she enjoyed the spring of the immaculately cut turf beneath her sandal-clad feet, then felt faintly dizzy

1

for a second as she inhaled the rich odours from her abundantly stocked flowerbeds. The roses, the sweet peas, the scented shrubs.

Good God, it was summer, she was as fit as a fiddle, she had no commitments and there was nothing at all that she *had* to do! The wood pigeons were cooing while honey bees were hovering over the roses and the pelargoniums, and she too shared their unquestioning contentment.

At the bottom of the garden a little lychgate led through into the copse beyond, and the path beyond it led down towards the river. As Claudia passed through, she felt another rush of satisfaction. This was also her land and she could enjoy her stroll in perfect peace without meeting other walkers. This new feeling of hers had a delicate quality to it, and she wanted to examine and analyse it, not have it popped like a balloon before she could savour it. She would be wanting new people around her soon, she was sure of that, but for now she felt more comfortable alone or with just her closer friends.

The copse on a summer's afternoon was a magical place to be alone. The dappled shade was green and fresh and cool; alive, yet tranquil, and dense with a brooding quality of expectancy. It was the sort of place one might imagine sprites and elves could be found, although it was only the pigeons, the rustling leaves and the nearby river that chattered to each other.

Not that it hadn't been a nice place for company too, she thought, waiting for a pang of pain, then smiling when, thankfully, it didn't come. Only happy memories surfaced. Herself and Gerald, on another post-prandial summer walk, both tipsy on good wine and feeling silly and rather randy. They had rolled in the undergrowth and actually fucked here, beneath an old tree that stood to her right. They had climaxed noisily among the ants and twigs and mud.

We were good together, she thought, taken all round. Her smile turned wistful. Of course, there had been

2

rough patches – the difference in their ages and Gerald's devotion to business matters had meant that frantic fucks in the bushes were quite infrequent – but it was only the cheerful times that were printed in her memory. She imagined she could see where the grass and the ferns had been squashed down and feel the good earth beneath her back as she celebrated life with her lover, her husband.

But it wouldn't be with Gerald the next time, would it? Her dear old husband was dead, and had been for eight months. She would have a new lover in the copse one of these days, though, when the time was right. And her husband's smiling shade would cheer them on.

Don't be weird, Claudia, she instructed herself, treading boldly onward, and stepping over the occasional root or straggling creeper that had strayed across the path. In the relative quiet of the woodland bower, she gradually became aware that the water sounds ahead were changing. The leisurely flow of the river was still a reassuring susurration in the background, but there was a louder, more arrhythmic splashing too – the sound made by a human occupation of the water. Where the river bellied out, diverted by an island of rocks, there was a wide, inviting pond, and from the sound of things, someone was bathing there.

Claudia frowned. It wasn't that she begrudged people access to the land – it wasn't clearly marked as private property or fenced off in any way. It was just that she felt protective of her hard-won little store of equilibrium and her sudden and self-nurtured bud of happiness.

Despite her qualms, though, she moved on. You're going to have to break out some time, Mrs Marwood, she told herself, and it might as well be now. She could almost feel Gerald behind her, pushing her forward.

But just as she was about to burst into the clearing and reveal herself, a dose of sixth sense told her to hold back. Slipping her hat off, she held herself quite still, her breathing shallow, then risked putting out a hand to draw aside the greenery and take a peek into the open area beyond.

Sitting on a rock where she often sat herself to dangle her feet in the pool, was a naked man, dangling his feet in the pool. Tall and young looking, he had a longish mop of curly mid-brown hair, and he was gazing down intently into the stiller area of water around his ankles. Whatever he saw there had produced a frown on his face.

Once she had got over the initial shock of the young man's nudity, Claudia allowed herself to breathe properly again and study his appearance more closely. He was very handsome, she quickly realised. Quite beautiful, in an eccentric sort of way. But there was something wrong, something disturbing or distressing him. He had obviously been responsible for the splashing she had heard, because his pale skin was gleaming with water, but now he was staring, in a fugue, at his own reflection. His angular but boyish face was certainly one Claudia would have happily stared at for as long as he would allow, yet the manner in which he was contemplating himself was in no way narcissistic. More than anything, he looked worried to death – almost afraid of his own attractive features.

And you've taken a beating too, haven't you, stranger? thought Claudia, noting that the young man's smooth, lightly muscled body sported several spectacular bruises in the area of his ribs and thighs. As he put up a hand and brushed his soft, wild hair back off his brow, she saw that there was also a nasty red graze on his temple. When he touched this gingerly and winced, she winced with him, but when, after a pause, he rose slowly and gracefully to his feet, what she saw made her forget all thoughts of pain.

Oh yes! Oh yes, yes, yes!

Claudia felt a crazy urge to wolf-whistle, but kept the sound as a silent tribute inside her mind. Whoever this mysterious stranger was, his body was familiar to her senses. He had exactly the kind of physique she had

4

always preferred in a man. Spare and lean, but strong looking, with fine, straight limbs and a chest that was deep and nicely defined but free of hair. His swinging penis was substantial and distinctly perky. Claudia would have liked a better look at that particular part of him, but he chose that moment to jump back down into the water.

Under cover of the aquatic commotion, Claudia crept a little nearer and sank into a more comfortable semi-crouch. In spite of her concern about the young man's injuries, her overwhelming feeling as she watched him was excitement – a delicious, clandestine devilment that sped through her system like a fortifying wine. He was so gorgeous, so appealing, so unaware of her. She felt as if she was stealing pleasure from his winsome, youthful body.

You ought to be ashamed of yourself, woman, she chided, grinning hugely and feeling even more recovered than she had done earlier. She was a widow, and getting a little too close to middle age for her own liking, but the sight of this man, so innocently vulnerable yet so tempting, filled the female core of her with a sudden jolt of yearning.

Who are you, mystery man? she thought, feeling her own body come alive beneath her cotton dress and minimal summer undies. And what are you doing here in my little bit of river?

After a few moments, what he was doing became quite evident. As Claudia watched from her hiding place, her heart hammering madly and her fingertips tingling with the denial of not touching him, the young man began a makeshift but strangely rigorous toilette.

First, he ducked his head, then rose again, rubbing at his tousled hair and making the motions of shampooing it. He washed his face carefully too, running his finger-tips over his jaw as if he were monitoring the length of his stubble. His regretful shrug indicated that he gener-ally preferred to be clean-shaven, but as there was clearly nothing he could do about it, he began to dash water over his arms and back and shoulders, again and again and again; so much so that Claudia wanted to race back to the house and return with towels and shampoo and shower gel, and all the fragrant, expensive grooming products that a man so fastidious would clearly relish. He even scrubbed frantically at his teeth and his gums with the pad of his forefinger.

When he had attended to his upper body to his satisfaction, the young man moved towards the bank into the shallower water, in order to wash himself just as thoroughly below the waist.

Claudia held her breath again. Believing himself alone, her cleanly young god was completely uninhibited, and after working his way up over his legs and thighs, he began massaging water freely over his buttocks and genitals. Claudia watched wide eyed as he meticulously scrutinised and dowsed himself; then shared his wry but unexpectedly sunny smile when the inevitable physical reaction to this occurred.

It took her all her time not to sigh, then gasp, as the stranger's wet penis swelled into a long, stiff erection between his fingers. As he handled himself, his lean young face became more tranquil, losing the expression of fear and worried sadness that had seemed to haunt it. In the midst of her own arousal – a rush of wet heat between her legs that was so sudden and so copious it shocked her – Claudia realised that caressing himself was as much a comfort to the young man as it was an act of sex. He seemed reassured by his body's own responses.

But that took nothing away from the eroticism of his performance.

As the stranger's eyes closed and his head tipped back, Claudia felt as if a gate she had been pushing against had finally swung wide open. The feelings that had been coming back gradually were suddenly all-consuming. Watching the flashing fingers of the young man in the river, she gave herself permission to reach down and clutch her groin.

She wanted to laugh. She wanted to cry. She wanted to lie back, throw her legs apart and make herself come until she couldn't see straight. But most of all she wanted to thank her mystic stranger.

That bud of happiness was now an open flower.

Chapter Two
One Fine Day

*T*he storm had arrived. At least, the thunder and lightning part was here, and the cleansing downpour probably wasn't far behind it.

Not that Claudia was particularly worried. Thunderstorms sometimes troubled her, especially if they were violent and Wagnerian, but tonight her mind was fully occupied, principally with the mysterious naked stranger from the river.

She couldn't seem to shake the image of him. It was a soft-focus movie that played continuously in her head. First he would stare at himself, then he would wash, and finally he would masturbate. She could still hear his broken cry of triumph as his semen hit the water like strands of white silk; she could still see him stagger, then collapse on to the soft earth bank, his eyes closed and his pale chest heaving with the sweet release of tension.

You should have climbed out from behind that bush and introduced yourself, you fool, she told herself, rocking in the scented water of her bath and thinking how much *he* would have enjoyed her creamy, moisture-enriched soap and the tang of her aromatherapeutic bath oil. She tried to envision him in the bath with her (it was quite a big one, and there was plenty of room for two), his hands moving on *her* body this time, not his own.

8

Her own hand drifted towards her crotch, and she was about to part the soft blonde mat of her pubic hair and touch herself again when an especially loud peal of thunder stayed her fingers.

'OK . . . Enough for now,' she said, laughing softly and agreeing with the heavenly moderator who had decreed, by the crashing of the elements, that to masturbate to orgasm three times in the bath was quite enough for the time being, thank you very much! There would be plenty of opportunity later, if she still felt that old, familiar urge.

No chance of not feeling it, Claudia thought, rising out of the water and reaching for a towel from the heated rail, if I can't stop thinking about my randy stranger from the river.

She had restrained herself at the time, for fear of disturbing him. She was a noisy lover, with a tendency to squeal when passion overwhelmed her, and it had been such a long time since she had last had an orgasm that she didn't think she could experience one in silence.

After his own orgasm, the stranger had appeared to fall asleep where he had dropped, his long body as still as the dead and his arms stretched out in a vaguely cruciform attitude. Claudia had watched him for a little while, feeling a sense of relief when she saw his chest rising slowly, then falling, as he breathed.

Who the devil were you, little boy lost? Claudia asked now, fluffing her short, streaked blonde hair, and thinking of the strange man's turbulent brown curls.

Who *are* you? She repeated the thought and wondered where the beautiful sleeper was now. It could well be that he was still close by. She hated the idea that he might be sleeping rough somewhere but if the river was his bathroom then his bedroom ceiling was most likely the open air.

And *what* are you? She questioned him silently as she stood naked before her mirror and smoothed a light nourishing cream into her face. Part of her attention was on her own body, her own 'too solid flesh' which was just a tad more curvy than she would have preferred but which, for a woman in her forties, still looked reassuringly girlish. The other, larger part of her mind still pondered the enigma of the stranger.

Yes, what was he?

A tramp, or a New Age traveller, perhaps?

But he looked too young, really, for the former, and much, much too clean for the latter. New Age caravans did travel through the village sometimes, on the way to the ancient standing stones on the nearby heath, but these were people in large numbers. Her bathing stranger had most definitely been a solo.

What if he was an escaped convict? Or even a runaway mental patient? Claudia shivered, even though the bathroom was warm and steamy. She wondered again if the man was still close by.

Screwing the top firmly on the moisturiser jar, she dismissed the more menacing explanations. Her mystery man had seemed confused, almost disorientated in a way, but basically he had appeared to know what he was doing. And the clothes of his she had caught sight of – a long, dark jacket and pale-grey trousers airing over a bush and socks, shirt and underwear drying on a stone in the sun – didn't look like prison or institution issue. Unless, of course, they were stolen.

Thunder grumbled again, like giant boulders being tumbled in a gully, and Claudia reached for her red silk kimono and slid into it. Tonight, she had rejected her usual towelling dressing gown as frumpy and boring, and the shimmering crimson robe – a gift from a Far Eastern business trip of Gerald's – was the appropriate choice for her self-indulgent mood. The silk was cool against her skin, yet stirring, and as she went down the stairs to make her preparations for a evening of sensual pampering, it swished and swirled like a living breeze around her thighs.

Besides, he was much too nice to be a criminal, she pointed out to herself, taking a bottle of white wine – a good 1990 Auslese that she was really looking forward to – from the fridge. Although he could be disturbed, she appended, selecting one of her favourite Riedel Sommelier wine glasses, and taking that and the dark, German bottle into the sitting room. It wasn't strictly normal to do one's bathing in a river.

Anyway, it was all purely academic now, reasoned Claudia, as she poured her wine, settled back on the sofa, and set her CD choice to play, using the handset. She would never see him again. She would never know what he looked like with his clothes on.

The ineffable strains of *Madama Butterfly* filled the room, just as the first sweet sip of wine blessed her palate. It was just as choice and fruity as she had hoped it would be, and with its flavour came a comforting rationalisation. The young man from the river was most probably nothing at all like the mysterious romantic presence she had created for him, but she could still preserve him as such in her fantasies. She would put him to work for her until a real-life lover came along.

Thunder rolled again, and he seemed to be with her, moving over her, his body cool yet virile. She put aside her glass so her hands could be his. She imagined him touching her neck, then her shoulder, then her breast, his long fingers curving to mould her rounded contour, sliding the bright stuff of her silk robe against her nipple. The little crest of flesh hardened immediately, and she seemed to hear his chuckle of delight, even though she had no true idea what his laugh might sound like. Sliding apart her robe, she held herself how he would hold her, circling her thumb in a slow and tender rhythm. She wished that she had heard more of his voice, so she could imagine him whispering endearments and little words of admiration. In her fantasy, of course, she was just right for him.

Moving her legs restlessly, she let her thighs slide apart, as if it were he who had nudged them open, impatient to reach her hot and honeyed centre. He would caress her belly for a few moments, teasing her, twirling strands of her pubic hair around his fingers; then he would probe delicately between her labia and find her clitoris.

Drawing a deep breath, Claudia duplicated her phantom lover's action, and at that same moment, thunder cracked across the sky and the fluid, soprano voice of Butterfly launched superbly into the aria '*Un Bel Di, Vendremo*'.

'One fine day . . .'

Claudia smiled as she swirled her finger, creating brilliant sensations that rippled and danced through her belly. The lyrics were about the return of a lover – the shallow, faithless Pinkerton – but to Claudia they spoke more of an arrival. Someone had arrived in her life today, even if he was fated to be purely a shadow-player in her mind, an icon of self-pleasure, a magic gift for her to cherish.

Sighing, she shifted her bottom on the sofa, feeling the delicious excitement massing in her loins beneath her fingertip. Soon. Soon she would allow herself to come again.

The thunder rolled and the sweet, operatic voice soared . . . and suddenly someone was hammering furiously and repeatedly at the front door.

Her heart pounding nearly as hard as the unknown caller's fist, Claudia snatched her fingers from her crotch and leapt to her feet, almost knocking over her glass of wine in the process.

She glanced at the clock. It was almost ten. Who the hell was trying to bash her door down at this time of night? Snatching her robe together and knotting the obi protectively, she darted out into the hall and stood there shaking.

Thunder crashed again, and over the sound of a rising wind, the thumping on her door panels redoubled.

She knew instinctively who it was out there.

This is insane, she thought, as she padded barefoot along the hall. He could be dangerous. Violent. Homicidal. These could be her last moments of life.

Ignoring all this, she turned the handle and flung open the door.

And there, with his wild brown hair flying around his face in the wind, his stunning blue eyes wide with fear, and wearing quite the most bizarre and unexpected suit of clothing she could ever have imagined, stood her fey, enchanted stranger from the river.

'Please! Help me!' he cried frantically, just as another peal of thunder rent the heavens and lightning forked electric-blue and seemed to reach for them. Then, accompanied by his shriek of pure terror, his eyes rolled upward in their sockets and he fainted. Pitching forward, he crumpled like a length of cloth into her arms.

With no time to ask questions of him, or of herself, Claudia caught him, and sank down, carried by his weight, to the hall floor. Luckily, she managed to tuck her legs under her as she went, and ended up half kneeling, half sitting on the doormat, with the stranger's head cradled in her lap.

Well done, Claudia, she thought. Nice catch. Now what the hell are you going to do with him? She looked down into his familiar but unknown face.

Up close, her wandering refugee looked slightly older than she had earlier estimated. Late twenties, she put him at, or perhaps thirty. Younger than she was, but not by too much.

Too much for what? the devil's advocate inside her countered, amazed that she could still be having erotic thoughts about the poor man when he was out cold.

And yet she *was* having them. She couldn't control them. His head, crowned with its stormy halo of curls, was nestled closely against her pubis, and she could feel his warm breath on her thigh through her flimsy robe.

As well as her split-second ruminations about his age, Claudia also realised that the stranger was even better looking up close. His hair was very soft, and his unconscious face was as serene as an archangel's. The right man at the wrong time, she thought wistfully, her fingers hovering tentatively over his sculpted lips and the strong line of his jaw. Or, she appended, the wrong man at the right time, which was just as bad.

But was a time ever right or wrong?

Giving in to temptation, she stroked his head, letting her fingers comb lightly through his hair and brushing the lovelocks back from his brow so she could assess the severity of his wound. Almost immediately he responded, stirring a little, scrunching up his face and groaning faintly.

'It's all right. It's all right,' said Claudia, trying to calm him, gripping his shoulders as he began to rise and struggle, 'You're OK . . . You're safe. Nobody's going to hurt you.'

Shaking her off quite easily, the stranger sat up, his eyes still closed as he gingerly felt his head. When the lightning flashed again, he let out a screech of fear and threw himself back into Claudia's arms.

'Hey, hey, hey!' she said soothingly, patting his back and smoothing her fingers over the black velvet coat that he was wearing, 'Don't worry . . . It's not that close,' she lied. 'We're quite safe here.' The way he continued to shake told her he didn't quite believe her.

Despite her continued efforts to pacify the newcomer, Claudia felt far from calm herself. She was sitting here on her own doorstep, in the beginnings of a rainstorm, with her silk kimono pulled half off her, holding her new fantasy object tightly against her body. He had spoken a sum total of three words to her so far, but she already had his trembling, slightly stubbled cheek pressed intimately against the bare curve of her breast.

'Hush, it's all right,' she said again, at a loss as to what to do next. There were things she wanted to do, like kiss him and touch him and much, much more, but that was from her dreams, and what was happening now was real.

Thunder pealed again, and the man in her arms cried, 'No! Oh, no!', and tried to cover his ears with his hands, dragging Claudia's kimono further off her in the process. Rather ineffectually, she tried to close the garment without pushing her panicked charge away. 'No! No!' he said, shaking his head as if the thunder was within his skull and he was trying to eject it. For a fleeting instant his parted lips brushed her skin.

They couldn't stay where they were because the rain, cool and refreshing as it was, had started to slice down quite heavily now. So, still tugging at her kimono, Claudia engineered her way to her feet, trying to help the stranger on to his at the same time.

'Come along. Let's get inside, shall we?' she suggested to him, alarmed by the way he was swaying. He stood for a moment, hands over his ears and his eyes screwed tightly shut, then he seemed to pull himself together, and nodded in silent agreement. After pushing the door shut behind them, Claudia was relieved to find that he followed her lead along the hall into the sitting room.

Astoundingly, when they got there, *'Un Bel Di'* was still playing. The whole melodramatic performance on the doorstep could not have taken more than a minute.

'Sit here,' she said to her unusual refugee, pointing to the sofa, and he crossed the room and sat down obediently. Leaning back, he closed his eyes and sighed wearily, his chest heaving as if he had just completed a marathon.

Claudia just stared at him.

Who are you? she wanted to demand, but he seemed in such a state of shock and distress that it would be unkind to interrogate him immediately. Even so, she still almost asked him who he was dressed as.

Down by the river, she had been so entranced by the naked man that she had paid only cursory attention to his scattered clothing. But now, his strange outfit intrigued her.

What she had taken for a jacket was in fact a long Edwardian frock coat in black crushed velvet, which he wore with grey trousers, a black and grey striped brocade waistcoat and a wing-collared shirt that was unfastened to show his chest. Slung around his neck was a rather mangled length of heavy grey silk which appeared to be the remains of a cravat. The whole ensemble was crumpled and dusty – especially the shirt – and there were grass stains on the pale cloth of his trousers, but he still projected an aura of forlorn elegance. He couldn't be a New Age traveller. He looked more like an escapee from the Victoria and Albert Museum, or a Tussaud's mannequin, touched by God and come to life.

Suddenly he sat up, then winced again as if the action had made his head hurt. 'I'm so sorry,' he muttered. 'I'm intruding . . . I'd better go.' He made a half-hearted attempt to stand, but started swaying precariously again, and flopped down. Claudia hurried towards him and knelt down by his side.

'You've been hurt,' she said, looking upward into his face. He was clearly very muddled, but still looked angelic. She wished he would open his eyes again, but he seemed to be drifting in and out of consciousness. She touched his arm. 'I'd better send for an ambulance or something . . . You need attention.'

His eyes snapped open again. They were a pale, clear, almost glass-like blue, and when they fixed on her a pang of pleasure stirred inside her. 'Please, don't go to any trouble. I beg you!' He covered her hand with his other one, and the pang of pleasure became a flexing serpent of desire, 'I'll be all right . . . I just need a moment's sit down. I'll go soon . . . I won't bother you any further.'

Claudia gnawed her lip as he slumped back again, his eyelids fluttering closed. Medical scrutiny was surely what he needed, but in her heart of hearts she really didn't want to ring for help. She wanted him alone, just with her, for a little while longer. She wanted to look at him and enjoy her precious living treat.

Liar! said the voice of the coiling snake of lust. You don't just want to look. You want to touch him! You want to make love to him! Take advantage of his beauty while he's vulnerable!

Stop this! she told her own subversive emotions, even though she knew that the lustful voice spoke truly.

16

'Can I get you anything?' she asked quietly. She glanced at the wine bottle but realised alcohol was probably a bad choice right now. 'Some coffee? A glass of water? A cup of tea?'

The crystal-blue eyes snapped open again and became part of one of the sweetest, most spine-melting smiles Claudia had ever seen.

'Tea would be wonderful,' he said in heartfelt tones. 'I would love some . . . Please.'

'Coming up,' said Claudia, rising somewhat shakily. 'Shall I turn the music off?' she asked, as he seemed about to doze off once more.

'Oh no,' he murmured, opening his eyes again and looking up at her appealingly. 'It's lovely. One of my – ' He stopped short, frowning. 'I like it very much . . . I'd love to hear "One Fine Day" again. If you don't mind, that is?'

Still mentally reeling from his smile, Claudia would have sung the aria for him herself if she had possessed the voice for it, but settled for re-selecting '*Un Bel Di*'. Feeling somewhat shell-shocked, she left him listening and made her way to the kitchen.

This must be the most stupid thing you have ever done, she thought, as the kettle was boiling and she was assembling the tea things. You've invited an unknown man into your home at night, and even if he isn't a murderer or a rapist, you've still left him completely alone in a room full of valuable antiques and collectibles. He might already have made a run for it with the Moorcroft Pansy vase, or Gerald's favourite tortoiseshell snuff box. Or he might like modern things, and have done a flit with the Bang and Olufsen CD player!

Don't be ridiculous, she told herself immediately. She could still clearly hear sad Butterfly's lament!

Placing chinaware, milk, sugar and a selection of biscuits on her best silver tray, Claudia found herself suspended between reality and her dreams.

She was preparing tea as if she had the vicar's wife waiting for her in the sitting room, whereas in actual fact, her guest was a man whose name she didn't know and who she had never set eyes on before that afternoon, when she had watched him cavort naked in the river and rub his sensational penis until he climaxed. She couldn't imagine a situation more bizarre.

Yet when she returned to the sitting room, her guest was still with her, as large as life, although he now appeared to have fallen asleep again. He had kicked off a very modern if scuffed and scraped pair of loafers – which didn't seem to be part of his fancy-dress outfit – and was curled up in a foetal position on the sofa, with his clasped hands beneath his cheek like a dozing cherub's.

There must be an inverse relationship between vulnerability and sexiness, thought Claudia, wanting to touch him so much that the tray shook in her hands and the cups and spoons began to rattle violently. The music was still playing in the background, but the clatter of the crockery woke the sleeper.

'Oh dear,' he said softly, straightening up and slipping his black-socked feet back into his shoes, 'I'm sorry. I dozed off. Please forgive me.'

'It's all right,' replied Claudia, setting out the tray, and suddenly very conscious of the way her kimono was apt to float and reveal portions of naked skin as she moved. In addition the silk was so sheer that her erect nipples stood out clearly. 'You . . . You're obviously exhausted.'

Taking refuge in the small rituals of a very English tea ceremony, Claudia didn't know what else to say. Could she come right out and ask if he was a vagrant? And if he wasn't one, how could she ask him what he had been doing bathing in the river, without revealing the fact that she had watched him there? The poor soul wasn't offering any information about himself, for the simple reason, she suspected, that he was too shattered and too confused to realise that an explanation might be called for.

She decided not to press the issue for now.

'Milk and sugar?' she enquired.

Instead of the straightforward answer she was expecting, the stranger appeared to have to think very hard about the way he took his tea. He clenched his fists against his thighs and stared intently at nothing for a few seconds, then looked up at her, his handsome face stricken with bewilderment.

'I don't know,' he said finally, shaking his head and making his soft curls bob and dance.

Claudia stared at him and felt the inklings of a disquieting suspicion. Could it really be *that*? Could this lovely, befuddled young man be the victim of something so fundamental and frightening?

'Try it just with milk and see,' she said, pouring milk into the first cup of tea and passing it to him. As she watched him take a sip and sigh with appreciation as if it were the first decent brew he had tasted in a millennium, Claudia's mind went winging back over the years to her childhood, and to an incident that had occurred during her first attempts to learn to ride a horse.

She had been a natural rider but had become too cocksure one afternoon and been bucked off, landing on her head. Thankfully, she had sustained no fractures and no permanent injury, but for a truly terrifying fortnight she had not had the slightest inkling of who she really was, and no memory of her life before the fall. Luck had been on her side, though, and after those two scary weeks she had woken up one morning and just remembered it all again.

Drinking a little of her own tea, and watching the stranger cradle his cup and stare into it as if some profound eternal verity was to be found floating in the English Country House blend, she considered the significance of the ugly graze that was partially hidden by his dangling kiss curls.

Was her beautiful man from the river an amnesiac?

And if he was, what could she do to help him?

Help him? Who are you kidding? You want to rape him!

Feeling horrified by her own seditious urges, yet also

19

revelling in them, she stared at his long legs in his creased grey trousers. His thighs were strong and lithe; she had seen them. And at their apex, his sex was vital and tempting.

Oh God, this was all so sudden! She had begun this day in perfect ordinariness – not feeling too bad about herself and her widowhood – and now she was an erotic predator on the prowl. Almost. And it was him – her pretty, confused stranger-boy in his weird, antiquated clothing – who had been the catalyst. She hardly dare look up, because a sixth sense told her that he was now looking back at her.

What the hell! She met his eyes. She had been right; he was looking.

'You're very kind,' he said, giving her a small but still exceptional smile. 'This tea is marvellous. Just what I needed. I – I didn't realise how much I liked it.' His brilliant eyes clouded, as if he were thinking again.

'Are you OK?' enquired Claudia, putting her cup down then rising and moving towards him like a drawn moth seeking the danger of a flame. 'I can't help noticing you've grazed your head. Do you have a headache?' She sat down beside him on the sofa, and before she could stop herself, she was lifing his hair away from the mark on his forehead.

It was his turn to rattle his cup in his saucer.

'Sorry,' said Claudia, snatching back her hand. 'I didn't mean to startle you, but that graze looks nasty . . . It must hurt.'

'It's fine, thank you,' he said, putting down the cup and saucer, then making as if to rise. 'You've been very kind,' he said again, 'but I shouldn't impose on that kindness any further.'

No! You can't leave! cried Claudia in silence, while in reality she said, 'It isn't an imposition at all.' He was halfway out of his seat now, but she caught him by his velvet sleeve and pulled him down again. He obeyed her with a small, perplexed twitch of his beautifully modelled lips. 'In fact,' she went on, unwilling to let go even of just his coat, 'you're obviously very tired. You should get some rest . . .' Here we go! Say it, Claudia, say it! she thought. 'Why don't you stay here the night? I have a guest room all made up. You're very welcome to sleep there if you wish.'

A succession of emotions crossed his face: fear, temptation, gratitude, others less definable.

'I – I – ' he began, then closed his eyes again, rubbing his face with his hand. 'If you're certain it's no trouble? I would be very grateful. I'm just so tired.' And it was true; he looked totally exhausted.

'It's no trouble, I promise you,' she said, her heart singing because he had been so easily won over. She rose, then reached down to take his arm and lead him. 'Come on, I'll show you where the room is. You look as if you could do with getting your head down straight away.'

'Thank you. Thank you very much. I think I could,' he said, his voice soft but strangely resonant. He allowed himself to be led from the room.

Claudia could hardly speak for excitement as she escorted her unexpected house guest upstairs. Cool it, she told herself. He's worn out. This is just a Good Samaritan act. Nothing else. Nothing's going to happen.

'Is there somewhere I can wash first, please?' he asked, as Claudia pushed open the door to the guest room, which was always ready for occupation. In the early days after Gerald's death, her closest woman friend, Melody, had often stayed over to keep her company, and Claudia had got into the habit of keeping the bed made up.

'Don't worry, this room has its own little bathroom.' She switched on the light, and pointed to the room's other door. 'You'll find towels and soap and everything you need.' For some reason she wasn't quite sure of – sentimental attachment, she supposed – she had also put one or two of Gerald's toiletry items in the guest bathroom's cupboard. 'And I'll bring you some of my husband's pyjamas and a robe.'

21

'Won't he mind?' enquired the stranger, sounding suddenly very focused and a little alarmed.

'No . . . I'm sure he wouldn't. If he was here.' The guest looked even more alarmed. 'I'm a widow. My husband died eight months ago.' Her companion's jaw had dropped now, and his face was a picture of empathic distress. 'But don't worry. I'm over the worst,' she went on, suddenly realising that today of all days, that was unequivocally true. 'Time has a habit of making things get better.'

The stranger still looked a little dismayed, but as Claudia made as if to leave in search of the night attire, he darted forward, grabbed her hand, then lifted it to his lips and soundly kissed it.

'Thank you,' he said, then kissed her hand again before releasing it. 'You don't know what this means to me. I don't know what I would have done. I – '

'It's OK. I'll get those pyjamas.'

Claudia turned and almost ran from the room, suddenly afraid of the dramatic response she had invoked in him. He was very beautiful, but if he *was* an amnesiac, he could be mentally unstable in other ways. She wondered again what the hell it was she had started.

When she returned with a pair of Gerald's royal-blue cotton pyjamas, plus a robe and some slippers, the bedroom was empty, but the frock coat, trousers and shirt were folded neatly over a chair, with the shoes set side by side underneath it. There was the sound of running water coming from the bathroom.

He's naked again, she thought, allowing herself the luxury of remembering. Naked in my house, such a beautiful young man. Her heart began to pound and she felt quite giddy. The silk kimono felt like fire against her skin, and she wanted to tear it off because its minimal weight was stifling. A great wave, something like fate or inevitability, seemed to be rushing towards her. Dropping the night things, she ran out of the room, almost afraid of what was happening to her body.

Strangely, her composure returned to her quite

quickly. She went around the house, closing up and making ready for the night. She went to her own bathroom, cleaned her teeth, spent a penny and fluffed her hair. Then she found herself spraying on some perfume, looking intently into her mirror, scrutinising herself for flaws or anything that might –

Might what? she demanded, turning her back on her reflection and walking resolutely into the bedroom towards Gerald's photograph. Put a younger lover off an older woman?

Her husband's smile seemed knowing and encouraging. As she put the frame back on the dressing table, some trick of the light on the glass made him appear to wink at her.

As she stepped out on to the landing, thunder rumbled. It was in the distance now, but still powerful and symbolic.

That settled it! She had her token excuse, if she had ever really needed one. Her guest was storm-shy, and the lightning made him frightened.

Chapter Three

The Man with No Name

He was awake, and sitting up in bed, actually watching the storm. He no longer seemed quite so afraid of it.

'Hello. Is everything all right?' Claudia asked him, peering cautiously around the door when he had answered her knock. She gestured towards the sky outside, which obligingly lit up with a distant bolt of lightning. 'Is the storm still bothering you?'

'Not so much any more, thank you.' He gave her a small shy version of 'the smile', which still made her quiver. 'I think both it and I have calmed down a bit now.'

Knowing exactly how foolish she was being, because in his new, more rational state he could well find her attentions embarrassing, Claudia closed the door and walked across to the bed. The stranger gave her an unfathomable look as she approached, which almost made her turn and run, but when she reached him he smoothed his hand across the coverlet at his side. Claudia took this as an invitation, and settled down facing him, with her kimono arranged carefully over her thighs. Too great a display of flesh might alarm him.

You stupid bitch! she told herself, as the stranger regarded her levelly, and she felt her loins melt like

24

honey on a stove. He's young and he's beautiful. Even if he is some kind of runaway, or mentally disturbed, why the hell would he want you? And yet something in her heart told her she was doing herself an injustice, and a gross one. Her nascent self-confidence reminded her of her powers.

'You must be wondering what the hell is the matter with me,' said her companion softly. 'Beating your door down in the middle of the night ... Screaming and fainting and cringing ... I hope I didn't frighten you too much?'

'No, not too much,' answered Claudia, her pulse and hormones in turmoil. Gerald's pyjamas seemed to fit the young man perfectly, and their rich blue was undoubtedly his colour. It made his smooth, milky skin almost luminescent in the lamplight, and turned his eyes into twin chips of aquamarine. Against the white pillows, his damp hair appeared black.

'You're certainly a bit of a "happening" though,' she said, clenching every muscle in her body to control herself. She wanted to lunge at him; to kiss him and caress him. 'It's not every night that a handsome young man dressed as an Edwardian love poet throws himself into my arms.'

The stranger laughed; a simple act that affected Claudia profoundly. She knew that at any second she was going to do something unthinkable, like tearing off her kimono and throwing herself into his arms. If he would have her.

'I wish I could explain everything,' he said, shrugging. 'The clothes, the screaming. Everything. But I can't.' He looked at her seriously, his face a complicated montage of emotions. She sensed that he had been genuinely flattered by her reference to him as 'handsome', but that he was also still a little desperate and confused.

'The thunder was just the last straw.' He sat up straight, then reached out and grabbed her hand. 'I don't know what's happened to me ... It's ... It's all a huge blank ... A blur.' His fingers were like steel around

Claudia's, but even the pain of his grip was exciting. 'I remember bits of yesterday, and today. All mixed up . . . But I can't remember anything else! Not a thing.' His eyes were shining now, and his mouth working with the effort of holding back his distress. 'This must sound so stupid! You won't believe me . . . I don't even remember my own name!'

'But I *do* believe you,' said Claudia, twisting her hand out of his grip, then reversing the process to take his hand in hers. 'The same thing once happened to me. I fell off a horse, banged my head, and I didn't know who I was for two weeks.' She paused, felt her own body shaking, then looked down and realised that she was caressing his hand with her thumb. 'But it all came back to me . . . And I'm sure the same thing will happen for you.'

'I hope so,' he said, suddenly sounding a little better. He looked down at her thumb, still moving against his skin. 'I would have liked to at least have been able to introduce myself.'

Ah, the social niceties. Her mind was red with lust, and she had almost forgotten them.

'My name is Claudia Marwood.' She twisted their fingers into the conventional grip of greeting, and her companion did the honours, shaking her hand.

'And I'm – ' He grinned and shrugged.

'The man with no name?'

He smiled again, then scrunched up his face, as if a physical effort might prise free elusive knowledge. 'Is that from a film?' Claudia nodded. 'Well, I've just remembered my first fact. Thank you!' Leaning forward, he suddenly touched his lips to hers.

It was like being hit by the lightning outside. The fleeting contact of his mouth was electric, and filled Claudia with such a wave of passion that she couldn't breathe for a moment.

This is insane! she thought. She was making a complete idiot of herself. 'I'd better go now and let you get some rest,' she said, and made as if to get up from the bed and run for it.

The hold on her hand turned to steel again. A carefully gauged, velvet-covered steel, but steel nevertheless.

'Stay.' His voice was husky, already changing. 'Please!'

She should have asked why, but she knew why. In the dim light, his blue eyes were steely too, and alive with a message that was unmistakable.

'Are you sure?' she asked, then had to smile, knowing that under any other circumstances this was a question the man would ask.

The stranger nodded, answering her smile with a beautiful and very male one of his own. 'At the moment it's the one single thing in the whole world I *am* sure of.'

Claudia was imprisoned by him. At the centre of their stillness, she felt the balance of power tilting on its fulcrum; her lost boy had found his way and taken command.

'Let me turn the light out,' she said faintly.

'Must you?' His voice was teasing now: deep and intense, but flirtatious.

'Yes, I think I must,' insisted Claudia, fighting not to go under entirely. She drew a deep breath when he released her, then she reached out and flipped off the lamp.

'I can imagine you,' he said, as she slipped off her robe, feeling glad of the darkness to hide her confusion. It was a long time since she had bared her body for a man, and even longer since she had been naked before a new lover rather than her husband.

The stranger lifted the covers, and shaking with nervousness and longing in equal parts, Claudia slid into bed beside him.

'Don't be afraid,' he said, and then she was in his arms, her bare skin against the cotton of his pyjamas, her mouth sought by his for their first true kiss.

Expecting boyish haste, she was astonished when he began to kiss her quite slowly. His lips were gentle and mobile against hers and the pressure they exerted complex. Without thinking, she opened her mouth and his tongue darted forward, accepting her gift, searching and finding her own tongue with its tip. He tasted strongly of spearmint, the toothpaste she had left for him, and she wondered why she had never realised how such a common flavour could seem so exotic.

His hold on her was measured too, hands flexing just enough to keep her against him; no grabbing, no groping, no force. His body was warm and firm through the cotton that covered it, his erection a hot brand against her thigh.

Suddenly, his self-control seemed to rip away the years from her. She became the impatient adolescent, surging against him, anxious to explore his body and touch and caress it. She scrabbled at the buttons of his pyjama jacket, trying to bare him. She wanted to taste and devour him.

'Hush!' he whispered, reaching between them and taking both her hands in his. 'There's no hurry . . . I'm not going anywhere.' He gave her fingers a little squeeze, then eased her on to her back and made her lie still, her arms at her sides.

'You're very lovely, Claudia,' he said, letting his long hand settle at last on her breast. 'So soft and warm. You make me feel so safe here.'

His fingers cupped her curves, first one, then the other, as if he were weighing and assessing her, the touch light and infuriatingly playful. Claudia longed for him to squeeze her; to be rough and forceful, to take her breath away, to ravish her. She shifted her thighs, trying to rub herself against him.

The stranger laughed softly. 'I never realised I was so desirable. Did you want me this much when you were watching me by the river?'

Shocked to her marrow, Claudia began to struggle, but the stranger was too quick for her, stopping her mouth with his lips and stilling her body by the simple expedient of pressing his own down potently upon it. Somewhere miles away, the thunder rolled again.

He knows I watched him! How could he know that? Who is he? thought Claudia frantically. She felt fear, and yet the fear excited her even more. Her body seemed to be burning underneath him and her nipples were so engorged that they were hurting, chafed by his weight yet sending sublime bolts of feeling to her groin.

The stranger could be a consummate trickster, she realised, the confusion and amnesia just a smooth and very clever act. And yet she didn't care. Her vulva was on fire for him, hot as hell and running with silky fluid. His thigh was between hers now, and his pyjama leg was wet where it pressed against her crotch. It was obvious that she was so aroused she couldn't think straight. He laughed again, the sound vibrating in her mouth.

Claudia broke away. 'How did you know it was me? Why didn't you call out? Say something?'

'I wasn't sure I was right,' he said more quietly, almost penitently. 'It was just a feeling ... I didn't *know* there was anyone there.' He sighed and grew still. 'Everything was so weird ... I could have been hallucinating ... Imagining things.'

The lost boy was back again, although against her leg, his penis was still a man of iron's.

'I shouldn't have been spying on you,' murmured Claudia, putting her arms around him and feeling him shiver in response and move against her. 'I should have made some noise or something ... Given you a chance to cover yourself.'

'I would probably have run a mile,' he answered, his equilibrium, momentarily lost, now returned. He rocked slightly, caressing her with his erection and sliding it closer to her sex. 'But I feel much better now. More together. More used to you.'

It was Claudia's turn to chuckle. 'Yes, I think you can be of some use to me.' She reached down and clasped him through the cotton pyjamas, feeling a rush of lust, and of confidence, when he gasped.

The young man was bigger and harder than Gerald had ever been, although her late husband had possessed a penis to be proud of. Claudia quivered inside. Her vagina fluttered as if to express its hunger, demanding she get on with the entertainment she had promised it.

How good could he be, this man who had stumbled into her life out of the storm? It was readily apparent to her that between the sheets, at least, he was surprisingly sure of himself, and he had the natural grace and the body of a good lover. And he wasn't a callow boy, despite his spaced-out behaviour when he had fallen into her arms. She sensed again that he could well be older than he looked, and excitingly experienced in the ways of physical love.

Time to find out.

Releasing his cock, she took his hand and drew it down between her legs. His face was against her neck now, and she felt him smile, slow and knowingly, against her skin. At her crotch, his long, rather tapered fingers began delicately combing the soft hair over her pudenda, parting it neatly, then pressing inward between the tender lips it covered.

He touched her very lightly, hardly more than a brushstroke, on her clitoris – and Claudia cried out, the tiny organ was so sensitised. She had known she wanted him, but she hadn't known how much. The almost ethereal contact had brought her heart-stoppingly close to orgasm, and she lay there panting, astonished by her own reaction.

'More?' enquired the stranger, against her throat. Claudia heard the familiar note of masculine arrogance in his voice, and she wanted to laugh with delight at how complete and diverse his approach was. He seemed to move from foundling to superlover in almost an instant.

'Yes! Much more!' she said fiercely, then grabbed his head, digging her fingers into his soft, tousled curls, and pulled his face down to hers so he could kiss her while he fondled her sex.

Again, the delicate, drifting touch; again the response out of all proportion. His fingertip lingered longer this time; too long for Claudia to be able to contain herself, if she had ever wanted to.

Climaxing, she cried out with joy against his gentle kissing lips and felt her vagina beat and pulse like a racing heart. He circled his finger, making her orgasm extend like a long, exquisite note, or a cadenza. She cried out again, her body jerking as she clapped her hand over his, and felt the minute flexing of his tendons as he cleverly caressed her.

'You ... You – ' she gasped, arching upward, riding the fabulous wave. 'Goddamn you! Who the hell are you?'

'I don't know! I really don't!' The stranger laughed, looking down into her face from just inches above it, his eyes like pale fire in the darkness. 'And right this minute, I can't say I care!'

And as she climaxed once more, and even harder, he kissed her again.

Moments – or what could have been hours – later, Claudia moaned, 'Enough! I need a minute or I'll have a heart attack!'

Obligingly, the stranger withdrew his hand and let it rest upon the sweat-sheened curve of her belly. The touch seemed compassionate, almost protective, the pads of his fingers resting on the operation scar that was masked by her pubic hair. In some other situation, Claudia might have been anxious when he traced its lightly puckered length, but she was still floating too much to care about anything. Lifting her weighted eyelids, she looked up.

The stranger had flung back the covers and was lying on his side, half propped up on one elbow, studying the movement of his hand upon her flesh. Her dark-adjusted eyes saw his serious expression, and the long, gleaming line of his torso where he had unbuttoned the jacket of his pyjamas.

'This must have hurt,' he said, nodding to the little cicatrix.

'Yes it did, but not for a long time . . . And I hardly think of it now.'

'I'm glad,' he said, regarding her steadily again, his light-blue eyes so vivid they almost frightened her. Then, leaning down, he kissed the little scar and the soft hair that tangled across it like a veil.

Claudia shuddered and he immediately straightened up again. 'Do you want me to . . .?' He left the question hanging, but she knew his meaning.

She did want him to, but she could also see the aroused state of his body; his erection pressing hard against the blue cotton of his pyjama bottoms. It was his turn, she decided, reaching out to touch him.

'Let's save that and concentrate on *this*,' she said, running her finger over the hard length of his flesh beneath its thin, cotton covering.

'I'd be delighted to,' he said impishly, unfastening the button and letting his stiff cock spring free. 'Is it as impressive close up as it was from a distance?' He hefted himself playfully, as if offering his manhood to her as a choice *objet d'art* for her approval.

'Of course it is, you vain creature!' she said, laughing and reaching for him, using his penis to tug him – very gently – towards her. He gave her the marvellous smile, then squeezed his eyes shut, sighing. 'But do you know what to do with it?'

'That's one thing I *can* remember,' he replied, deftly extricating himself from her grip, then sliding over her again. 'It's coming back to me very clearly now.' He poised himself, hovering, the glans of his cock just touching the entrance of her vagina. 'Is this right?' he enquired, pushing a little, the very tip of him finding its niche with perfect ease. He rocked his hips and a little more of him slid inside her. As he held himself above her, his face was like a pale, beautiful mask in the darkness: his eyes unblinking, his lips parted, his expression half fierce, half loving. He looked like a god; a demon lover; transcendental.

Frozen in the act of being possessed, Claudia felt a dizzying unreality overtake her.

What if her adorable stranger were even more of a happening than she realised? An angel, an alien, a supernatural being sent to pleasure and enchant her? He had the looks for the part, and the mystique. Even his weird clothes were romantic and other-worldly.

'Oh, please,' she murmured half to herself, thrusting upward, grabbing at him, wanting him even more for his strangeness. He slipped in a little further, his presence commanding and his girth a challenge to the moist tightness of her channel. His eyes were still wide open, observing her face and reading the lineaments of her soul as he took her.

'For God's sake, fuck me, whoever you are!' she cried out, dying for him to invade her.

'Gladly,' he growled, as he completed his incursion.

There was no unreality about the stranger's penis inside her. He was all too real. Claudia felt a sudden urge to cry again, as she had by the river. At last! She had a man inside her. Living, breathing, hot and hard. She didn't know his name, but her body seemed to have known his for ever. He fit into her so accurately he might have been made for her; he felt more right for her than Gerald had ever done, although her husband had never disappointed.

Deliciously impaled, she tried to move beneath her nameless lover, but he held her still and tamed. She scrabbled at him, wanting to hug him tighter and explore him, but by some sleight of hand and body, some physical trick she could not unravel, he quelled her struggles. He pinned both her hands above her head, with only one of his, and used his other hand, at the small of her back, to clasp her close to him.

'Hush,' he murmured again, kissing her throat and

33

then her shoulder. 'Be still. Let our bodies get to know each other.'

'But mine does know you!' she wanted to shout, but somehow all she could do was pant and gasp. He was subduing her by just holding her and being inside her. His inaction was somehow vigorous and all-enveloping. He just had to be there; he didn't seem to need to move.

'You're wonderful. You're wonderful,' he chanted softly, his voice catching as if he too was feeling the happy urge to weep. Claudia felt his long eyelashes brush her cheek as he kissed her jawline, then her ear.

And then he did begin to move, so slowly, so very slowly, allowing her to feel the whole length of him sliding smoothly in and out of her. She savoured the strange blend of friction and slickness that was his very essence in motion against hers.

How could a young man exert such control over his own so obvious desire? She had expected haste, clumsiness, frantic thrusts and fumbling; yet he was so deliberate, so in charge of both himself and of her. She realised she was starting to come again, her loins melting in the age-old, unmistakable implosion. Losing mastery of herself, she thrashed in his hold, her body filled with a gorgeous, blinding violence; yet he gentled her, stopping her shouts with his mouth and bottling the fire inside her to increase it and enrich it.

But when she had reached a plateau, relaxing into a long, dreamy orgasm that seemed warped and extended into a condition rather than an event, the stranger seemed to step up another gear. Flexing his supple body, he began to thrust more authoritatively, pounding her with a delicious force and fury. His kisses became powerful and devouring.

'Oh God!' he shouted, releasing her hands so he could slide both of his beneath her to grab her buttocks and plunging into her as if he were trying to become her.

Engulfed in passion, Claudia felt consciousness slide sideways and fragment. She was a swirling feather being carried on a torrent, a dancer spinning down into infinity. But just as velvet darkness claimed her she felt the sensation of moisture on her face. Tears. Not hers, but the stranger's, warm and salty; the happy weeping of a sweet soul in release.

'Oh Claudia!' he cried, and came inside her.

The stranger woke in the darkness, and for the first time in hours – or days, or weeks? – his predominant emotions weren't terror and a blank sense of dislocation. His first question wasn't an agonised 'Who am I?'

The question now, he realised, was 'Who is *she*?'

He was lying in a wide, comfortable bed, swathed in fresh, clean sheets that smelt of some flower-scented fabric softener, and wearing a pair of equally clean but somewhat tangled cotton pyjamas. Beside him lay a woman, soundly sleeping.

And he had memories! Recent ones, albeit, but recollections which filled him with the much-needed emotion of contentment.

'Claudia,' he said, under his breath, not wanting to wake her.

Yes, her name is Claudia.

He turned to his sleeping companion, and discovered she was beautiful. Dawn's light was filtering through the curtains and falling on a face that was fine-featured and serene and hair that was short and streaked several shades of blonde, its texture thick and shaggy and the cut flatteringly feathered.

Sitting up very carefully, he looked down on her. She had tiny lines at the corners of her eyes, the imprint of laughter, and though she wasn't a girl, she seemed exquisite and ageless. The drawn down-sheet revealed her lovely, rounded breasts.

We made love, he thought, wonderingly. Then he smiled, feeling – knowing – with satisfaction that the smile that played around the corners of *her* lips was attributable to him. He wanted to kiss her but it seemed a crime to disturb her rest. He wanted to make love to her, but he wanted her to be awake and actively wanting him as he took her. He didn't want to steal pleasure like a child filching sweets.

The cosy room around him looked familiar only in the fact that it was the one he had fallen asleep in. This was Claudia's home, he knew that. He remembered arriving here last night; he remembered a storm, and a horrific, half-blind panic that seemed more like an animal's response to the elements than that of a reasoning human being. He remembered Claudia's warmth and kindness; he remembered his instant and quite alarming desire for her.

But when he tried to picture what lay beyond the room and the house, the fear and the sense of blankness closed back in around his mind. There were only confused fragments available to him, and most of them brought pain in their wake.

Only one recollection was pleasant. He remembered being beside a river and seeing sunlight on the flashing water. With the picture of dancing light came a curious sense of eroticism. He felt a wild urge to laugh, but clapped his hand to his mouth to contain it, not wanting to wake his pretty Claudia from her slumber. He smiled, though, remembering what he had done and what he had felt beside that river.

It was strange how sex seemed so definite, so constant, so reassuring, when everything else in his present, and in his past, was insubstantial at best and effectively non-existent at its worst. When experiencing pleasure – and when *giving* it too, he acknowledged with a smile – he had substance, he was himself. A man. A person. Even if he had no inkling of who that person was.

He covered his face with his hands. One thing he had learnt over the last mangled and tangled expanse of hours was that when he pushed, when he tried hard to remember, he always felt worse – and excruciatingly tired. Weariness suddenly bore down on him again, and in this soft, inviting bed, there seemed no reason left on earth to fight its grip.

He felt far less fearful of unconsciousness now, he

realised, as he lay down again and turned his head on the pillow to face the lover who was also his literal saviour.

He might have no name, but at least he wasn't alone any more.

'Claudia,' he whispered, then rejoined her in the consoling vale of sleep.

Chapter Four
House Guest

*I*t had taken Claudia all her time not to wake him as
soon as she woke.

When a shaft of morning sun falling across her face
had roused her, she had lain still for a few seconds,
wondering if her senses were playing tricks with her.
Then she pinched her own thigh, instead of that of the
angel who lay in bed beside her.

Her handsome young stranger – her lover, she
thought, rolling the innocuous little word across her
tongue – had been sprawled across his side of the bed,
his hair all tousled and his smooth, pale face gently
smiling. He had been fast asleep – as he still was now, a
little while later – but a perfect icon of innocent temptation. Claudia had pinched herself again, to make sure
that he was real, and she still bore the dark bruise upon
her thigh.

You were inside me last night, she said to him silently.
You touched me. You made love to me. I adore you.

Oh dear, this is far too drastic and far too soon, she
thought, as she placed some clean clothing over the end
of the bed for him. Luckily, the newcomer was of a very
similar build to her Gerald, and though her late husband
had been well into his fifties, he had possessed the taste
– in casual clothes – of a much younger man; not to

mention the good looks to carry them off. As Claudia had not yet had the heart to send anything of his to a charity shop, there was plenty to choose from for the stranger. She had picked out denims and a soft white shirt for him, along with boxer shorts, clean socks and a pair of deck shoes.

Steepling her fingers to stop herself reaching out and caressing him, Claudia took another yearning, lingering look at her sleeping beauty. His long, rather elegant face; his soft, crazy hair; his sculpted lips. Those lips had kissed her with complete assurance last night, despite the fact that only a short while earlier, those same lips had framed a cry of fear.

And she could still hear his heartfelt groan as he had climaxed.

Come away, you old lech, she told herself, gathering up the clothes the stranger had arrived in, for laundering, then turning her back on the very image of temptation.

She almost ran down the stairs, her tread light. She didn't know how much good a hectic session of love-making had done her amnesiac house guest, but its benefits to herself were outstanding.

Her energy levels were even higher than they had been yesterday, and when she had stood naked before her mirror, after her shower, she had been convinced she could see a glow upon her skin. There was a naughty light in her brown eyes and a recurring smile upon her lips, and she had the aura of a woman who had been well and very beautifully fucked. She was a walking cliché, but she certainly wasn't complaining.

You're mad, Claudia, she thought, stuffing the stranger's shirt, socks and underwear into the washer and imagining them swirling around intimately with her smalls while she raced back upstairs and swirled intimately around their owner.

Yes, it was a kind of blissful madness, but given the chance to go back to yesterday and change her choices, she wouldn't alter a thing. Not one second of it. Even if the stranger did turn out to be an actor and a con-man

– which was still a possibility, her ever-cautious side counselled, despite his air of total plausibility. She was a rich widow living alone, when all was said and done. Perfect pickings for someone young, clever and as gorgeous as he was.

Ignoring her qualms, and still reliving the marvels of last night, Claudia made coffee then sat down at the kitchen table to enjoy it. In a little while, she decided, she would take him some of the tea he seemed to like so much – and serve herself to accompany it, hopefully! – but for now she would allow the man his sleep.

Her coffee finished, she examined the velvet frock coat he had arrived in.

The coat was beautifully made, and bore the hand-stitched label 'Hawkes of Savile Row', which suggested it could be a genuinely well-kept antique garment rather than an item of fancy dress. It was rather dusty, and looked at the moment as if it had been slept in for several nights – which it probably had been – but with expert cleaning it could be made as good as new.

As she smoothed her fingers over the lush nap of the velvet, she felt something hard beneath the surface, near the hem. Turning the coat over, she discovered a small tear in the lining of its inner pocket, and when she managed to work the hard object out through the hole, it proved to be a watch. A period fob watch to be precise; a very choice one that appeared to be made of gold. There was nothing to identify the stranger in any of the other pockets, either of the coat, the trousers or the waistcoat, which suggested he might well have been robbed or mugged or something, but the hypothetical thieves had clearly missed this hidden treasure. It had become caught somehow, and thus detached from its fob and chain.

Curiosity made Claudia flick it open, and she smiled when it proceeded to play a tinkly but melodious 'Blue Danube'. Twisting it around, she suddenly discovered that it was also engraved:

To my dear son Paul, on the occasion of his twenty-first birthday. Love, Dad.

Paul! Her lover's name was Paul.

'Paul. Oh, Paul,' she whispered, wishing the timepiece was magic and could whisk her back the requisite number of hours so she could sigh 'Paul . . .' as her mysterious lover entered her. So she could groan 'Paul' as he fondled her so beautifully that she climaxed repeatedly. So she could cry 'Paul!' in exultation, when they came together.

A sudden 'Cooee!', and a rapping sound, made her almost drop the watch. She stuffed it swiftly into her jeans pocket as a familiar figure came in through the opened kitchen door.

Melody Truebridge was the friend who, with loving kindness, had pulled Claudia through the first lows of her early widowhood and was now attempting to coax her back into revelling in life's joys. It seemed ironic that all Melody's attempts, no matter how well meaning, had failed, and that last night Claudia had achieved that very goal by other almost divinely granted means.

'Hey, what's this?' demanded Melody, tripping towards Claudia and plucking accusingly at the snug, cream T-shirt she was wearing with her jeans. 'I thought we were going to get all dolled up and have a posh day out shopping?' As conspicuously well groomed as she always was, Melody's smooth, young face was fully made up, and her platinum-blonde hair was carefully styled into a sleek, almost helmet-like, bob. Her suit was smart and tailored, and her heels high but chic.

Almost in uniform, thought Claudia sourly for a moment, wishing that Richard, Melody's husband, would stop seeing his wife as a business accessory for once. He was highly critical if Melody wasn't always turned out to within an inch of her life.

'Well?' prompted Melody.

'I'm sorry. I forgot,' said Claudia, smiling sheepishly. With her ongoing disapproval of Melody's marriage, and her recent and far more pleasurable preoccupations, it was obvious that she appeared inattentive.

'Are you all right, Claudia?' enquired Melody, her carefully made-up eyes wide as she sat down at the kitchen table.

'Yes, I'm fine. I've just had something on my mind,' said Claudia quickly, then looked down to see that she was still clutching the velvet frock coat. 'Something sort of cropped up.'

'What sort of something?' enquired Melody, her expression sharpening. For all her gentleness and amiability, the younger woman was keen witted and could see effortlessly through fibs. 'And what's this?' she added, reaching out to stroke the fabric of the coat. 'It doesn't look at all like Gerry's kind of thing. It looks more like fancy dress.'

Claudia was immediately in a quandary. What could she say to Melody? Could she tell her? They had shared so much; she knew all the younger woman's joys and troubles as intimately as she understood her own. But Paul was such a drastic innovation in her life, and he suddenly made her feel guilty, as if she had sidelined her trusted confidante in favour of intimacy with a stranger she couldn't rely on.

'It belongs to – to a friend.'

'A man friend?' Melody's pretty grey eyes were even wider now.

Claudia hesitated still. She wanted so much to share this, but –

'It is! It *is* a man!' said Melody triumphantly, grabbing Claudia's hand. 'You're blushing! Come on! Spill the beans! You old dark horse!'

'Less of the "old", if you please,' Claudia protested, realising she was already bright pink in the face, blushing as furiously as if her friend had come in and found her being made love to, by Paul, on the kitchen table.

'You know what I mean ... Now, come on. Give!' insisted Melody, forcing Claudia to look at her. 'When did you meet him? I only saw you two days ago and you never said anything then.'

Again Claudia wondered what she could tell her friend. Had she even the right to tell her anything? There were two in this midnight tango, after all.

And yet she felt compelled to speak. Melody wasn't just a casual acquaintance, she was a trusted companion. Her quiet, pacifying presence had kept Claudia together when her whole world had been on the point of crumbling.

'Well, this is going to sound a bit wild ... A lot wild, actually. But believe me, it's all true.' She went on to describe, in judiciously edited terms, the advent of the mysterious, outlandishly clothed Paul into her life. She did not detail his activities by the riverside, trying to suggest he had merely been paddling in the water; and neither did she mention the fact that she had gone to his room last night. Melody's pencilled eyebrows went up, however, and her sceptical expression revealed the fact that she didn't believe Claudia was telling her everything.

'Well, I'd say you were completely mad,' she told Claudia at last, grinning and shaking her head, 'on several counts. One being – ' she suddenly looked more serious ' – what you've done is very, very dangerous. Inviting a potential mugger or rapist into your house, late at night. And two – ' she lightened up, her eyes twinkling ' – if this Paul is *bona fide*, and as scrumptious as you say he is, I can't understand why you haven't laid a finger on him! He sounds just what I had in mind for you when I suggested you go out with Tristan.'

'Don't be ridiculous. I just put Paul up for the night!' said Claudia quickly. 'And you know I've got my doubts about Tristan.' Tristan Van Dissell was – or had been – a business associate of Gerald's, and a handsome man a good deal younger than Claudia. Despite that, Melody had proposed him as a possible 'first date'; an entrée back into the world of romance and relationships.

'Minor quibbles, and never mind him for now,' dismissed Melody, like an advocate rejecting flimsy, circumstantial evidence. She grabbed Claudia's hand. 'Just look at you! You're positively gleaming! Nobody looks as smug as you do just from playing the Good Samaritan!' She pulled Claudia closer, studying her. 'You've had him, you sly old thing, haven't you? Admit it!'

Still pink in the face, Claudia looked away. She was just about to frame some kind of answer when there was a flash of movement at the periphery of her vision. And as that flash gained a voice she spun around on her chair to face him.

'Good morning,' said Paul shyly from the kitchen doorway. He was immediately the focus of Melody's attention.

Seeing him again, her exquisite stranger-lover, Claudia felt lightheaded. Even in a pair of perfectly ordinary jeans and a plain white shirt, he looked as exotic and as 'different' as he had in his Edwardian finery. And the fact that his curly, tousled hair was still damp and roughed up from a recent towelling, and that the borrowed shirt was unfastened and hanging loose outside his jeans' waistband, implied exactly the degree of familiarity with his hostess that Melody had been trying to get Claudia to admit to. He looked every inch a kept man; there was no denying it.

Not that she wanted to deny it – especially when he gave her a warm, complicit and strangely intricate smile which expressed both nervousness and a quintessentially masculine bravado. Pride made Claudia want to sing, grab him and make love to him – even if he *was* only after her for her money!

She glanced from her lover to her friend. Melody was staring at Paul with undisguised sexual interest, and her pink-painted mouth had fallen open. Claudia was about to introduce them when the other woman took the initiative.

'And good morning to you too,' she replied, grinning. 'I'm Claudia's friend, Melody, and she's been telling me all about you.'

Paul stepped forward into the room and shook the hand that Melody held out. All the while he smiled that shy but glorious smile that was already becoming intoxicatingly familiar to Claudia and which now seemed to have a sudden and quite stupefying effect on Melody too.

'I'm – ' he frowned for a second, clearly fighting to drag up at least his name from his memory.

'Paul,' supplied Claudia softly, rising from her seat and moving towards him, fishing the watch from her pocket as she did so. 'I think your name is Paul. I found this caught inside the lining of your coat.' When she reached him, she flipped open the case and put the timepiece into his hand. He smiled at the pretty little waltz it played, then looked closer to read the inscription.

'Does it ring any bells?' she asked, when he said nothing but just stared at the words etched into the gold.

'I'm not sure,' he said eventually, flicking the watch shut, then open again, then shut, as if the action itself might trigger a memory. 'Paul ... Paul ...' he intoned slowly and thoughtfully. 'It doesn't feel *wrong*,' he continued after a moment, 'but I couldn't honestly say for certain that it's my name.'

'I like it,' said Claudia, realising she did, very much. 'It suits you.'

'Yes, it's a nice name,' agreed Melody, apparently shaking off her fugue and finding her voice again. 'You look exactly how a Paul should look.'

There was a brief but intense silence, and in it Claudia sensed Paul's fragile confidence teetering. He was still less than a day away from his arrival in terror and confusion.

'How about a cup of tea, Paul?' she said, pulling out a chair for him. As he sat down, she gave Melody a significant look.

'Well, is there anything you want from the shops, Claud?' Melody enquired, smoothly fielding the message. 'Perhaps I can drop those at the cleaners for you?'

She nodded towards the frock coat, waistcoat and trousers, which were now draped across another of the kitchen chairs. 'Taylor's are very good with special fabrics. I could ask them to deliver them when they're ready, if you like?'

A minute or two later, after some slight, inconsequential chat and a drama-school array of looks laden heavily with meaning, Melody was gone, taking Paul's clothing with her to be cleaned. In the hall, she had restated her warnings. 'Be very, very careful!' she had said, squeezing Claudia's hand. 'He looks heavenly but he might still be a dangerous lunatic.'

'I'm sorry, was that difficult for you?' Claudia asked when she returned to the kitchen after showing Melody out. Paul was still sitting where she had left him, staring intently at the watch as 'The Blue Danube' played.

He looked up at her, and her heart seemed to turn over inside her. He was smiling, that special between-the-two-of-them smile that seemed both knowing and blamelessly pure at the same time. Claudia was bound by it, completely captured. She felt possessed by a great and irresistible longing to reveal everything about herself to him, body and soul, in one blinding cathartic instant. She just couldn't believe that he was anything but honest.

Blushing again, her eyes flicked to his still-naked chest, and she found herself remembering the feel of it pressed against her breasts as he bore down on her and his penis forged its way inside her.

'A little, but not as bad it would have been yesterday,' he answered, flipping the watch shut and placing it on the table. Claudia blinked, trying to remember what the question was she had asked. 'Your friend's nice. She seems very concerned for you.'

'She is,' said Claudia shakily, turning away before she did something rash, like begging him to make love to her again. 'I sometimes wonder how I would have coped without Mel when my husband died. She kept me going. Kept me sane. Took care of me.'

'She's obviously got a kind heart,' observed Paul, his voice pensive. 'Even though she is unhappy about something . . .'

'What makes you say that?' Claudia turned to face him again, and saw him rubbing his forefinger thoughtfully along his moulded lower lip. It was a contemplative mannerism, but somehow profoundly erotic too.

'I don't know . . . Maybe it's a "lost soul" thing? Perhaps it takes one to know one?'

Possibly, thought Claudia, wondering at his powers of perception. 'She's not exactly happy all the time,' she told him, not wanting to detail her dearest friend's marital difficulties to someone neither of them really knew. 'I suppose you could say I take care of her a bit too . . .'

'I can't imagine anyone *not* wanting to take care of either of you,' said Paul softly, rising from his seat and moving across to where she was trying to fill the kettle for his tea, and not doing very well. As it clattered against the tap, he took it from her, placed it on the draining board, then slid his hands around her waist and hugged her to him.

'And I thank you for doing the same for me,' he whispered, kissing the side of her neck, his lips gentle but potent with meaning.

Claudia felt as if her knees had turned to jelly. She drooped back into his hold, her breath suddenly coming in harsh, deep gasps. All he had to do was be close and touch her in the most innocent way and she was as mad for him as a panting bitch on heat.

Not that his touch *was* entirely innocent. Between her buttocks, she could feel the knot of his genitals pressing against her through several layers of fabric. He was erect again, as hard and as fabulous as he had been last night. Unable to help herself, she pushed backwards against him.

Feeling a little dazed, she looked up and saw their ghostly reflections in the window over the sink. Her own image was glassy eyed and sluttish; her lips were parted and her nipples were two clear, telling smudges beneath her light T-shirt and her thin cotton bra. She couldn't see Paul quite as distinctly. His face was just a pale impression, where it was inclined over her shoulder as he pressed his lips to her throat, and his hair appeared as a wild, darker mass, a tangle of serpents against the sleek blondness of her crop. His long eyelashes were two crescents, a pair of silky, black fans; his mouth a flexing line as he kissed her.

'You give me this!' he said, his teeth grazing her skin as he rubbed his hard body against the cleft of her bottom. 'And I feel whole again. I don't need to know my name when I'm with you.'

Claudia leapt in his arms when he slid his hand down and cupped her crotch through her jeans. It was like being wrapped around by an electric fence; wherever he touched her, her body sizzled with energy. He laughed aloud as she shimmied against him, his chuckle intense and wicked as he kneaded her mercilessly between her legs.

'You make everything so simple for me,' he murmured, almost devouring her neck as he rubbed and rubbed her. The seam of her jeans was pressed tight against her clitoris, and she knew that her demon lover was aware of it.

'Oh Paul. Oh Paul,' she gasped, savouring his name as the lovely tension grew between her legs. He was stimulating her with his fingers and massaging her bottom with his cock. How close are you to orgasm? she wondered dreamily, as her climactic spasms began to ripple, then she cried out as their full force took her over. Her vulva was jumping and pulsing in his grip, and she knew he must be able to feel her reaction through the denim. He laughed again, as if confirming her supposition.

'Paul! Oh God, Paul, you bastard, you're adorable!' she yelled. She seemed to come and come and come for several minutes.

48

As her eyes fluttered open and she regained the ability to support herself, the first thing she saw was the kettle.

'What about your tea?' she said faintly, trying to straighten up.

'In a little while,' he said huskily, his voice sounding more domineering and older than it had done at any time so far. With a little bump of his pelvis, he reminded Claudia of his erection, then sliding his hands down to her hip bones, he held her still while he ground his cock against her bottom.

'There's something I need right now far more than tea,' he said, then had the grace to laugh at his own statement of the extremely obvious. Releasing her, his hands went to the button and the zip of Claudia's jeans.

A whole slew of inconsequential thoughts whizzed through her mind as Paul went to work on her denims.

He was going to have her jammed up against the sink. What a cliché – but how exciting!

And what time was it? Eight? Nine? Ten? If it was the latter, she should have had her breakfast by now and be doing the dishes before her cleaning lady arrived. Oh God, what if Mrs Tisdale walked straight in, as she always did, and found her employer being shafted against the sink by a total stranger? Mrs Tisdale was a dear old soul, and like Melody, she was always saying how worried she was for Claudia, being on her own. She would probably have rung the local police by the time Paul was finished!

And neither one of them had had any breakfast!

Such mundane considerations were blown away by the impact of Paul's fingers on her bare bottom. Within seconds, he had loosened her jeans, and now had both of his long, slender hands down inside them, and inside her knickers too. For a few moments, he just held her buttocks, a hand gripping each lobe, then he began to knead them and move them very slowly.

Claudia sighed, gripping the edge of the sink and bracing herself against it. She was aroused all over again by Paul's caress. He had gripped her bottom last night, while he was making love to her, but somehow now, in the presence of clothes and sinks and kettles, the intimate fondling seemed far more lewd and daring. She felt him circling the twin mounds of her flesh, stretching the tender groove between them, his little fingers rudely rubbing against her anus.

'You're so lovely, Claudia,' he murmured in her ear, at the same time gripping harder down below.

Claudia became too excited to keep still. She twitched her thighs, churned her hips, pushed against the hands that contained her, hoping to edge one of them down to stroke her quim. What would really be the nicest thing, she thought, would be for him to slide one hand down the front of her jeans, while still stroking her from the back with the other. She wanted to ask him to do that, but their relationship was too unusual, too tenuous. If she broke the spell, he might vanish like a dream.

But a dream with special powers, it seemed. Perhaps, she thought, as his right hand deftly relocated to exactly the part of her body she had wished it towards, the loss of his memory had created mind space for other abilities? He was either telepathic or just very, very clever. She shifted her thighs faster as, within her panties, he touched her clitoris.

'Again?' he queried, then without waiting for an answer, he pressed down gently on the swollen bud of flesh.

Claudia let out a high, yipping cry and climaxed with a force that was just as piercing. Throbbing with pleasure, she retained just enough sensibility to keep her arms braced and prevent herself pitching forward into the sink with its soapy water. Otherwise, she was help-less; her lover's puppet.

While she was still pulsating, still panting, still coming, she felt him swiftly peel down her pants and jeans as far as her knees, then with equal dexterity release his penis from his clothing. She was still in orgasm as he neatly slid inside her.

He wasn't gentle this time, and he wasn't slow. As if

fired by the novelty and danger of their situation, he fucked her quickly and powerfully. You've read my mind again, thought Claudia, her vulva beating.

Her mad, scary orgasm continued, soared anew, and her arms ached with the effort of keeping upright. She was bearing the weight and momentum of both of them, because Paul was busy with her breasts and her clitoris. After a few minutes of commotion, he shouted incoherently, his hands convulsing on her body while his penis leapt within it. Claudia bit her lip as her own sensations doubled.

They should have ended up on the floor, but somehow a miracle recovery prevailed. They found themselves laughing like teenagers as they scrabbled to right their clothing.

'I shall never be able to look at washing up in the same light again!' said Claudia, eyeing the soapsuds, whose silent deliquescence had accompanied their congress. The kettle stood abandoned on the draining board, but as she reached for it, remembering the tea she had offered an aeon ago, Paul took her hand and led her back to the kitchen table. Pulling out a seat for her, he made her sit down.

'Allow me,' he said, returning to the sink and the kettle, and flashing her his sweet, sunny smile over his shoulder. 'It's the least I can do under the circumstances.'

Claudia watched him move around her kitchen as if he owned the place. Pretty sure of yourself now, aren't you, young man? she thought, observing his neat, economical movements as he assembled the crockery and made the tea with the assurance of one who prepared it every day of his life. The correct disposal and timing of leaves and boiling water seemed to be something that had remained in his memory when both name and identity had apparently gone AWOL. Melody's whispered warnings returned to her. Could his little-boy-lost act be just that? A clever, almost award-winning performance?

She waited until he had poured them both some tea,

and she had tasted hers – which was even better than the tea she made herself! – before she tackled him.

'So, Paul, what are we going to do with you?'

He gave her a very straight look, completely without guile. It made her blush as if she were the one under the spotlight of suspicion.

'I don't know,' he said slowly, then unexpectedly he began fiddling with his cup and his teaspoon. The sudden return of his confusion put Claudia off balance too. He was so changeable; she didn't know where she stood.

'I don't know where to start,' he went on, 'or where to go. I don't even know where I am, really . . .' He laid down the spoon, raised his cup to his lips and took a sip. A fleeting look of pleasure crossed his face.

'Well, what do we know about you so far?' said Claudia, setting down her own cup and placing her hands palms down on the table. She would be firm, take a hold of this conversation. 'Your name is Paul, you're over twenty-one, and you like tea, *Madame Butterfly* and sex.'

'Oh, it's a bit more than that,' he returned, his pale eyes glinting. 'I enjoy most classical music, I think . . . I adore tea, and I *love* to make love. It seems to be the only thing I can do, and that I know I'm good at!' The pendulum of his confidence had swung again.

Claudia tried to hold fast, to be objective, although her body's instant response made that difficult. Even so recently sated, it was beginning to react again.

'As for where you are . . .' She looked around her, which was easier than looking at him, and made a vague gesture to encompass their surroundings. 'This is my home, Perry House, and it's situated at 162 Green Giles Lane, Rosewell under Berfield, in Oxfordshire. We're about sixty miles from London, ten from Oxford, and the river you were paddling in yesterday is the Little Ber, which eventually flows down into the Thames.'

'And from whose bank you watched me,' he reminded her, looking a little arch.

'You were on *my* land, I'll have you know!' she cut back at him. 'Trespassing. I'd say I had every right to watch you.' She could feel herself succumbing more and more to his presence with every second that passed. It was frightening, and she continued to struggle. 'Stop trying to distract me,' she said evenly. 'Now ... Do you know *when* this is? What the date is?'

He frowned, although he still seemed unchastened. 'I have no idea ... The middle of summer?' he suggested.

She told him the date, and he shrugged. 'That seems to feel right.'

'Is there anything else you do remember? Anything specific? An event. A name. Anything.'

Paul put down his cup, took a deep breath, and appeared to screw up every mental faculty available to him. Claudia felt a pang of remorse for pushing him, and for her doubts. The look of stress on his face made her heart twist.

'I can only remember bits of things,' he said at last, his voice rough as if he were close to tears of frustration. He began playing with the corner of his shirt tail; first smoothing out the material, then pleating it between his long and elegant fingers. 'Impressions. Fragments ... I remember someone hitting me. And kicking me.' He dropped his shirt, and pressed his hand briefly to his side, where Claudia knew there was an extensive and many-coloured bruise. 'I remember a place with lots of people ... Cars in a car park. Everyone was staring at me. Their eyes seemed huge ... Weird. As if they were out of focus.'

'Was this recent? Or do you think it's something from before whatever happened to you happened?' Claudia's concern deepened. Paul was visibly shaking now, and as she watched, he covered his face with his hands.

'Recent. I think.' The words were a little muffled. 'And I remember being in – in some kind of cafeteria. I must have had some change in my pocket. I think I ate something ... Had some tea ...' He dropped his hands and gave her a lopsided smile. 'Yes, I remember that clearly. It was disgusting. Then after that I washed my face ... I was in a cloakroom. I frightened myself to death, looking in a mirror. My face ... It didn't mean anything to me.'

That meaningless face was anguished now, and feeling so sorry for him, Claudia reached out and took his hand. It felt rather cool. The jumbled and fragmentary tale went on:

'After that, I remember walking and walking. Perhaps I stopped and slept somewhere, I don't know ... The next thing I really remember is being on the riverside, and from there on everything seems clearer. I bathed, and ...' He looked straight at her, and managed a smile. 'When my things were dry, I put them on, curled up and went to sleep again. The next time I woke, it was getting dark, and I seemed to be at the epicentre of a thunderstorm. When I saw the lights of your house, I just ran for them.'

So it could have been anyone, thought Claudia, looking at the handsome face and the beautiful body of the man who had literally fallen at her feet, then risen and revitalised her.

By pure chance ...

And yet she didn't believe that. Fate, karma, luck, whatever it was, had brought him to her at precisely the moment when she needed him. He was her catalyst; he had been *meant* to regenerate her sexuality.

'And the rest you know,' he said simply, his hand stirring in hers.

Claudia felt her soul stirring too, as his long fingers curved around hers, evoking other curvings and other enfoldings. For two pins, she would have drawn him to her again and encouraged him to do that thing he did with such confidence. But there were practical matters to consider.

'Well, it occurs to me that there are two things we should do with you now,' she said, trying to sound at least focused, if not strictly business-like. 'You obviously haven't eaten properly in some time, so first, I should

cook you a hearty but healthy breakfast. The second is
that I think you should see a doctor. And quickly. You've
obviously sustained a head injury of some kind.' She
glanced quickly at the abrasion on his forehead, which
still looked quite fearsome. It was partially hidden by
his curly hair, but its potential danger could not be
ignored. 'It might be serious.'

Paul surveyed their linked hands. 'A doctor?' He
frowned, his brow rumpling as if the word was either
completely foreign to him, or had some special, perhaps
ominous, significance. 'I don't think I want to see a
doctor. At least not yet. My head doesn't hurt at all,' he
went on, reminding her of a stubborn child who
wouldn't let his skinned knee be cleaned up. 'Didn't you
say that your memory came back of its own accord in a
fortnight? Mine might do the same.'

'And it might not,' contradicted Claudia, faint suspicion uncoiling once again.

'I don't want to be poked and prodded and questioned. Treated like a freak!' he said with sudden vehem-
ence, snatching away his hand.

'It wouldn't be like that,' said Claudia, thinking of her
own GP, who was an excellent clinician but a brisk, no-
nonsense old fellow who got straight to the point and
asked many, many questions in a direct and sometimes
caustic manner.

Then, just as she began to consider the possibility of
going to a hospital Out-Patients Department, where
treatment would be equally brisk but far more imper-
sonal, another option suddenly presented itself.

She remembered a brief conversation at Gerald's
funeral, and a pleasant but rather odd phone call not
long afterwards.

'I know I'm not your GP, but if you ever need someone
to talk to, please don't hesitate to call me. Either at the
cottage, or at my London surgery. Even if it's just for a
chat . . . I might be able to help.'

And she might at that, thought Claudia, grabbing
Paul's hand again and making him look at her.

'Look. There might be another way,' she said earnestly, thinking quickly as she spoke. 'I know someone . . . She's a doctor, but she's a sort of friend too. If I give her a call, will you at least agree to meet her? I can promise you she won't treat you like a freak.'

Chapter Five
Doctor's Orders

The trouble was, the physician could well turn out to be more of a freak than her prospective patient, thought Claudia, smoothing down the front of her soft, ochre-coloured cotton skirt as she hurried through the hall after lunch.

There had always been a lot of loose talk about Beatrice Quine MD in the village of Rosewell, and as she opened the front door, Claudia found it easy to understand why people were so fond of speculating and telling tall stories.

'Well, hello! I always knew that you'd call on me one day but I never expected you to look quite so well when you did,' said the doctor, giving Claudia a long, warm look, then sweeping confidently past her into the hall. 'What can I do for you? Tell me all about this handsome stranger of yours.'

Closing the door, Claudia suddenly found herself a good deal closer to Doctor Quine than she had expected to be. The other woman had stopped short, turned around, and was now standing barely a couple of feet away, smiling. Before Claudia could catch her breath, she was being kissed soundly on both cheeks, continental-style, and her nostrils were awash with a dizzyingly exotic perfume. After a second, and having thoroughly greeted – and disorientated! – her hostess, the doctor stood back, rocking on her heels, with a mischievous look of enquiry upon her face.

The only conventional thing about Doctor Beatrice Quine's appearance this fine afternoon was her old-fashioned and rather battered-looking medical bag. It was an ordinary item, very normal and quite reassuring, while its owner was far from it. The doctor was extra-ordinary, and Claudia felt suddenly intimidated, but in a strangely pleasant way.

Beatrice Quine was a woman of unusual beauty. Probably about Claudia's own age, or possibly a little older, the physician had chosen to eschew the usual sober, suited style of a serious professional woman, and was instead wearing a thin white vest and an eye-stopping pair of lilac chamois-leather trousers. Her narrow feet were exotically sandalled; a heavy, beaten silver slave bangle embraced her upper arm, and she wore a massive and complex-looking watch – obviously a man's – around her other wrist. Her long, luxuriant, almost violently red hair was drawn back in a single waist-skimming plait, and to say she made an impact was to understate by light years.

'Please ... please come this way, Doctor Quine,' stammered Claudia, feeling ridiculous for being so obviously and embarrassingly awestruck. After all, Bea-trice Quine was only another 'woman of a certain age', like herself; just another female with all the same accoutrements and hang ups. Why then, did the hand-some doctor make her tingle so?

'Oh please, it's Beatrice!' said the doctor gaily, as Claudia escorted her to the sitting room, still feeling completely thrown by her own, involuntary responses.

This is so weird! she thought. Unbelievable. The way I'm reacting is the same way I did when I first set eyes on Paul. What's happening to me? This is all completely crazy!

'What a divine room!' exclaimed Beatrice, walking into the centre of the sitting room, giving a little twirl and making her long plait swing out in an arc behind her. 'You have so many lovely things,' she went on, taking a seat on the sofa without being asked. It was clear the good doctor was used to being accepted with open arms and intimate familiarity wherever she went.

'*I* like them,' said Claudia uncertainly, wondering whether to sit down beside her self-possessed guest. Beatrice appeared totally relaxed; she had already put aside her bag and settled deep into the cushions, crossing one chamois-clad leg over the other and draping her arms along the back of the couch's upholstered back – and Claudia was presumably expected to sit next o her.

'So, this "patient" of ours . . .' encouraged Beatrice Quine as Claudia sat down gingerly. 'Where is he, by the way? In bed?'

'Er, no,' murmured Claudia, more thrown than ever by the doctor's disturbingly unprofessional emphasis on that last word. Beatrice's brilliant eyes were twinkling rather significantly too. It was as if she already knew about all the events that had occurred since Paul's arrival, including the encounters in his bed and in the kitchen. And yet Claudia was quite convinced she had revealed no inkling whatsoever of anything untoward.

'No, he's taking a nap on the couch in the conservatory,' she went on, no longer able to meet her companion's soul-piercing green-eyed gaze. 'He seems to need a lot of rest and sleep . . .' Had she blundered again? Seemed to imply something? She sensed a further sharpening of the doctor's interest. 'He's fine, though, when he's awake. He doesn't seem at all out of it, or disorientated . . . Well, not now, at least. He was rather shaken up when he first arrived.'

'Well, that's a good sign,' replied Beatrice, her voice suddenly business-like again. 'The need for sleep could be a result of trauma . . . but then again, if you say it's possible he's been wandering about the countryside for a few days, it could just be simple exhaustion.' When Claudia risked a peek at her, the doctor did indeed look quite serious, her fine brow furrowed in concentration. 'You say he has a head wound?'

'Yes, a nasty graze, but there's no swelling or obvious bruising.'

'Hmmm . . . Things don't sound too serious, but you can never be sure. The brain is a curious organ. It can sustain what seems like a horrific injury, and the patient can recover completely . . . and yet a slight knock can have serious repercussions – ' Beatrice paused at Claudia's look of horror. 'Don't worry!' she said quickly, reaching out and laying her long, beautiful, but very plainly manicured fingers on Claudia's bare arm. 'I'm sure that isn't the case here. If there was a bad problem, it would almost certainly have shown up by now.'

Claudia felt confused – and horrified with herself. Paul could be in the throes of a terminal brain seizure, right at this moment, and yet all she could think of was the delicate touch of Beatrice Quine's fingertips on her forearm. The contact was like fire; a static charge. It was as special, in its own way, as the first time Paul had laid hands on her the previous night.

'Are you all right?' enquired Beatrice, cocking her head a little to one side. 'I didn't mean to frighten you . . . I'm sorry.'

Claudia was not all right, but she nodded and smiled, very aware that Beatrice's hand was still resting lightly upon her arm, fingers curved, skin soft and excitingly warm. She was also aware of the doctor's increased closeness, and the proximity of her beautifully shaped breasts, so perfectly displayed by the white vest and an obvious lack of brassière.

What would it be like to caress her, thought Claudia dreamily, as if she were floating aloft on a cloud of Beatrice's spectacular perfume.

She raised her eyes, almost in slow motion, and found Beatrice frowning. 'Are you sure you're OK, Claudia?' the doctor asked.

'Oh, er . . . Yes, thanks,' stammered Claudia, wishing she could shake off the mind-fuddling disruption of

Beatrice's fingertips. 'I think I'm suffering from a little
sleep deprivation myself. It was rather late by the time I
got Paul settled last night . . . and I was worried about
him.'

'Of course you were,' said Beatrice, her tone a little
questioning as she finally withdrew her hand and
reached for her black bag. 'But really, though, I think
you should consider Paul a very fortunate young man.
A less hospitable person might have turned him away,
set the dogs on him, called the police.' She rose and
made an elegant sweep around her with her free hand.
'Instead, he found you. And you took him into your
beautiful home and made him welcome . . . If I was lost
in a storm, this is exactly the kind of place *I'd* want to
find shelter in.'

A vision of Beatrice wet through, in a thin satin frock,
fainting on the doorstep, confused Claudia even further,
and it was only with a supreme effort of will that she
didn't sway as she too stood up. 'You'd be very welcome,' she said, without thinking, then blushed pink
when the doctor slyly grinned.

'Thank you. That's very nice of you,' Beatrice said
softly. 'Now, may I see my patient?'

'Of course,' replied Claudia, very aware that her voice
was coming out rather more huskily than she intended.
'I'll show you where he is.' She made an abrupt gesture,
and walked ahead, becoming angry with herself for her
own reactions. This was all too stupid. What on earth
had got into her?

A perfect stranger, that's what! she told herself ruefully as she led the way to the conservatory. Paul had
not only 'got into' her in the crudest and most primal
sense of the expression, but he had entered her life on
other levels at the same time. He had reactivated her
somehow; completed a circuit which had already been
close to forming. He was the jolt that had set her senses
back in motion.

And here he was. With the greatest of care she pushed

open the conservatory door and held her own breath as Beatrice gasped behind her.

'My God! What an angel!' the doctor breathed, resting her hand on Claudia's shoulder as the two women surveyed the recumbent young man.

Like Claudia, Paul had showered and changed since their wild encounter against the kitchen sink. He now wore a pair of Gerald's chinos and a plain but very full white lawn shirt, which for some reason he had left open and unbuttoned again. His long, slender feet were bare, too; his toes pointing endearingly towards Claudia and Beatrice as he lay full length, apparently sleeping, on a battered chaise longue placed beside an opened window. A more complete picture of enticement, Claudia could not imagine. She wanted to stroke his tousled hair, kiss his naked chest, caress his cock.

'I can quite see why you took this one in, you lucky thing,' Beatrice continued, in a whisper. 'I do wish he'd turned up at my cottage.'

There seemed to be no really adequate response to that wish, so walking as quietly as she could in her soft-soled deck shoes, Claudia escorted her appreciative companion to the side of the chaise – and to the handsome, almost unearthly young man who lay on it. It felt like sacrilege to interrupt his peaceful slumber.

'Paul,' she whispered, leaning over him and squeezing his shoulder cautiously. 'Paul, wake up!'

The blue, blue eyes snapped open, and the whole of his tranquil, almost graven, face lit up at the sight of her. He smiled his beautiful smile, then before she could protest, he had reached up, curved a hand around the nape of her neck and drawn her down so he could kiss her on the lips.

For an instant, she stiffened, bunching her muscles ready to struggle against him, then a heartbeat later, she relaxed and let him master her, enjoying the whole-body thrill that came just from his kiss. As his tongue teased hers, she imagined Beatrice watching them, and felt her pleasure flare up at the thought of it. Let the sexy doctor see that she wasn't the only mature woman in the village who indulged in excesses of wicked sensuality. Why should Beatrice Quine corner the entire market in younger lovers?

When his free arm snaked around her back, and she felt herself almost falling over on to him, Claudia decided reluctantly to rein in his enthusiasm. 'Steady on,' she murmured into his ear, extricating herself. 'There's someone here to see you ... It's my friend, the doctor.'

To her credit, Beatrice had not made a sound during Claudia's brief but incendiary entanglement with Paul, and now her expression remained quite neutral. But when she stepped forward, her face became all smiles.

'Beatrice Quine. An MD for my sins ... Pleased to meet you,' she said, holding out her hand.

Total confusion passed like an eclipse across Paul's handsome features, but with a surprising equilibrium, he quickly replaced it with a broad smile of his own. Rising lithely to his feet, he took the doctor's outstretched fingers and squeezed them.

'Paul ...' Releasing Beatrice's hand, he shrugged his shoulders. 'Well, Paul "Something or other". I can't remember the rest at the moment.'

'Oh, it'll come back soon, don't you worry,' Beatrice said, her voice sounding reassuringly confident and knowledgeable, although Claudia was at a loss to know how the other woman could be so sure, even if she was a physician. Doctors were like that, though, she reflected. And they got away with it because you wanted to believe them.

'Right then,' Beatrice went on briskly, setting down her bag on the nearby wrought-iron table, then snapping it open. 'Sit down, Paul ... I'd like to take a look at you.'

I'll bet you would!

The retort came to Claudia spontaneously, though to her relief, she didn't come out and voice it. Watching Paul instantly comply with the doctor's orders, she felt a plume of confused emotion shoot through her. She felt dismissed and excluded. Jealous. To make things worse, the sense of envy was unfocused. She could just as easily be jealous of Paul, as of Beatrice.

'I'll be in the kitchen, if you need anything,' she said, forcing her voice into a pleasant, amenable shape as she made her way to the door.

'Thanks. This shouldn't take too long,' said Beatrice with an acknowledging nod. She was already seated and reaching into her bag for her stethoscope.

As Claudia paused at the door, she met Paul's glance and saw a small, strange smile on his face – an expression that reflected her own curious melange of feelings. She saw guilt and excitement. Male power, and the fear of a lost and scared young man. And suddenly she didn't feel quite so jealous any more. Whatever Beatrice did to him, whatever liberties the sensuous and cavalier doctor took in the course of her examination, there was an essence of Paul that would remain exclusively Claudia's.

On reaching the haven of the kitchen, she had a sudden craving for a bracing shot of brandy. Her feelings and her reactions were so unsettling. Pouring herself some mineral water instead, and slipping in ice cubes and lemon, she placed the glass on the kitchen table, then sat down astride a reversed kitchen chair – arms folded across its back, her chin settled upon them – and tried to centre herself by watching the bubbles rise through the fluid. It was a strange activity, but observing the minute spheres of gas defying gravity had often brought tranquillity in the past.

It didn't work today, however. Instead, she saw day-dreams in her San Pelegrino.

The first was memory, not a flight of fancy.

Paul had made love to her over there, by the sink that now gleamed and smelt so wholesomely of pine. She could still feel a ghost of his presence inside her, his fierce young penis thrusting and jerking triumphantly. In hindsight, she viewed their coupling like a scene from a soap opera or a television movie. Handsome youth shafts prime-time woman among the pots and pans. It was an old chestnut but oh, how she had enjoyed it.

And you would do it again, right now, if he was here, wouldn't you? she accused herself, very aware of the erotic tension in her body. Leaning back a little, she touched her nipple through the fine cotton of her camisole, feeling pleasure shoot through her and make her gasp. The little crest was as hard as the stone of a rare, exotic fruit. She could feel its tight puckeredness through the flimsy tan material.

She was wet too, she realised; nectarous and ready. Rocking a little, to and fro, on the hard, wooden seat, she experienced another delicious spasm, this time in the humid niche between her legs.

'Oh! Oh my God!' she hissed, reaching down to slip her hand beneath herself and press her palm against her crotch.

What was happening to her? She had never been this fired up with constant desire, even in her headiest early days with Gerald. It was as if Paul's body were calling to her even as she thought about him, stirring her senses remotely, almost touching her.

And not just Paul's body. She could see, no, almost feel, Beatrice too. Taste the vitality of her. Feel herself as one with the other woman's knowing, voluptuous nature.

Just what was the good doctor doing to Paul? Claudia wondered. Rationally, she knew that Beatrice would be conducting a perfectly standard medical examination, but certain facets of her mind were suggesting far different scenarios – procedures more outlandish, and perhaps forbidden.

She seemed to see Beatrice and Paul, but not in her sun-dappled conservatory. With her eyes focused on the rising, rippling bubbles, she envisioned a stark white consulting room somewhere, its floor and walls tiled and antiseptic. Beatrice sat behind a futuristic desk of glass and metal, and Paul sat before her in a rigidly moulded steel and plastic chair. Still clad in his white shirt and chinos, he looked nervous and exquisitely boyish, while the doctor's clothes had changed, and her mien was regal, yet impassive. Obligingly, as if to improve Claudia's view, she rose from her seat, then slid out from behind the desk.

Don't be silly, Claudia told herself, blinking at her own imagination. She wouldn't wear *that* for a consultation!

Beatrice the clinician had on a long, white coat, the universal garb of all doctors, but beneath it, her dress was a form-fitting white silk cheong-sam. The soft luminescence of the lightly brocaded Eastern fabric gave her an aura of both purity and worldliness; and while its knee-length skirt was modest, the sensuous cling of the whole garment was arresting and blatantly sexual, especially in combination with sheer, seamed black stockings and a pair of elegant black calf-skin high heels. The effect of such discreet glamour was both undeniable and electric, and within the dream, Paul's wild blue eyes were filled with hunger.

Neither of the imaginary protagonists said a word, as was often the case in such daydreams, but for Claudia's part, actual spoken language was superfluous. Standing before Paul, Beatrice leant forward, her hands on his arms, and appeared to whisper something in his ear. His immediate response was to blush vividly and move uneasily in his chair, and when Beatrice released him and leant back against her desk, he rose to his feet, the movement cautious and shaky. After a second's pause, he began to remove his clothes.

First came the white shirt, which he dropped on the chair behind him, then he kicked off his shoes and peeled off the socks he had worn beneath them. Claudia wondered momentarily where this footwear had come from – he wasn't wearing any now, in the real world – then focused steadfastly on the rest of his disrobing.

His cheeks still pink, Paul hesitated again, his long fingers toying nervously with the narrow pig-skin belt that held up his chinos, but with a slow grin, Beatrice nodded that he should proceed.

Paul's throat flushed crimson, but even so he obeyed the physician, unbuckling his belt with only the slightest fumble, then stepping gracefully out of his trousers and throwing them over the chair, with his shirt. He gave Beatrice one last supplicating look then, but she nodded again, and hesitantly he slipped down his boxer shorts.

The condition of Paul's penis clearly betrayed his state of mind. Its tumescence showed how much the dazzling presence of Beatrice affected him; but the fact that it was not fully erect yet clearly illustrated his nerves, too, and his awe of the white-clad physician.

You aren't so shy with me, my lad, thought Claudia, momentarily distancing herself from her own visual fantasy. Did this indicate some secret desire within her? A need to be dominant with him?

She made a mental note to explore this new avenue later, but for the moment, she was enjoying her young lover's strange scenario with Beatrice.

The good doctor began her examination in the most innocuous and unremarkable of ways – by donning her stethoscope and listening intently to her patient's heart and chest. It was only Paul's complete nakedness the set the procedures apart from pure routine.

Or so it seemed at first, because after a moment or two, Claudia noticed how much Beatrice's fingertips were lingering as they skimmed the young man's body. She was testing the smoothness of his skin as much as the regularity of his heartbeat; the resilience of his musculature as much as the depth of his respiration. It was only a matter of time before his cock came under scrutiny.

And when it did, Paul let out a gasp of shock. Still no words, just an excited exhalation as his firm flesh leapt and stiffened. In Claudia's glass the tiny bubbles continued to rise.

Ah yes, I know what that feels like, she thought, as the image of Beatrice, too, made a subtle sound of satisfaction. It was easy to remember the sensation of that sprightly young rod throbbing softly in her fingers; to feel its heat and the velvety texture of the skin that enrobed it. Moaning soundlessly, Paul threw back his head and bared his teeth, his fists clenching at his side as the woman clad in white manipulated his penis. Beatrice whispered in his ear again, and though Claudia knew not what it was the doctor had said, she sensed it was something tantalising and obscene – because Paul trembled finely and shook his tousled mop of curls.

Beatrice murmured again, giving Paul's cock a small, coaxing squeeze as her lips moved inaudibly against his ear, and a second later his handsome face twisted in what appeared to be both chagrin and ecstasy.

'I can't!' he seemed to say, although in her dream state, Claudia still heard no structured utterance.

Beatrice appeared to be persistent in her encouragement, and after a moment, she released her intimate hold, took Paul's right hand in hers, then folded it securely around his penis. Paul hesitated, then reluctantly began to masturbate.

Claudia had seen this, of course, in real life, but even so, Paul's self-pleasure was enchanting, and even more so for the phantom presence of beautiful Beatrice. Licking her raspberry-pink lips as she watched him, the doctor took up a position behind her by now industrious 'patient' and stared down, over his shoulder, at his endeavours. As she was quite tall for a woman, and had her high heels to elevate her even further, she could observe him easily without having to stretch. Reaching around, with her slim white hands, she caressed his thighs.

It was like observing some exotic Latin dance, thought Claudia, wondering where in the world she was getting such ideas from. What she had conjured up was the gyration of two bodies in perfect harmony; a red-hot rumba, or a salsa that rudely mimicked perverted sex. Paul jerked his slim hips in time to the movement of his fingers – and close behind him Beatrice's pelvis matched his rhythm. She was pounding her silk-covered crotch against his buttocks.

Paul's lips moved soundlessly as he clearly approached his crisis, and against his pale neck his tormentor still murmured and chivvied at him. Beatrice was smiling, her own face as contorted as Paul's was. Claudia wondered what pleasures the doctor was experiencing. Her hard nipples rubbing against Paul's muscular back? Her mons pubis bouncing against his bottom, producing an indirect but insistent stimulation? Or was it more a mental thrill than physical? A rush of raw power induced by her complete control of Paul – a bodily delight that was rooted deep within her psyche?

This is insane! thought Claudia, still rocking, and still rubbing at her own sex. It's in *my* psyche, not Beatrice's. It's *me* who's getting off on controlling him and making him do things.

But why did she continue to see the visions? The sight of Paul's naked body jerking. The sheen of sweat on his pale skin as Beatrice's hand roved over his hips, his belly and his chest. The agonised judder of his pelvis as he reached his orgasm. The deft, near-impossible way that Beatrice enclosed his glans in her fingers at the very instant his semen spurted from it. The way she caught every drop of his essence, and as his knees began to buckle, conveyed it to his lips and silently commanded he consume it.

Help! I'm going mad! thought Claudia in a sudden panic, snatching her hand away from between her legs and in her haste knocking over the glass of water.

What a thing to think . . .

You're perverted, old girl, she told herself as she mopped up the spill, and placed the miraculously unbroken glass in the sink. You must have reached a funny age.

But as she made her way up the stairs – to change out of her sodden skirt and top – she grinned to herself. The idea of compelling Paul to taste his own semen was unlike any erotic urge she had yet experienced, but there was no denying the fact that it – and similar acts of mild coercion – were a powerful turn-on. If she hadn't upturned her water glass, she had no doubt that she would have had an orgasm herself by now. Either from friction, or from pure fantasy excitement.

And I'm still excited, she acknowledged, as she stood in the bathroom, peeling off the dripping skirt and preparing to slip into a fresh outfit and a clean pair of knickers. The briefs she removed were stained dark where her body's nectar had flowed in response to her reveries, the thin cotton stickily revealing. She was just on the point of touching her own fluid, and tasting herself as the dream-Paul had been made to taste himself, when it suddenly occurred to her just how long she must have been fantasising. It felt like hours.

Beatrice will wonder what the hell I'm doing, she thought frantically, scrubbing a towel over her naked body; not only to dry her skin from her dowsing, but to mop up the spicy perspiration of her arousal. Briefly, she debated having a shower, then imagined the doctor leaving the conservatory in search of her, strolling curiously through the house and discovering her up here sluicing off the betraying odour of guilt.

Claudia rubbed even harder, wincing with delight as the textured terrycloth abraded her puckered nipples and sent streaks of hot sensation to her clitoris. Without stopping to censure herself, or even to think straight, she positioned the bunched towel between her thighs and began a steady sawing motion.

'Oh God, oh God, oh God,' she moaned, as the wedge of cloth moved back and forth, back and forth, between her labia. The action was rough and crude but exactly what she needed. After a few seconds, she collapsed in a blinding orgasm, the pummelled flesh of her well-rubbed vulva pulsating with pleasure.

And as she lay panting on the bathroom floor, she heard her name being called.

Chapter Six
Cassis and Other Intoxications

'You must think I'm being extraordinarily presumptuous,' said Beatrice cheerfully as Claudia finally entered the spacious but cosy sitting room. The doctor was holding a crystal copita containing what was obviously a generous measure of sherry, and once again, she was leaning back, completely at home, on the brocade-covered sofa.

'I came in here looking for you, and happened to notice the decanter,' she continued blithely, taking a sip of the deep caramel-coloured liquid. 'And then I remembered how sensational Gerald's cellar always was ...' The beautiful physician gave Claudia a shame-faced grin. 'I'm sorry, I'm really far too forward, I know. It will get me into awful trouble one of these days.'

'No problem. I was going to ask you if you wanted a drink anyway,' replied Claudia, crossing the room to where the decanters stood on their silver tray. She had been very nervous about facing up to Beatrice again – and possibly having to explain why she was now wearing hot-pink culottes and T-shirt, instead of her other outfit – but the doctor's contrition seemed to provide a little psychological leverage. Claudia's confidence blossomed and she felt prepared to enjoy herself, but just as she poured herself some sherry and was about to join Beatrice, a sudden jolt of shock and guilt assailed her.

'Paul!' she cried, turning quickly and spilling a splash of sherry on the tray. 'What about Paul? How is he? *Where* is he?' She gulped a little of her drink, then – grateful for the fortification – she moved quickly towards the sofa.

'Don't worry. He's fine,' said Beatrice soothingly, putting her own glass aside and taking Claudia's out of her shaking fingers. 'He's still a little sleepy, but I don't think there's anything serious to worry about.'

'Nothing serious!' protested Claudia, feeling a different sort of guilt. She thought of the exertions she had more or less lured him into and the encouragement she had given him. 'But he's obviously suffered a head wound . . . And he's lost his memory, for heaven's sake! Isn't that serious enough?'

Beatrice considered her very steadily, and Claudia felt not only the tightening in the physician's long, graceful fingers, but the calming power in the other woman's lambent green eyes.

'I agree. We can't dismiss either of those things,' said the doctor quietly, her beautiful face composed, 'but neither should we overreact to them. I've examined Paul as thoroughly as I can in the circumstances, and to the best of my judgement, I can't see any indications of a major problem.' Beatrice went on to detail some of the tests she had performed, and while the procedures themselves sounded somewhat superficial, Claudia had to admit that she felt reassured. She had no concrete knowledge of how good a clinician Beatrice actually was, but somehow instinct told her the woman's skills were exceptional.

'It's my belief that Paul's memory will return of its own accord, and fairly quickly,' Beatrice continued, 'but I certainly don't think we ought to just leave it at that.' She paused, as if debating how to proceed. 'Look, I'm on the board of a small private hospital, not far from here. I could book Paul in for a check-up . . . There's a good neuro man I know who owes me a favour.' She gave a small, cat-like smile, and for a distracting moment Claudia wondered what that favour might be. 'I could get him to pop in and give Paul the once over. The hospital is small, but it's superbly equipped. Their MRI scanner would give us a much clearer idea if there's anything to be concerned about.'

It sounded an ideal solution, but yet again, Claudia experienced a muddled array of doubts.

For one, Paul had expressed such a reluctance to be examined in the first place; he might refuse point blank to visit a hospital. And the reluctance in itself raised another possibility, one which Claudia realised she kept conveniently pushing out of the way into a dark corner of her consciousness. Returning it to the light, however, she was forced to face up to it.

Was Paul on the level? Was his amnesia, and all that stemmed from it, authentic? Or was he just an extremely canny young man taking advantage of a middle-aged woman who was vulnerable, and ripe for a liaison?

I'm not middle aged! she thought fiercely, extricating her hands from Beatrice's and reaching down for her sherry. Concentrating on the glass, she lifted it to her lips, acutely conscious that the doctor was observing her every move.

And what the fuck does it matter if he is a con-man or a gigolo? she demanded inwardly, savouring the bracing kick of the rich, almost toasty-flavoured wine. He hasn't hurt me, and goddamnit, I can *afford* him!

'Goodness, I'd give real money to scan what's going on in *your* brain right now.'

Jolted from her deliberations, Claudia looked up into Beatrice's green eyes, which were alight with curiosity.

'What on earth were you thinking about?' persisted the doctor, rising swiftly in a flash of lilac and white, then returning to the sofa, with the sherry decanter, almost before Claudia could frame an answer. 'First you looked worried, then you looked grim, then you looked defiant.' The physician topped up both their glasses. 'It

must be something to do with Paul ... Do tell me.'
Placing the decanter within easy reach, she took an
encouraging swig of sherry, then chuckled softly and
knowingly. 'I know it's a cliché ... but you can trust me,
I'm a doctor!'

Claudia found herself smirking at the other woman's
audacity. Her doubts and confusion began to seem
mercifully less weighty.

'You know you said that there was probably nothing
serious wrong with Paul,' she began, still wondering
how to frame the possibility that her mysterious young
lover might be using her. It seemed very important not
to let Beatrice think her a gullible fool. For a reason she
was still a little reluctant to put her finger on and name,
she really wanted the dashing doctor to admire her and
to find her as impressive and sexy and bewitching as she
found Beatrice in return.

'Well, do you think it's possible that there's *nothing*
wrong with him at all?' she went on. 'That he's pulling
the wool over my eyes ... Taking advantage ...' She
paused again, looked around the splendidly appointed
room with its many well-loved treasures. 'After all,
Gerald did leave me fairly well off. And I'm alone. And
Paul is ... well ... You've seen him, for heaven's sake!
He's quite spectacular – and he's obviously very
intelligent.'

Beatrice didn't respond for several moments. Instead,
she sank back a little further into the upholstery, lifted
her glass of sherry before her and seemed to seek an
answer, and perhaps tact, in the amber fluid. For a
strange, illuminating instant, Claudia recalled looking
into her glass of mineral water, back in the kitchen, and
seeking – and finding – her own answers of a sort. Then,
in a vision within a vision, she saw the white coat, the
white cheong-sam and Beatrice's long, shapely legs in
fine black hosiery; and suddenly it seemed more important than ever not to look a fool in her companion's eyes.

When she eventually replied, Beatrice's voice was soft
and challenging.

'Would it be such a disaster if he *was* perfectly well?'

She knows! thought Claudia, feeling hot all of a sudden, but in a strangely welcome way. She knows exactly what I was thinking just now, and she agrees with me! A slow coil of unfolding desire stirred within her, but she could not differentiate whether it was for Paul or for the woman who sat beside her. The most exciting thing was that she couldn't even bring herself to worry which it was.

'Perhaps not,' she said cautiously, watching Beatrice sip her sherry, and feeling her heart race at the way the doctor's long, elegant throat undulated sensuously. 'It would depend on whether he's just a trickster of some kind, or a genuine criminal . . . What do you think? Be honest. Has he really hurt himself, or is it all an act? Is he bona fide . . . or is he . . . is he *bad*?' It sounded melodramatic, but it was difficult to phrase her thoughts again.

'Well, there's nothing faked about the graze on his head,' said Beatrice, still reclining. She recrossed her long, chamois-clad legs, and pointed a sandalled foot as if observing her pedicure. Claudia noticed that her toenails were painted fire red. 'I'm not the world's greatest judge of character sometimes,' Beatrice added, her mouth twisting wryly, 'but he seems sincere enough to me. And anyway, I've got a bit of a fatal weakness for bad boys. There's far more scope with them than there is with the good ones.' She turned and winked, then drank more sherry, with obvious relish.

Claudia laughed. The longer she spent with Beatrice, the more she liked her – in more ways than one. 'I'll give him the benefit of the doubt then.'

'I hope that's not all you're giving him the benefit of,' said Beatrice, giving Claudia a searching look from beneath her long, thick eyelashes.

Claudia was on the point of saying, 'I don't know what you mean', but she realised it was redundant. She did know what Beatrice was angling towards, and she knew that the other woman knew she knew. She gave the doctor the most candid look she could, then said, 'No, actually, it isn't.'

'Hah! I thought so!' cried Beatrice triumphantly. 'I suspected it when we spoke on the phone, and when I saw you together, well, that passionate clinch rather gave things away, you know. I just knew you had to have had him.'

Had him? Claudia supposed that was roughly what had happened, although it was difficult to define exactly who had had whom. It felt like six of one and half a dozen of the other.

'Well, as you say,' she observed quietly, 'he is rather spectacular . . . And I suppose I'm just as susceptible as the next woman.' She made it her turn to top up the sherry copitas, and was unsurprised when Beatrice showed no sign of refusing. She assumed the other woman had walked the short distance through the village from her cottage. 'I wasn't interested for a long time after Gerald's death. In fact, I wasn't sure if I ever would be again . . . But I'm ready now, and I know Gerald would be the last person to expect me to stay a dried-up old widow for the rest of my days.'

'You could never be dried up!' proclaimed Beatrice cheerfully, clicking her glass to Claudia's – and shifting a little closer on the settee as she did so. 'Which is probably why Gerald adored you so . . . He was a special man. The sort of man who could appreciate a special woman.'

'Thanks,' muttered Claudia, confused again, not least by the very tangible sense of a 'history' in the room. Gerald had made no secret of the adventurous sex life he had pursued prior to their marriage, and it was perfectly clear that Beatrice had – at some time – been a part of it. What surprised Claudia was the lack of a sensation of jealousy at the idea. She felt almost elated that she should have so intimate a link with Beatrice. After all, hadn't she found it easy and so very arousing to imagine the doctor erotically embroiled with Paul too?

'Is this the first time you've taken a younger lover?'

Beatrice's question was both matter of fact and teasing, and an arch, worldly quirk of her finely etched eyebrows made Claudia start to laugh again. 'I'm sorry, I'm such a horrifyingly nosy bitch,' apologised the doctor almost immediately, chuckling throatily herself. It was a moment of girlishness, of feminine bonding, but even so, Claudia couldn't suppress a pang of lust at the way Beatrice's uninhibited laughter made her brassière-less breasts quiver beneath her vest.

You're a beautiful bitch too, Doctor Quine, thought Claudia, still slyly looking at the other woman's ripe, lush body. It was amazing how comfortable such feelings were quickly beginning to seem.

'It's all right, Beatrice,' she said, running her finger around the rim of her glass. 'I don't mind. I suppose I started all this myself, really, in the first place.'

Beatrice didn't speak, but her sparkling green eyes begged importunately for secrets.

'Yes, Paul is the first younger man I've been with,' Claudia continued, 'but there haven't really been all that many of any age. I was a bit of a late starter, I suppose.'

'Me too, would you believe it?' Beatrice said with a smile. 'Although I've rather made up for lost time since . . .'

I'll bet you have! thought Claudia, wishing she could be as blatantly inquisitive as her companion.

'There's something uniquely satisfying about making love with someone younger than yourself, isn't there?' said Beatrice musingly, after a few seconds. 'I can still remember my first. Vividly.' Her voice was dreamy, reminiscent and potently promising. Claudia had the distinct impression that her mind had been read yet again.

'You mean in that being older, you feel more in control?' she queried, admitting silently that in her case 'out of control' would have summed her up better. Despite his supposed weakness – maybe even because of it – Paul had effortlessly taken the upper hand on both occasions.

77

'In general terms, I'd say yes to that,' replied Beatrice pensively, 'but for me it didn't quite happen that way. More the reverse, really, at the time . . . Although it *was* what I wanted, so I suppose ultimately I did call the shots.'

Intrigued, mystified, Claudia said, 'Tell me about it,' without even thinking.

'Her name was Cassis,' said Beatrice, her oval face alight with memories.

'*Her* name?'

Beatrice felt the familiar sexual frisson that she invariably experienced when she shocked someone. She had been leading up to the subject of lesbianism quite subtly for her, she thought, and her finely honed instincts about these matters told her that Claudia was almost *à point* already. But the final articulation always retained an impact.

'Oh yes, sorry . . . I never thought,' she said, shrugging lightly and enjoying Claudia's wide-eyed expression. 'Cassis was a girl, of course. I always forget that not everyone . . .' She let the explanation tail off delicately, then schooled her features into a look of concern. 'I haven't upset you, have I? Some people find the idea of same-sex lovemaking repellent, I know.'

'It's all right,' said Claudia, taking a quick sip of her sherry. Beatrice noticed that a flattering blush was creeping up the other woman's throat and face. 'I don't have any prejudices. Please . . . Go on. Cassis is such an unusual name. Is it real?'

Goody! thought Beatrice exultantly. The time was not yet quite ripe to make an overt proposition to this delightful and so promising woman, but at least the path ahead was far from stony.

'Oh, I don't think so,' said Beatrice, thinking back to another promising woman, albeit one of a quite different nature to the warm-hearted Claudia. 'She was a punky sort of girl then, about nineteen or twenty, and she tinted her hair a wild shade of blackcurrant-purple. She worked

78

in a bar, too, and her trademark drink was a truly wicked kir.' Almost immediately, Beatrice imagined she could taste the fruity power of the liqueur crème de cassis, only to have it replaced by the heady flavour of Cassis herself, and the pungent spiciness of her demanding young quim.

'How did you meet?'

How had they met indeed? Beatrice was tempted, for the sake of looking better in Claudia's eyes, to glamorise the sequence of events, but in the end, she decided to be honest. Well, fairly honest.

'I saw her one evening when I slipped into her bar for a drink. I'd had a long, tiring day, making home visits to some fairly high-powered and obnoxious patients, and I really needed to let my hair down and unwind.'

The patients had been mostly older women, blue-rinsed dowagers and carping hypochondriacs, a thoroughly undesirable lot with whom she had been obliged to be strictly professional and tactful. When they were all behind her, she had longed for the company of a very different kind of woman, and made her way to her favourite dyke bar, with her spirits and libido rapidly rising.

'She barely spoke to me that first time,' she said, giving Claudia an almost bashful little look. 'But I was smitten the moment I saw her . . . I felt such a fool. I was thirty-five at the time; successful, prosperous, supposedly assured-looking. And there I was, virtually drooling over a scruffy little nymphet who couldn't be bothered to give me the time of day. I was convinced that she thought I was pathetic.'

And it had been that way for any number of weeks. Beatrice recalled going back to Bar Sappho time after time, trying to play it cool but ending up gawping at Cassis – as she flitted lightly and efficiently around behind the bar – like a starving dog at a particularly succulent chunk of meat. There had been the reward of an occasional cool smile, and a word or two as Beatrice had received her glass of kir, but these had only served to make her hotter and hotter and hotter.

'Then one day, there was a bit of an altercation,' said Beatrice, already thrilling to the memory of what the fracas had led to. 'Some men . . . Yobbos. Lager louts or whatever . . . They came into the bar, very, very drunk, and when they realised what kind of place it was they became abusive. I was just on the point of slipping quietly to the payphone and calling the police when Cassis vaulted over the bar and set about them.' She could still see that slim, elegant body, and the way Cassis had launched herself gymnastically across the room. 'She was magnificent! She threw them out, one and all. Put the fear of God into them, as if she'd been a Russian shot putter four times her size . . . But somewhere in the mêlée, she hurt herself. Sprained her wrist quite badly . . . And it was her right wrist too. Her cocktail-mixing hand . . . Somebody said, "Is there a doctor in the house?", and suddenly I knew all my prayers were answered!'

She had found herself alone with Cassis in a tiny flat above the bar, and the confined space had only made her more and more aware of the girl's slim body, her firm, rounded breasts, and the delicious prize that lay at the apex of those peerless, black fishnet-encased thighs.

'I could smell her sex,' Beatrice heard herself blurt out, expatiating graphic detail long before she had intended to. Beside her, she was vaguely aware of Claudia, open mouthed. But it was too late to hold back now. The power of memory impelled her to storm onward.

'She didn't wear perfume, I realised, and I think it was deliberate. She wanted women to be able to smell her arousal. To want her.' Beatrice took a sip from her newly refilled copita. 'And I certainly did.'

Cassis had been perfectly aware of that desire too, Beatrice recalled. The younger woman had revelled in it, and while at first she had been grateful for Beatrice's medical expertise and her practical assistance, she soon became more and more imperious.

'Get me a drink, Beatrice.' 'Unfasten my boots, Beatrice.' 'Take me to the bathroom.' 'Pull down my tights and knickers. I need to piss . . .'

Recalling Cassis's orders, Beatrice found it hard to believe her own servility. The almost-painful stimulation she had received from subsuming her own will and performing the most menial and intimate tasks for the porcelain-faced, gothic-haired young goddess. She had experienced a piercing quiver of feeling in her own sex when she had passed soft toilet tissue between Cassis's labia to cleanse her. She had almost come herself when the girl had bade her, in a soft but smokily implacable voice, to masturbate her to orgasm.

'Come on, Beatrice . . . You're so clever. So knowledgeable about the workings of the human body. Show me what a brilliant therapist you are. Get your lily-white hand down between my legs and bring me off!'

'My God!'

Claudia's exclamation brought Beatrice back to the present with a sudden jolt – back to the present and a state of high arousal. For a moment, she was tempted to just lean across, press her lips to those of the beautiful widow beside her, and forget the past. She had a mad, singing urge to expunge her memories of Cassis and reach down between Claudia's smooth thighs instead. She had a powerful feeling that the welcome would be equally as humid.

But rare as it was, Beatrice admitted, her own good sense prevailed. The perfect moment would be here quite soon, she was certain of that, but it hadn't arrived quite yet.

'I was enslaved. I couldn't help myself,' she said, returning to her narrative. 'I did exactly as she ordered. And she was so wet. As lush as a hothouse peach . . . She had the juiciest quim of any woman I've ever touched.'

Beatrice could virtually hear Claudia ask the question, even though the other woman didn't speak. How many women have you touched then? She decided not to elucidate, and continued with her tale of what had happened in Cassis's poky bathroom.

'She sat on the toilet seat, and I had to kneel down beside her on the linoleum-covered floor. There was hardly any room, and I was wearing a tightish skirt. It was cold and uncomfortable, and the place was dirty . . . But I was so besotted, and so completely excited, that it was difficult to breath.'

It had been awkward to worship at the shrine of Cassis's womanhood, but she had managed somehow – twisting her arm and hand at an almost impossible angle, and negotiating the limited access that a tangle of pushed-down tights and panties had afforded her.

'More! Harder! That's it! More!' the dark, tyrannical waif had ordered, pumping her hips and making Beatrice's task even harder. Between the violent motion and the extreme slipperiness of Cassis's abundantly lubricated flesh, it had been difficult to maintain pressure and friction on the sweet spots: the girl's plump clitoris and her tender vaginal opening. Beatrice smiled to herself, remembering her initial clumsiness – and Cassis's colourfully expressed scorn – and then how quickly she had established a dextrous rhythm. It wasn't for nothing that she had at one time considered being a surgeon; she had lightning hands, precision instruments of muscle and bone.

'She soon came,' said Beatrice, her calm voice belying the furore she felt within. Between her vivid memories of Cassis and the warm, fragrant presence of the rapt woman beside her, she felt charged with a living field of hot desire. Her breasts were tingling, and between her legs, her silk G-string had ridden up into the sensitive niche between her sex lips. It would take little more than a wriggle or three to make her climax.

Contain yourself, Bea, she told herself sternly. It's still too soon! Much as she was aching to come, dying to ease the building tension, she knew that if she did so there was no way she could hide it. There were women of her acquaintance who could have a monumental orgasm in a public place without a facial muscle even twitching – but Beatrice knew she wasn't like that. She was a groaner, an ecstatic thrasher, a born exhibitionist.

And so she kept still and went on with the story. It was tantalising to wonder how close to coming Claudia was, though.

'One orgasm wasn't enough for that little madam,' continued Beatrice, aware that her voice had wavered slightly on that most significant word. But all those years ago, Cassis's voice had done more than waver. She had shouted as loud as Beatrice herself liked to do; she had yelled, issued commands and cursed and blasphemed as her lean and limber body jumped with rapture.

'Show me your hair, you gorgeous bitch,' the dark girl had ordered, and Beatrice trembled now at how exquisite obedience had been. With a few quick moves, she had released her cape of hair from its temporary confinement in a chignon, aware of Cassis's juices on her fingers as she did so.

In a few seconds there had been yet more of Cassis's essence on her hair. Pulling savagely on Beatrice's scalp, the younger woman had grasped a thick, red tress in her uninjured left hand and jammed it roughly against the vee of her own crotch. With an uncouth sawing action she had employed it to mop her vulva, dragging Beatrice's head back and forth cruelly in the process.

'But why did you let her hurt you? Surely you could have stopped her?'

Claudia's quiet voice sounded new, almost unfamiliar somehow, and Beatrice realised it was virtually the first time her companion had spoken during the narrative.

'But I didn't want to stop her,' said Beatrice, turning to look into Claudia's puzzled brown eyes. 'And the fact that she was hurting me was part of the excitement. A big part of it.' It was clear that whatever sex games Gerald Marwood had played with his spouse during their life together, the two had never progressed as far as erotic sado-masochism. 'Admittedly, it's not usually my scalp I'd choose to be punished ... but it did make an interesting variation.'

'Oh, I see,' said Claudia, fiddling with her sherry glass, a nervous, half-excited, half-appalled smile playing around her lips.

But do you see, Claudia? Beatrice wanted to say. Can you imagine what it's like to want someone you desire, someone you want enough to be melting for, to punish you? To chastise you, either frivolously or with absolute severity, for some totally imaginary transgression? Would you bare your lovely bottom for me – and I know it must be a wonderful one! – and let me spank it? Or beat you with something? A ruler? A hairbrush? A leather strap?

But maybe Claudia wasn't the one who would suffer? Beatrice had a momentary but heart-shaking vision of her new friend poised in the act of bringing a long, thin switch down across the muscular buttocks of the pale, mysterious Paul.

The picture was fleeting but it was almost Beatrice's undoing. She bit her lip and took a deep breath to resist her massing pleasure.

It was a relief, and serendipity, and also, perhaps, a bit of a disappointment, when a sharp but melodious beeping – from the vicinity of her left wrist – suddenly fractured the precarious moment. The pre-set alarm on her elaborate watch was demanding attention ...

Claudia jumped and almost spilt her sherry. Being so absorbed in Beatrice's bizarre tale of the domineering and odiferous Cassis and so eager to hear more, an intersection of the real world, in the form of the doctor's watch alarm, was a shock so keen she felt a physical wrench from it.

'Oh shit! I'm so sorry! I have to go now,' cried Beatrice. Quaffing the last of her sherry, the doctor sprang to her feet and cast about for her battered black bag. When she spotted it, she hesitated for a second, then gave Claudia a swift but passionate hug before retrieving it.

'Look, I really am sorry about this, but I have to see someone shortly. And . . . Well . . .' She glanced down at her becoming but bohemian outfit. 'I can't go dressed like this!' As if galvanised, she strode towards the door, and the hall, and the world beyond Claudia's sitting room, and their magical cocoon of feminine intimacy.

Crestfallen and strangely bereft, even though Beatrice hadn't actually left yet, Claudia followed in the doctor's wake and the trailing aura of her strong and musky perfume.

At the front door, Beatrice said, 'Don't worry too much about Paul. If he has genuinely suffered amnesia, he's young and basically healthy, and the odds are he'll make a full recovery before long.' She paused, giving Claudia a tigerish, conspiratorial grin, then reaching out to gently stroke her face with fingers that felt deliciously cool, yet inflammatory. 'And if there's nothing wrong with him . . . Well then, he's even *more* fit and healthy, and I urge you to make the most of him! I'll be in touch soon about the hospital tests. Probably tomorrow . . . If I sweet-talk one or two people, there should be a window for him in the next few days.' She trailed her hand down Claudia's throat and across her shoulder, and then caressed the full length of her bare arm and gave her hand a squeeze. '*Ciao*, Claudia, it's been wonderful to meet you. We'll get to know each other a little better soon, I hope.'

And with that Doctor Beatrice Quine was on her way, sailing down the path, her Amazon-red plait bouncing against her back to the womanly cadence of her confident, long-limbed walk. As she closed the gate behind her, she looked around, smiled once, then sped off down the lane without another backward glance.

My God! Two seductive strangers in the space of as many days. What's happening to me? Claudia thought, staring towards the spot where Beatrice had disappeared around the bend in Green Giles Lane. The changes that had begun yesterday afternoon, as she had set out on her fateful walk towards the river, were still occurring and growing progressively more radical; and whether she liked it or not, she was putting out a whole new set of signals.

Her heart pounding, she turned and strode towards the conservatory. And Paul.

Chapter Seven

The Patient and his Treatment

With a struggle, Paul managed to remain motionless. He couldn't imagine anything much worse than Claudia discovering that he had been sneaking around spying on her. It was an affront to both her kindness and their intimacy. But after having encountered Doctor Quine, a sense of curiosity had overcome him. He had just had to know what the two women were like when they were alone together.

The examination had been over fairly quickly, and despite her outré appearance, it seemed that Beatrice Quine was a serious and efficient clinician, with a bedside manner that was both unimpeachably professional and almost maternally reassuring. Listening to her low, milk-and-honey voice, and feeling the diagnostic touch of her long, capable fingers, it had been almost possible to forget that she was disturbingly lovely, and that her nipples were clearly visible through her thin white vest. Almost possible, but not quite. The way he had responded to her had made him feel hot and guilty, and more than that, despicably traitorous. Only a few hours ago he had been making love with Claudia.

To take his mind off sex, Paul tried to anchor his attention to Beatrice's assessment of his health, and to her suggestions. The prospect of tests, tests and more tests was certainly cooling to the ardour, the only compensation being that he would not have to face the rigours and the indignity of the National Health Service. Strings would be pulled for him, it seemed, which was marvellous, apart from the fact that he wondered how on earth he could recompense the beneficent Beatrice for pulling them. He already owed such a huge debt of obligation to Claudia.

When the examination was over, he feigned fatigue to allow himself time alone to mull over his predicament, but once Beatrice had left, he found formulating a solution to be an uphill task. His brain felt fogged and intractable; the only subject he could focus clearly on was sex.

He found himself remembering the sensation of pushing into Claudia's welcoming body, that morning in the kitchen, then speculating whether Beatrice would feel as tight and as delicious a fit for him. What would it be like to try first one woman, then the other? Then have the sumptuous pair of them on either side of him, in a wide, double bed?

Dear God, man, what's got into you, for pity's sake? he demanded silently of himself. Why was the flesh all he could think of? Was it because his intellect was currently so sadly deficient?

What's going to happen if I never remember? he thought, sitting up, swinging down his legs on to the floor and observing ruefully that he had an enormous erection. I'll have to be a gigolo, he told himself almost hysterically, letting his hand fall inevitably against his crotch. It seems as if that's all I'm going to be fit for!

Yet despite his qualms, there was comfort, once again, in his arousal. In a world of looming MRI scans, blank expanses where memory should be and faces that were beautiful but completely unfamiliar, it was consoling to touch a known quantity, his rigid manhood. It seemed to be one of the few of his physical and mental processes that hadn't been compromised or changed. Or become unsettling and strange to him.

Impatient with the sense of powerlessness that afflicted him when he was apart from Claudia – and suddenly, from Doctor Beatrice too – he leapt up and paced the conservatory on bare, noiseless feet. His aching groin troubled him, yet he felt restless and unable to simply lie back, relax and stroke himself. His clouded mind was filled with images of the two women he knew were now together, presumably discussing him. He tried to juxtapose them: blonde Claudia with her fine-featured, intriguingly quizzical face and her delicious shaggy-elf haircut; and the dramatic, bravura Beatrice with her fire-red plait and her square-on, challenging look. Both were fabulous, and painfully desirable to him, despite their differences, yet somehow he couldn't put them both in the same frame together. Each was enough to satiate him; in combination, it was an obvious case of overload.

Yet he had to see them. Together.

Every door and every floorboard seemed to creak as he made his way towards where instinct told him the women would be, yet he knew this was just as much his imagination as his fantasies were. His feet were bare, and he wasn't making any noise. When he reached the sitting room, the door there was a little ajar. He could hear Beatrice talking softly from within.

The doctor was telling a story, by the sound of it – a yarn from her past about someone she had been sexually involved with. After a moment, it became apparent that the someone had been a woman.

Yes! thought Paul, exultation pouring through him like a wave as his hopes and suspicions were vindicated. As his shaking fingers slipped to his crotch, he focused on Claudia.

His saviour was sitting still and rapt, a surprisingly chaste distance from the more animated figure of her companion, the raconteuse. Her eyes were brilliant, and her expression shocked, but wondering.

She's not horrified, thought Paul, the revelation exciting him even more. She likes it, he thought, giving his genitals a subtle squeeze.

The doctor's narrative was a hot one, completely explicit, with no punch left unpulled. Paul wondered for a moment whether she was mythologising herself, spinning an exotic line to entrap the woman beside her, yet for all the description's wildness he could well believe it was a record of a true event. He knew Beatrice no better than he knew anybody else at the moment, but instinct told him she lived her sex life on the edge. It also told him that she was deeply in lust with Claudia and planning to seduce her.

But not today, thought Paul, with some regret. It was patently clear that the beautiful doctor was restraining her impulses.

And what did her intended victim think? Was she ready? Did she appreciate Beatrice's self-control, or was she impatient?

He noticed that Claudia was no longer wearing the soft, flattering tan outfit she had been wearing earlier, and he pondered for a second why that might be. She was wearing a zingy pink T-shirt and culottes now, and wishful thinking suggested it was because she and Beatrice had already made love – and fastidiousness had compelled her to shower and change afterwards. But scrambled as Paul's thought processes were, he knew his hopes were an impossibility, because only a few minutes had elapsed since the doctor had left the conservatory. There would have been no time for the two women to strip and entangle, kiss and fondle, sob and writhe and gloriously come.

Don't! Do *not* do this! he told himself desperately, then he gnawed his lip as beneath his fingers his swollen cock tingled. But the damage had been done. As Beatrice's husky voice described the rest of her erotic encounter with the barmaid Cassis, it was another first contact that Paul seemed to see.

The place was the bed upstairs, where he had slept and been pleasured last night; the time was the future, hopefully soon; and the two lovers, coupled and caressing, were Beatrice and Claudia. They were lips upon lips, breast to breast, pubis to pubis; their hands were frantically roaming, their fingers exploring. As he seemed to watch, they fell apart, like the two halves of a tightly fitting shell, only to recombine in a top-to-tail pattern, kissing each other's sex. Their bodies were jerking and convulsing with passion – when suddenly something beeped.

Paul almost staggered, the shock and the sense of dislocation were so great. Subconsciously, he realised the sound was that of an alarm watch, but he didn't stop to either see or hear that confirmed. By the time it was turned off he was sprinting lightly but soundlessly to the haven of the conservatory.

And here he was, a few minutes later, trying to present the impression of a man deep in the sleep of the innocent, while the soft footsteps of the benefactress he had so shamelessly spied on came closer and closer and closer . . .

Paul appeared to be asleep when Claudia stepped into the sun-dappled conservatory. He was lying in the same vulnerable, almost foetal, position as she had found him last night when she had returned from making tea. His feet were bare, his hair was rumpled and his face was seraphic.

He's faking it, thought Claudia, smiling to herself as she approached the old chaise longue. She didn't know how she knew, because her beautiful stranger's face was perfectly tranquil; but the same – possibly imaginary – gut feeling that kept niggling her about his amnesia, or lack of it, now told her Paul was hiding something else from her.

Strangely enough, the idea of his duplicity was exciting. It was as if the game of sexual brinkmanship she had played with Beatrice had inspired her. There was a lot to be said for walking a fine line of danger.

'I know you're awake,' she said, standing over him, feeling extraordinarily empowered.

Paul's eyes flashed open, and he unfurled his long limbs and sat up on the chaise, automatically making room for Claudia to sit down beside him. He didn't say anything or offer any lame excuses; he just looked at her warily, as if waiting for a judgement.

'So, how do you feel?' she asked, enjoying his expression of slight befuddlement when the question wasn't quite what he had expected.

'OK. I think . . .' He stared down at his bare toes, and wiggled them, as if checking his motor skills. 'A bit apprehensive about these tests I have to have. But I suppose it's better to know the worst. I could be sitting here with a time bomb in my head. Fine one minute . . . and the next, "Zap!" Cabbage city.'

He seemed genuinely worried. There was fear in his face, and his body was tense. Despite her suspicions of a moment ago, Claudia placed her hand on his arm and squeezed reassuringly.

'Well, Beatrice didn't seem to think so. I'm sure the tests are just a precaution.' She felt a tremor pass through his body, but couldn't tell whether he was still fearful or her touch had affected him. The feel of his firm flesh through his shirt sleeve was certainly affecting her. 'I was frightened when I lost my memory, but everything turned out all right in the end. I may not be Einstein – ' She grinned encouragingly ' – but I'm certainly not a vegetable!'

'I bet you're delicious though,' he said, turning slightly towards her and looking up slyly through his thick, dark eyelashes. He put his free hand over hers on his arm.

Claudia's heart thumped wildly. He had changed from consternation to seduction in the blink of an eye. She was in peril again and she found it exhilarating. Striving for cool, she returned his glance levelly.

'Do you remember anything yet?' she asked, keeping her voice as unruffled as she was able. 'Any flashes?

Any inkling of who you are? What you do? How old you are?'

Paul gave her his devastating smile in a clear call of 'touché'. 'Not really,' he said, his hand still curved possessively over hers, as if he wasn't prepared to yield his ground entirely, 'and I have *tried* to remember. Honestly.'

'I believe you,' she said, extricating her hand, afraid that the fact that it was she who was trembling now would undermine her. 'It must be more difficult for you than it was for me ... I was just a child. I had less to remember. And children are content just to *be*. They don't consider themselves defined by what their occupation in life is. They're not troubled by a need for "purpose" and "direction" and suchlike.'

'What's *your* purpose in life then?' challenged Paul, his chin coming up.

Bastard! thought Claudia, forced to smile. He was as sharp as a blade. His mental fog clearly didn't extend to his perception of human nature.

'I'm not sure I have one just yet,' she said honestly, experiencing a curious lack of anguish over the statement. A few days ago she had been sunk in futility. 'But something will turn up soon. I can feel it.'

Sitting with this beautiful young man, in a sunlit conservatory, surrounded by greenery and her carefully chosen flowers of blue and white and yellow, Claudia suddenly felt herself to be at a fork in the road. Her urges were divided.

On one hand, she knew that they could spend the rest of the afternoon in a warm, soul-searching conversation; that she could share her worst fears and her most tremulous hopes with him, and that he would understand and help her just as much as she could, and would, help him.

But the other prong of the fork led to an entirely different form of therapy, one she sensed would be just as effective and perhaps less premature than a 'talking cure'. She looked at Paul's long, narrow, square-tipped fingers, his sculpted mouth and the pale but powerful musculature of his bare chest where it was revealed by his open shirt. She looked too at his groin, and saw a growing disturbance beneath the creamy linen of his chinos.

Her direction was already chosen for her. Reaching out, she slid her hand into his curly brown hair, at the nape of his neck, and drew him to her.

Paul's mouth yielded instantly, even though Claudia knew his lips were strong and mobile and that he could probably kiss her into submission with effortless facility. Pressing her advantage, she slid her tongue between his teeth and explored him as slowly as her own impatience would let her. His body remained inert, and his arms were still at his sides, but he made a small surrendering grunt in the depths of his throat.

Yes! thought Claudia, kissing harder – so hard her own jaw almost pained her – and pushing Paul back against the shabby old cushions. She had never felt such a sense of control before in her life – even when she and Gerald had played their light-hearted little bed games, and supposedly she had been 'dominating' him. If only for the moment, this was real power. Paul might have any number of tricks up his sleeve, and be nothing like the misplaced person he had led her to believe him to be, but right now, right here, she knew – in the very pit of her being – that he would do absolutely anything she commanded him to. Hero or villain, he was hers for the taking.

Pulling away, gasping, she put her mouth to his ear and murmured, letting the fire that surged inside her do the talking.

'I'll give you a purpose, Paul. A direction while you're waiting to get your life back.' She kissed his neck, felt a pulse beating crazily, and fought an urge to bite him like some born-again vampire. Drawing back, she held his head in both her hands, then darted forward again, looking intently into his face and almost laughing when his blue eyes fought to focus.

94

There was no need to tell him what the purpose was, or ask him if he wanted to pursue it. The fact that his pupils were huge and black, and his breathing fast and ragged, provided the answer. She kissed him again and his arms rose up around her.

'Touch me, Paul,' she told him, when they broke apart again, both panting after a long and complicated engagement of lips and tongues. 'Make yourself useful to me before I change my mind.'

'Gladly!' he answered, with a low, male chuckle that made her insides flip-flop deliciously. 'Oh so very gladly,' he growled, tugging at her pink top and wrenching it out of the waistband of her culottes. His long, slim hands made perfect cradles for her aching breasts.

'Yes!' she cried, articulating her triumph this time as he squeezed her with exactly the degree of forcefulness her body hungered for. Powerful fingers and thumbs rolled her nipples back and forth between them, and for a second – in between waves of sensation that threatened to precipitate an early climax – she entertained the notion that her lover might be a sculptor, the way he used his hands. Or even a baker, she thought, laughing with delight as he enthusiastically kneaded her. Arching her back, she thrust her bosom towards the treatment, feeling him dip down and roughly kiss her shoulder as an answer. Her laughter turned to moans, expressions of a passion that alarmed her, as he nudged aside the neck of her T-shirt, and applied his mouth to her bare skin with an even greater vigour.

Paul clearly had no qualms at being compared to Nosferatu. He nipped at her throat, again and again, and the imprint of his strong white teeth was sharp and thrilling. As he bit her, he pulled her nipples, and worked and squeezed her.

Claudia had never experienced such an uninhibited and dynamic sexual mauling. In return, feral with her own desire, she raked her nails down his tense, hard back and tore his shirt. Gerald's shirt, she thought detatchedly, and as the fine cotton ripped she imagined her husband's applause at the sheer abandon of her performance.

So close to orgasm already, the ferocious ache between her legs became unbearable. 'Touch me, I said!' she commanded, wrenching Paul's flexing right hand from her breast and dragging it insistently down her body. 'I want it there!' She jammed his fingers between her legs. 'Get on with it! No messing about!'

Clutching her vulva firmly, Paul drew back a little way and gave her a hard, almost angry look. Then he laughed, his long face wild, his lips reddened from kissing and biting her, and began to massage her, at breast and crotch, while glaring, with unalloyed devilment, right into her eyes.

Oh God, what have I done? she thought, both helpless and ecstatic as her body fired and she fought to hold his gaze. She was in orgasm; she was in terror; she was drowning in a sea of brilliant, burning blue. And inside her sex, her muscles clamped in jerks of pleasure.

'Fuck you, Paul! Who the hell are you?' she cried, still climaxing.

'I don't fucking know!' he growled, releasing her genitals then hugging her close to him. 'I don't fucking know,' he repeated, almost sobbing, and rocking both their bodies.

Claudia believed him – for now. It seemed the easiest thing to do while slumped in his arms, with the most intimate parts of her body still trembling exquisitely.

For a while they stayed quite motionless, although the air around them seemed to vibrate in a stunned, shocked silence. Paul was breathing deeply against her, but she sensed a tautness in him, a vortex of emotions he was having difficulty quelling. For her own part, she felt numbed, but in a state of wonderment. Her own actions, and reactions, had quite astounded her. She felt shaken up, but also satisfied and impressed. As Paul's hand began to move gently on her back, she looked over his shoulder, through the glass into the garden beyond. A bird swooped across the lawn, and a butterfly seemed to follow it. In the afternoon sunshine, the familiar scene had never looked lovelier.

Presently, the two of them pulled apart and studied each other ruefully.

'I'm sorry – '

'I'm sorry – '

They both laughed as their apologies coincided. Giving his thigh an encouraging pat, Claudia bade Paul say his piece first.

'I'm sorry,' he reiterated, shrugging his shoulders and sighing. 'I was rough. I got carried away ... I behaved like a pig.'

'*You* behaved like a pig?' Claudia looked at him, so sweet and tempting, and felt the hunger that he had just sated so comprehensively for her begin to stir again. If anybody's behaviour was porcine, it was hers. It was only a few minutes since she had last had an orgasm, and already she was longing to sample another. 'I think it was me whose behaviour was piggish. I was outrageous. I've never said anything like that before. You must think I'm a harpy!'

'I think you're wonderful,' said Paul, his features calm and straightforward, his stunning eyes as pellucid as blue glass.

It wasn't the first time Claudia had heard herself described as 'wonderful', but only with Gerald had she ever felt it had been meant honestly and truly.

Until now.

She could see no guile in Paul's clear gaze, no hint of flattery or hyperbole. For some reason he did think of her as wonderful. And feeling so good, about herself and her body, she tended to agree with him.

So she simply said, 'Thank you.'

'My pleasure,' said Paul, looking down at his own crotch, and grinning. He was hugely erect beneath the cream fabric of his trousers.

'Clearly,' she said, answering his smile with one of her own. He had gratified her needs, but his own tumescence remained unattended. It would be *her* pleasure to rectify

97

that shortfall. Her smile broadened as she laid her hand across his crotch.

Beneath the fine cloth he was firm and fine and lively, and when she gently palpated him, his eyes closed as if the light pressure was too much for him. Claudia was very much aware of her perception of him as an angel again. His pale face glowed like an icon's and his softly curling hair was reminiscent of a score of well-known religious images. Even his bare chest looked both sacred and profane. What she felt for him was so dangerous it scared her.

'Oh!' he gasped, wriggling a little, and for a second Claudia was alarmed that she might have brought matters to a premature conclusion. But his flesh stayed hard, and his smile remained intact.

'Please . . . I want you,' he whispered, his eyes flicking open as he tried to sit up and reach for her.

'Hush!'

Releasing his penis for the time being, Claudia dashed away his hands, then took him by the shoulders and inclined him towards her. Without much dexterity, she unbuttoned the cuffs of his torn white shirt, then slid it off down his arms and over his hands as if she were undressing a little boy, but in a hurry. It fell behind him, in a crumpled mass, forgotten.

Paul's eyes widened when her hands went to his belt, but obeying her unspoken orders, he did not attempt to assist her in undressing him. He merely lifted his bottom when she said 'Hup!' and dragged his trousers and his briefs down to his ankles.

Oh what a lovely, lovely thing, thought Claudia as they both surveyed his cock. It had bounced up vigorously on its release from his clothing and now swayed slightly to and fro above his darkly furred groin as if the weight of its reddened glans was almost too much for it. Claudia licked her lips, unconsciously preparing to fellate him – but the call of her voracious vagina was far too imperious. Fumbling with her own buttons now, she tore off her culottes and peeled off her knickers.

In the second before she took him, she smelt her own juices, and saw the dark and sticky stains on her under-garment, then she was sinking down, riding his rigidity, her heartfelt sigh descending and gusting as her body lowered.

'Oh God!'

'Oh God!'

As their voices played echoes again, she laughed with happiness.

Paul laughed too, and the involuntary movement made his erection lift inside her. She felt completely filled, divinely impaled and almost uncomfortable in the way his bigness stretched her. Flexing her vagina she watched him try and rend the upholstery.

'Oh God!' he cried again, his pelvis bucking. 'You *are* wonderful! Bloody wonderful . . . I – ' His teeth began to chatter as his body leapt and hammered.

No, I'm not . . . I'm a voracious harpy, you silly boy! thought Claudia in the last instant that thought was possible. Then, utilising his sturdy male hardness while it still existed, she almost bounced up and down until she joined him in orgasm. The position was strained and difficult, with her folded legs at awkward angles, but in her world of heat and pressure she barely noticed the creaks and protests in her limbs. There was only a burning, living light that scorched her inner core with rapture – and the writhing angel that struggled beneath her, in her thrall.

It was a little while before she was able to unfurl her cramped legs and lift herself off him. Her knees com-plained a little, and she experienced the sharp stab of a slight pull in one thigh muscle, but apart from that she felt awash with vital energy.

'Dear Lord, just look at me!' she muttered, catching her reflection in the glass a few feet away. Her hair was mussed, her face was glowing, and she was naked from the waist down, with her freshly put-on T-shirt marked and crumpled. Looking down she saw a film of perspiration across her thighs and her pale bare belly, and the tell-tale glint of yet more moisture in her pubis.

What a fright, she thought, but somehow her own lewd and dishevelled appearance gee-ed her up even more. She felt fit, young and daring. Beatrice Quine would be proud her!

More than proud, a subversive voice inside her announced. She would want you, Claudia. With you looking like this, the good doctor would fall down on her elegant knees and kiss the same damn place that Paul has just shafted!

It was an outrageous idea, but the face in the glass smiled at the thought of it. Claudia put her hand to her mouth, which her muscular encounter with Paul had bruised a little, and imagined Beatrice's lips there, kissing her better. She smiled some more.

A sound halfway between a groan and a contented sigh refocused her attention. Paul was slumped at an angle, just as she had left him, like a beached merman who had been ravaged by a warrior princess. His shirt was a crushed rag beneath him, and his trousers and briefs were still around his ankles; he looked as indecent as Claudia felt, but equally as blissful.

No harm done, obviously, Claudia reflected, quashing the little twist of suspicion that reared its head. Should a man suffering from shock and concussion really be able to perform as such a wonderful lover? Who could say?

Who even cares! the echo of Beatrice Quine proclaimed merrily, and right now, with her quim still singing, Claudia agreed with her.

Paul moaned again, smiling in some sort of semi-somnolent daze, and stretched slightly, wriggling his bottom against the chaise. He had to be aware of his rude state of display, Claudia was convinced of it, yet he seemed to glory in showing her his penis. Not that she minded admiring the flaccid but still entrancing organ, recalling the feel of it, full and rampant, deep inside her. As if it had heard her, the fleshly length stirred, like a sleepy, blushing serpent.

'Slut!' Claudia muttered cheerfully, reaching for her knickers and culottes. She wasn't quite sure who she was talking to – herself or her beautiful, exhibitionist lover – but that was another thing she was too replete to bother about.

As she zipped up, then stepped back into her footwear, two disparate bodily sensations impinged on her awareness. She was ragingly thirsty and she had a strong desire to urinate. Giving the still drowsing Paul a lingering last glance, she left the conservatory.

Her bladder satisfied, and refreshed by a quick wash, clean knickers and a spritz of perfume, Claudia almost floated back down the stairs towards the kitchen. There was much to be said for the services of a younger man – even when one did most of the sexual work oneself! – and the more she had of Paul, the younger and younger she felt. Beatrice was quite correct. What did it matter if he *was* a gigolo?

He'll probably want tea, she thought, eyeing the china pot and cups set out ready on the tray. She was already lifting the kettle to fill it when she realised that what she wanted herself was something far more frosty.

'Well, nuts to you, Paul Whoever-you-are!' she proclaimed defiantly, and opened the refrigerator. 'Why should I indulge you every time? Isn't it enough that you get my gorgeous body?' Within a minute or two she was putting the finishing touches to a tall jug of St Clement's, dropping in ice and freshly sliced orange and lemon.

'I thought you might like a change from tea,' she announced, nudging open the house door and stepping into the conservatory.

But when she lifted her eyes from the tray, she nearly dropped it: highball glasses, Waterford jug, the lot. The patio doors to the garden stood open in mute testament, and both the sleeping Paul and his tangled clothing were gone.

Chapter Eight
Progressive Therapy

*B*lank panic flooded Claudia's system, coupled with a disappointment so bitter she could barely absorb it. She had known this might happen, that he might fly the coop as suddenly as he had arrived in it, but even so, the actuality of it cut her deeply. She felt betrayed and very angry; foolishly used.

And then rationality clicked in, bringing concern and some serious guilt with it.

Even the most heinous of villains wouldn't go on the run in a torn shirt and bare feet. The pair of trainers Paul had been wearing earlier were still lying abandoned, kicked on to their sides, beneath the chaise, and if he had sought out other footwear she would have heard him ascend the stairs. Which meant that if he really was gone, he must have suffered a relapse of some kind and wandered off, in a fugue, lost and disorientated. Setting down her tray with a dangerous wallop, she shot out into the garden.

Her sense of relief, however, when she saw Paul at the far end of the lawn, crouched down and studying the plants in her herbaceous border, was so strong that she almost felt angry with herself. It was ridiculous to have become so attached to him, so soon, regardless of how beautiful his body was and how marvellously he used it. To become obsessed was dangerous; she couldn't build her life around him.

'Are you all right?' she enquired lightly, as she got near to him, determined not to show how alarmed she had been just a second ago.

'I'm fine . . . Thanks,' said Paul, straightening up and turning towards her, his smile glowing yet almost boyishly bashful. 'Are *you*?' he added, the modesty gaining a subtle, impish edge.

'I think so.' She met his eyes and stood for a few seconds, hands on hips, surveying him challengingly. It wasn't antipathy she felt towards him at that moment, and the vibes she received from him weren't exactly defiant, but there was a kind of clash, and it was deliciously exciting.

'I've made us a cool drink,' she said, turning towards the conservatory, conscious of him watching her closely. 'Not tea, I'm afraid. I fancied a bit of a change.' As she led the way inside, she could hear him following, his tread near silent as his bare feet kissed the grass.

'That looks splendid,' Paul said, as they stood over the tray bearing the St Clement's jug, glasses and a couple of dishes of cocktail nibbles she had added. Lunch seemed an aeon ago, and she had suddenly felt hungry.

'But could we drink it over there?' he asked, nodding towards the white-painted wrought-iron garden chairs and table, which stood at the far end of the garden, on the other side of the path to where Paul had been admiring the borders. As if she had already answered him, he took command of the laden tray.

'Of course,' replied Claudia, obscurely irritated that Paul was suddenly directing the situation again. For someone taken in on charity, he had a remarkable knack of getting his own way.

But when they were seated, and she was being mother with the iced and fruity mixture, she had to admit that they were in the right place to enjoy it. The afternoon was well worn on by now, and though the sun still shone, it was low and mellow, and the air was balmy.

'Delicious!' said Paul, his eyes closing with pleasure as he sipped his drink through one of the straws that Claudia had stuck whimsically into their glasses. They were striped and seemed to express her sudden mood of out-of-time holiday.

She made no comment but watched him for a while as he took long, almost greedy pulls of the St Clement's, and in between raised his long, pale face towards the dying sun. He looked more content, by far, than a man in his overall situation had a right to, but despite the implications, that made Claudia happy too. She decided not to question, for now.

'I saw a squirrel while you were inside,' said Paul, after a little while. He put aside his glass, sat up and gestured towards one of the beech trees at the end of the garden. 'It just ambled across the grass as if it owned the place, then suddenly took off and scooted up that tree.'

'Yes, we get a lot of them. It's the proximity of the woods.'

'We?' queried Paul, his blue gaze focusing quickly on her face.

'Force of habit,' said Claudia, putting down her glass, wondering whether to top it up, but feeling just too lazy to bother.

'Do you think of him all the time?' asked Paul, picking up his glass again and fiddling with the straw. 'You must miss him.'

'I don't . . . and I do,' she answered. 'That is, I don't think of him all the time. Not any longer.' And especially not now! she thought. 'But I do still miss him. We had a good life together. He was a fair bit older than me, but it didn't make any difference that counted. If you know what I mean?' She slanted him a sideways glance, as she reached forward and finally topped up her glass.

'Yes, I think I do,' he said rather smoothly, holding out his own glass to be refilled.

Cocky little bastard! thought Claudia, although she still felt compelled to laugh. He thinks that's why I was so eager to sleep with him – because I was missing the regular sex I had with Gerald.

Their eyes met and Claudia tipped her glass to him. 'And for your information, Mister Mystery, I was *not* dying of frustration until you arrived. I haven't really needed . . . needed "it"!'

Paul raised his eyebrows, grinned, then took a sip of his drink, his mobile lips pursed almost suggestively around the straw. 'Oh, so it's just me you did it for,' he observed, after a long, pensive drink, 'as a kind of progressive therapy for my amnesia.'

'Cheeky tyke!' she said, debating whether he deserved a glass of St Clement's down his front. It really wasn't his fault, though. She knew her own leading remark had started this.

'I'm sorry,' said Paul, putting down his glass and twisting in his chair to look at her. 'I'm being flippant and stupid. And really, neither of our situations are anything to be flippant about.' His expression grew grave, and with that, almost poetically beautiful. Claudia felt her insides quiver. 'You must have been very lonely.'

Though she wanted him, she sensed he was being serious, and she knew exactly what he must be feeling. His own loneliness was different, but just as affecting as hers.

'It hasn't been so bad. I've got friends.'

'Like Melody and Beatrice?' He gave her a look that was superficially innocent and perfectly bland, yet in the blue depths of his eyes something else stirred.

Claudia returned his look, then glanced quickly around her. The idyllic summer's afternoon scene appeared exactly the same, and the heady garden scents were just as delightful as they had been a moment ago, but she sensed another lightning change in the colour of the mood between them. The pendulum was swinging towards sex again, as it had inevitably seemed to do in the less than twenty-four hours they had been acquainted.

'Melody is the only one I'd really call a friend,' she

said, wondering where it was that their conversation might lead. 'I've known her years. Since she was a girl. We've become really close.' She paused slightly, catching another flash of increased interest in Paul's expression. 'But as for Beatrice, I hardly know her. I only really spoke to her for the first time at Gerald's funeral. She was his friend, really, not mine.'

'Oh, I see.'

Did he? Claudia thought that quite probably he did. She decided to be provocative. Two could play at his game, and she had a sudden, acute inkling of where he had been leading with his specific mention of Melody and Beatrice. The demon! It was as if he had read the very thoughts she had been entertaining earlier when the sultry doctor had first stepped over the threshold!

'What do you think of Beatrice then?' she asked, trying to sound diffident. 'I should imagine she has quite a bedside manner.'

'She's very impressive,' was Paul's evasive reply. 'What do *you* think of her?'

Claudia tried to frame an equally unrevealing response, but as she did so, Paul took a drink from his glass, and from its cold surface a droplet of condensation fell on to the smooth plain of his uncovered chest. Mesmerised, she watched the tiny spheroid begin to trickle slowly downward, over his pale midriff in the direction of his waistband. In her imagination his clothing disappeared all of a sudden, and the drop of water continued its progress, running down across his belly until it reached his pubis.

'The same. You've summed her up perfectly. She *is* impressive.'

'Is that all?'

'She's compassionate. Knowledgeable. Wonderful at her job, I suspect.'

Is that all?

He didn't say it again, but nevertheless Claudia seemed to hear the words.

'She's beautiful. Very sensual. Very bold. She's got a

106

fabulous body and she wants everyone to know it.' She saw the lights in Paul's eyes leap and flare. 'She seems so young, but I know she's several years older than I am.'

Paul laughed lightly. 'How old are you, anyway?' he asked, with an admirable lack of the usual embarrassing toing and froing that some men indulged in when trying to discover a mature woman's age.

Claudia considered lying. She had no idea how old Paul was himself, but she estimated him to be a good ten years younger than she was, at least. 'Forty-two,' she said, after a pause.

'Really?'

He sounded genuine. Was it a line? she wondered. She waited for him to say words to the effect that she didn't look 42 but he didn't.

You're too clever for that, aren't you? she thought, watching him drink again, his mouth snug around the straw, his throat undulating. Further protestation would have been too unsubtle.

'I'm surprised at you saying Beatrice isn't your friend,' he said, after his swallow. 'You looked as if you knew each other well. As if you confided in each other. I could imagine you being very close indeed.'

Claudia's nerves prickled. He was at it again; implying, suggesting. And how –

'I don't know what you're talking about,' she rounded on him. 'You only saw us together for a few moments.' A vague memory came to her as she spoke; something she realised she had either barely registered, or perhaps even suppressed. A moving shadow that she had espied, out of the corner of her eye, as she had been seeing Beatrice Quine to the door.

'It only takes a few moments,' he said, as cool as could be. There might have been a tiny flash of discomfiture in his expression, but Claudia had to admire his self-control. He was clearly going to bluff his way through any suggestions, spoken or otherwise, that he might have eavesdropped on her conversation with Beatrice.

She decided to call his bluff – but not on the issue of being spied upon.

'Perhaps you're right,' she said, picking up her own drink, drawing a meaningless pattern on the side of the tall glass, then setting it down again, untasted. 'I do feel close to Beatrice, in a way. It's a sort of instant thing. An immediate attraction. If she were a man, it would almost be love at first sight.'

There! Try that! Is that what you wanted? she challenged him, silently.

'Love?' He whistled softly. 'As much as that?'

'Well, perhaps not quite – '

'Affection?'

He was still playing. Still sitting there, toying with her, tempting her; both flirt and victim in one breathtaking package. She watched him put his glass down and regard her very evenly. For an instant she imagined him in an invisible pair of sunglasses. His expression was camouflaged somehow, as if there were a veil over his eyes' intense blueness, not dimming them but rendering them unreadable.

Suddenly, Claudia wanted the game to be over. It was less than an hour since he had been inside her, when she had ridden him on the chaise in the conservatory, but to her great astonishment she already wanted him again. And yet she didn't seem to possess the same momentum she had then. In a way she couldn't quite fathom, Paul had taken control of their unspoken interactions. It was up to him to call the shots this time; it was up to him to either seduce or to command.

'I think the word that you're looking for is lust,' she said, her voice almost a whisper. Hating herself for her own wimpishness, she hoped she hadn't overstepped the mark.

'I hoped it might be.'

When Paul stood up, unfolding his slender frame from the garden chair, Claudia realised she had been holding her breath. She drew in air, with relief, as he reached out and took her hand. 'Tell me all about it,' he said, drawing her up out of her own chair and leading her quite quickly towards the door into the house. 'Tell me about this "instant thing" you have for Beatrice . . .'

And so she did tell him.

As he almost dragged her up the stairs, his narrow fingers tight around hers, she told him of the subversive thoughts that Beatrice's dark nipples had inspired when she had first seen them through the doctor's thin white vest.

'They looked so firm . . . so tempting,' she said, as Paul pushed open the door to the guest room – to *his* room – and drew her inside. 'Like little ripe fruits. I wanted to suck them and bite them.'

'Go on! Tell me more!' he urged, raising her arms above her head and almost manhandling her out of her T-shirt.

'I wanted her to take all her clothes off, so I could see what she looks like naked.' She giggled. 'And to see if her hair's natural, or whether she dyes it!' She sighed with pleasure as Paul gently caressed her own nipples, touching them as delicately as if they were precious fruits too.

'I wanted to kiss her all over. To smell her, and to lick her,' she went on, extemporising wildly and feeling both proud and shocked over it, while Paul proceeded to relieve her of her footwear, her culottes and her panties. Standing back, he left her naked in the illuminating glare of the still-bright early evening sun.

For a moment, Claudia wanted to hide herself. This was much more of a revelation than last night, or on either occasion today. There was no protecting darkness now, nor a partial clothing to alleviate her fears and appease her modesty. He could see all of her now: every curve; every bump; every dent. Every niggling physical feature she felt that the years had been less than kind to; all the imperfections his own perfection rendered prominent.

'Oh God!' he cried rawly, dragging off his own clothes. 'Tell me more!' he begged, throwing aside the bedding, then rambunctiously tumbling her backward on to the mattress.

So she told him more. She made up bawdy stories of a kind that would never have occurred to her before, and recounted them to him as they rolled and squirmed and rutted.

By the time they had finished, her mind was fuzzed, confused and drifting. But her flesh was replete, and her drowsing spirit was drenched in bliss.

'The one thing that Beatrice can't provide you with,' murmured Paul sleepily, as Claudia stirred, and the back of her hand brushed against his subsiding penis.

'True,' said Claudia, amused that even he, her unique and illusive stranger, was prone to the same phallocentric notions as the most common of men. 'But I'm sure she could match a man in any other way. She strikes me as a woman who knows all there is to know about sex and eroticism.'

'Yeah, that's the impression I got too,' said Paul, his hand moving slowly, almost soothingly, on Claudia's flank, in an action that was more companionable than amatory.

'Why, did she make a pass at you?'

'No. Sadly not,' Paul replied, stretching his long body. They were both still uncovered, but the light had grown dim. Claudia wished she could see him a little better. 'It's probably unethical or something.'

'Probably . . .' Claudia sat up, turned to face him, and touched his cheek to make him look straight at her. 'Would you have succumbed, though, if she had done?' His long dark lashes fluttered bashfully. 'It's all right,' she continued, watching him blush. 'I won't say I wouldn't have been jealous. But it's not as if you and I have sworn eternal fidelity or anything, is it?' She paused, as a rather breath-catching concept occurred to her. 'You might actually be committing adultery by being with me, you know. What if you're married?'

'I suppose I could be,' he observed, frowning, then turning his face to kiss Claudia's palm, 'but if I do have a wife, I have absolutely no recollection of her.' He kissed her again, and again, his lips moving up to taste the inside of her wrist. 'About Beatrice,' he said, causing Claudia to grin at the blatant change of direction. 'All those things you just told me. Did you mean them? Would you really have sex with her? I'm not saying I wouldn't be jealous, if you did . . .' He looked up, smirking against the skin of her forearm. 'I'd just want you to promise you'd let me watch you!'

'Bastard!' she chided, with genuine affection. 'You men are all the same where two women are concerned.'

'Well, at least that's something about me that's normal,' said Paul cheerfully. He kissed her right in the crook of her elbow, parting his lips to lay his tongue against the vein there. 'You still haven't told me about you and Beatrice, though. Whether you really meant it, or whether it was just some sexy bullshit to turn me on.'

'It was both,' she said, squirming slightly as he threatened to bite her. 'Although for some inexplicable reason, I've never considered other women sexually alluring until now. It must be something *you've* done.' She took him lightly by the hair, and made him meet her eyes again. 'I never fancied a woman until I met you.'

Paul gave her a look of mock affront.

'You know what I mean,' she said, drawing him to her and kissing his lips.

'And what about Melody?' he enquired, when they had separated and he had pulled her companionably into his arms. 'Would you consider her as a lover? It's obvious that she adores you.'

'I beg your pardon!'

The idea seemed preposterous; obscene almost. Her feelings towards Melody had never been anything other than purely affectionate and supportive. She had looked upon the younger woman almost as a daughter, or a much younger sister. The comfort they had given each other had always been purely platonic. It had never occurred to Claudia that it could be anything else.

And yet . . .

111

Melody was beautiful: even now, forced as she had been into a mould of her husband's making. The hard, glossily groomed look that he preferred for her was all wrong for the delicacy of her features, for her youth and her dreaminess. Claudia could remember another Melody. A lovely naiad-like girl with soft, dark hair that had a hint of a wave, and a face that was exquisite without the need for any make-up. There had been – and still was – a youthful vulnerability about Melody that spoke strongly to Claudia, the grown-up.

My God! she thought suddenly, looking at Paul, who was still waiting for an answer, his blue eyes huge and wicked with speculation. It's the same thing with him! The same spark that attracts me. The same quality of helplessness combined with strength. They could almost be siblings, and I *do* want the pair of them . . . I do!

'I'm right, aren't I? You do want her,' persisted Paul, moving against her with an erection that was already renewed and lively.

Claudia turned away, momentarily nonplussed. It was embarrassing, almost terrifying, to be read so easily – and yet it excited her. It also seemed strangely apposite. Melody, too, had the same knack of sometimes knowing what others were thinking – or at least what Claudia herself was thinking.

'In a way,' she conceded, 'although it had never occurred to me until this moment. We've been friends and confidantes for years, despite the age difference. But there's never been any sexual attraction before.'

'Maybe you just didn't recognise it as such,' said Paul, assuming an air of sagacity that Claudia found extremely sexy. 'Although judging by the way she looks at you, she's known about it a *long* time.'

'How come you're suddenly such an expert on personal interactions and relationships?' demanded Claudia, reaching down to take him in hand.

Paul moaned softly and bumped his hips to push his flesh into her grip. 'God knows!' he said, through gritted teeth, still squirming. 'Instinct or something. I seem to know all sorts of things, but not any of the facts that would really be most use to me. Like my name. Who I am. Where I come from.'

Claudia made as if to pull back. The moment might be spoilt now.

But Paul would not allow her to release him. He folded his fingers around hers and continued to rock.

'I'll tell you something else, too,' he said, his face twisting and contorting as his pleasure clearly mounted and his cock seemed to expand inside her hand. 'Melody's unhappy . . . Very unhappy. And if you made love to her it might distract her from her problems.'

'How in the hell do you know that?' Claudia demanded, still caressing him, and at the same time wondering how on earth he could carry on an analytical conversation – about someone else! – when he was being stimulated and well on his way to orgasm. Even she was having serious trouble concentrating on both Paul's stiff penis and the unsatisfactory nature of Melody's marriage. Either one was worth the whole of her attention.

'I just know!' he gasped. 'I can tell . . . It's in her eyes.'

Which was true, although how Paul had found time to observe this in just a few minutes acquaintance was quite remarkable; almost uncanny. The depth of his perception was amazing, especially for one in the midst of such a trauma of his own. There was so much to him, and every moment revealed yet more.

But I can't go on like this right now, thought Claudia suddenly. Her body was screamingly alive and turned on. She was wet and swollen, and ready for her lover. There would be other opportunities, later, to discuss Melody.

'Can we talk about Mel later?' she said softly, rolling on to her back, releasing his penis, and using both her hands to urge and guide him towards her.

'Yes . . . Yes, of course,' said Paul, his voice faltering a little as he poised himself between her thighs. She felt the silky head of his manhood butt against her, homing in, with blind accuracy, as if it were a key seeking a lock it had opened for years. 'Forgive me ... I'm with *you* now.' He swivelled his hips and pushed, and 'with' became 'in' in one long glide. 'This is the wrong time to be discussing another woman!'

'I'll forgive you,' panted Claudia, wrapping her arms and legs around him.

It was a long time before either of them spoke a word.

The trill of the telephone woke Claudia from her slumber, and it took her several moments to remember exactly where she was.

Looking about her, she saw the familiar accoutrements of her sunlit cream and oak bedroom, and wondered for a moment why on earth she wasn't elsewhere. It didn't seem natural, somehow, to be here, in her own four poster, surrounded by pale lace and fine fabrics and the accumulated collectibles of her marriage to Gerald. A plainer milieu was much more what she had expected – specifically that of the guest room, with its blue decor and far simpler furnishings. And its neat divan bed, currently inhabited by Paul.

The phone continued to protest, and cursing herself for not switching on the answering machine, Claudia reached out for the bedside extension, then muttered 'Yes?'

'Hello? Claudia? It's Beatrice!' the doctor said, her voice as bright and crisp as the fine morning outside. 'I hope I didn't disturb anything,' she went on, not laughing but sounding as if she might like to.

'No. Not at all. It's just that I think I've slept in a bit,' said Claudia, sitting up and rubbing her face and then her hair with her free hand. Yes, what the devil time was it? she wondered. The sun was already climbing high in the summer blue sky.

Beatrice made a resonant 'hmmm' sound which seemed to say 'Pull the other one!' then continued, 'Well, it'll probably have done you a power of good!'

'If you say so,' replied Claudia, then, realising how ungracious she sounded, she said, 'Sorry, I think I'm still half doped . . . Is there some news about Paul's hospital appointment?'

'Yes! Excellent news!' said Beatrice. 'I've managed to get them to fit him in this afternoon – if that suits the two of you, of course.'

'Oh yes, that'll be absolutely fine. It's very kind of you to go to all this trouble,' Claudia said, all the time wishing – and feeling guilty about it – that she and Paul could be left to their own devices just a little bit longer. It was only a matter of time before he remembered, then left her.

'No trouble at all. I'm happy to help,' Beatrice assured her, and Claudia had the feeling that the woman really meant it. For all her outrageousness and devilish sexual reputation, Doctor Quine was thoroughly caring and genuinely kind.

The appointment was for 2.30pm at the Ainsley Trust Private Hospital, which Claudia had never visited but had heard various friends speak of in highly glowing terms. She had a general idea where it was and, with Beatrice's instructions, had no doubt she could find it fairly easily. The doctor would meet the two of them, in reception, at 2.15.

'And tell Paul not to worry,' she exhorted Claudia, her tone gentle and reassuring. 'David Colville's brilliant. He's the best man in his field, but I doubt if he'll find anything ominous. I'm convinced that it's just a matter of time.'

Time, thought Claudia, after Beatrice had rung off. That little matter of time. How much of it *I* have . . . There may not be much, so I'd better not waste any.

But had she wasted last night, perhaps? She and Paul hadn't slept together, mainly because by the time they had finished making love, bathed, then eaten a scratch meal together, both dressed in bathrobes, it had become apparent that Paul was exhausted. His eyes had appeared heavy and slightly smudgy, and once or twice he had rather shamefacedly smothered a yawn. He had made no demur when she had shuffled him off to bed, and no demand that she join him when he got there. It had been both a great relief and a bit of a disappointment.

But we could still have just slept together, she thought, checking the time, then letting out a gasp of dismay. If they were going to make the appointment, they were going to have to get moving.

Deciding to get ready herself first, and then concentrate her efforts on Paul, she quickly chose some clothing, then began a swift but careful toilette, acutely conscious of the fact that she wanted to impress Beatrice, as well as look her best – and youngest! – for her lover.

She couldn't stop thinking that she should have spent the night with him. A warm body in her bed was something she had missed a lot since Gerald's death. For comfort. For reassurance, when the occasional nightmare woke her in panic. Just for sheer, animal contentment.

But it wouldn't have stopped at that, would it? she demanded, setting down her comb, as she had been flicking her short, amenable hair into its most flattering arrangement. She studied her hands as if she had never seen them before. These hands were voracious and unstoppable when placed in proximity with Paul's body, and if she had shared his bed, she would have found herself touching him in the night. She would have woken him, made demands on him, coaxed him into satisfying her when he sorely needed to sleep uninterrupted.

Better to have left well alone, she thought, squashing selfish regret as she stood up, then studied her reflection in the Victorian cheval-glass which had been one of Gerald's many lavish wedding gifts.

Not bad! she decided, liking the cream and navy button-through dress she had put on after a good deal of thought. It was sleeveless, mid-calf length, and nominally modest, but the implied access of the long line of square navy buttons seemed vaguely suggestive. Not enough to be tarty; just promising. Strappy sandals – not high but curvily constructed – only added to the provocative impression.

116

Idiot! she told herself. What are you expecting out of this? You're going to a hospital, chaperoning a sick friend who's having tests, not to a discreet hotel for an *après-lunch* liaison.

Even so, it boosted her confidence to look as if the liaison was an option. Smoothing down her skirt, she gave her image a rakish wink.

Chapter Nine
Classic Recollections

'What's the matter?' asked Claudia anxiously as she turned around and found that Paul had stopped dead. He was rooted to the spot, staring intently at the car – which she had backed out of the garage, while waiting for him – with a look of half anguish, half hope upon his face.

'What is it, Paul?' Claudia persisted, laying her hand on his arm when he still didn't move. There had to be something; something either very wrong or perhaps even very right. Gerald's lovely old classic Mark II Jaguar often induced gasps of admiration, and even envy, but it had never before struck anyone to silence.

'Paul!' She gave him a little shake when she felt him start to tremble. 'Tell me what it is! You're scaring me!'

When he turned to her, his eyes were huge. 'I once had a car like this,' he said, his voice just a breath as he stepped forward, unconsciously shaking off her grip, and laid his fingers on the Jag's smooth, steely paintwork.

He can't be faking this, thought Claudia, her heart twisting at the strange, stricken look on her companion's face. He was caught in an intense inner struggle, as if the memories were being physically wrenched from his grey matter. He was fighting hard, and he had never looked more beautiful.

'It was a wreck. Almost a write-off . . . But I'm sure it was this model, and this colour.' He drew his hand across the car's bonnet as if caressing it.

'That's good. You're remembering something. It could be very important,' said Claudia, moving to stand beside him, next to the driver's door. 'Does it bring back anything else? By association?'

Paul drifted away again, still trailing his hand over the bodywork, then examining the leaping beast, the Jaguar insignia, with his fingertips. After a moment, he walked around to the passenger door, then unfastened it, and bent to look inside the car. When he climbed inside, Claudia opened her own door, tossed her shoulder bag into the back seat, and slid in beside him. She wanted to prompt him afresh, but knew the moment was highly delicate. He was frowning again as he scanned the walnut dashboard.

'Yes . . . Yes, it does,' he said belatedly, still studying the clocks, the indicators and the radio. 'Sort of . . .' He turned to her. 'But it's difficult. Far away. Sort of muddy.'

'Don't force it,' she said, touching him again, and realising it was getting very difficult *not* to touch him. They were so close, in the car; it made her blood race. 'Be patient.' Oh yes, Claudia, do try! She drew her hand back, almost as if she had burnt it. 'Look, if you feel a bit shaken up, we can cancel this. I'm sure Beatrice and this specialist or whatever will understand.'

'No, it's all right,' said Paul in reply, turning to her, his face suddenly calm, almost beatific. 'I feel fine. I think I'm beginning to remember a little more . . . It's . . . It's sort of clearing up somehow.' He frowned again, but it was rueful, even a little amused. 'But whatever it is, I don't think it's anything very recent. It feels more like a memory of a memory, if you know what I mean?' He grinned – his perfect, angelic, boyish grin – and Claudia grabbed the steering wheel, rather quickly, to restrain herself.

'Yes, I suppose I do,' she said, with no real notion of

what she was talking about. 'Sort of . . .' The enclosed, leather-scented space was having a wild and alarming effect on her; concentrating Paul's magic into an aura that packed the punch of a rare, vintage brandy. Was she deluded to think she could concentrate on her driving?

'We'd better be off,' she said briskly, when Paul seemed to be making no move to fasten his seatbelt. He was just sitting beside her, glancing around the interior of the car, as if reorienting himself into a bit of his past he could now remember. He touched the dashboard, the leather seat at his side, even the evocatively shaped gear lever, then simply sat back, his attention obviously inward.

It would have been so much easier to concentrate and be objective about the journey and the events ahead if he didn't look quite so wonderful, reflected Claudia, feeling perplexed. From the selection of Gerald's clothing at his disposal, Paul seemed to have deliberately chosen the outfit most stunning and most flattering to him: a loose, creamy-coloured summer suit – which her late husband had worn but once, protesting that this was one purchase that really *was* too young for him – teamed with a white silk collarless shirt and a pair of beige leather loafers. With his wild hair, intense eyes and pale complexion, he looked like some later-day, almost 'designer' messiah. Claudia felt ashamed of how weak and irresponsible his beauty made her; she wanted to go to bed with him immediately and hang the hospital!

'Paul!' she prompted, then took action when he looked at her rather vaguely. Reaching over, she tugged out the seatbelt and drew it across him, her fingers shaking and making her fumble with the buckle. Her hands were far too near to his cream-clad groin for sense or comfort.

'Sorry,' he said, as she started the car, and with a smoothness and competence that astonished her, pulled out of the drive and into the lane, heading north towards Oxford and its environs.

'I was miles away,' he continued, still glancing around the interior of the car. 'I think – '

'Are you remembering more?'

'Yes. But it's in very specific bits. Mostly to do with this car ... or my car ... and things that happened in connection with it.' Without asking, he flipped open the glove box, as if searching for clues within it. The folded maps it contained, however, were clearly unrevealing. 'This car is beautifully kept,' he said, then smiled wistfully as if some fond memory had just come to him. 'The one I remember is, or was, a disgusting heap of scrap by comparison.'

'You probably had it when you were quite young, then. When you were hard up, perhaps?' It seemed logical.

'I think so,' said Paul, closing his eyes and fingering his temple just beneath the fast-healing graze.

Cruising the car along an open stretch of road now, with no traffic to speak of in front of or behind them, Claudia allowed herself to picture him younger. Much younger than he was now, in his late teens, perhaps, or early twenties. Would he have looked even more handsome? Or did the addition of just a few years add more distinction? Either way, she knew he would have been startling.

Against her will, she pictured the young Paul with a woman. A girl. She would be pretty and faultless and fresh; slim as a whip, yet sexy, with a streaming mass of wild dark curls. In bed, she would strain against Paul, her perfect body responding to his with all the life and pure energy of her youth. And he would thrust into her, yelling with pleasure, putting her through hoop after hoop of strenuous copulation, in the way that only the very young had the stamina for.

'Claudia! You're going a bit fast!'

Paul's voice, not sharp, but audibly concerned, shattered the image of thrashing limbs, and lithe, pumping bodies. Experiencing a jolt of visceral fear, Claudia concentrated hard and slowed the car.

'Sorry,' she said, focusing on her task. 'I was trying to make good time. I thought we could call somewhere for a bite of lunch. I know a nice place not too far from the hospital. I thought it might take your mind off the tests and whatever.'

It had been a vague thought in the back of her mind, but now it seemed eminently sensible. A bite to eat, with some good coffee, perhaps? Anything to keep the excesses of her imagination in check.

Paul made a thoughtful little sound, then said, 'Yes. Why not? That's a great idea.' He paused for a moment, and she saw him smooth his fingers rather edgily along the side seam of his trousers. 'And you never know, we might meet someone who knows me.'

And won't that be interesting? said the subversive voice of Claudia's lingering suspicions. As time went by, she was becoming more and more sure that everything he was telling her about himself was true, but up until two days ago she had always been a cautious individual, and a little residue of that wariness still remained.

They drove on for a little while in silence, Claudia applying as much of her attention as she could to the road and the manipulation of the powerful, classic car that she loved almost as much as Gerald had done. Paul was apparently deep in thought, or the retrieval of his errant memories, with a frown on his brow, one arm across his midriff, and one knuckle pressed pensively to his chin.

The quaintly named Mogander Arms was another classic – an old country pub which, despite its growing and increasingly trendy reputation for fine food, had still managed to retain a bit of the character that had made it popular in the first place. Pulling into the car park, Claudia felt a rush of reassurance from the prospect of the pub's pleasant, comforting ambience, and – despite the alarms and upsets that were attacking both her peace of mind and her libido – she realised she was quite ravenously hungry. Having what amounted to a toy boy obviously burned off a great number of calories!

'Let's sit here,' she said, leading Paul to a table for two, in the annexe to the rear of the main dining area.

There was a stiff breeze blowing outside, but here, in the shelter of the building but close to the open french doors to the beer garden, they had the best of both worlds: open-air eating yet protection from the elements.

They both chose the same main dish – a lightish concoction of pasta, roast vegetables and a herb and crème fraîche sauce – and voiced their selection almost simultaneously, laughing in a way that freed the tension which had slyly been building between them. Claudia would have liked to have ordered a bottle of wine – she would have liked it very much indeed – but asked for mineral water for the pair of them instead. She had to drive; Paul was due for hospital tests. After two days of near madness, she forced her old, accustomed sensibleness to prevail. It was amazing how peculiar that now felt.

Glancing around the room, Claudia quickly became aware they were under scrutiny. A trio of young women at a nearby table – twenty-somethings, involved in a celebration of some kind – were all darting what they probably hoped were covert looks at her and Paul from time to time. It was obvious they were agog with speculation.

Take a good look, girls, she felt like saying as she sipped her water, and tried hard not to let her watchers know she was aware of them. He's glorious, isn't he? she challenged them. He's a god, he's young, and he's mine! Well, at least for the time being he is.

Paul was still deep in thought, his long face cool and rather grave. Suddenly, he looked up and smiled, his blue eyes dancing.

'What is it? What else have you remembered?' demanded Claudia, reaching across to touch his hand as she caught his excitement.

Paul twisted his fingers to catch hers, then raised his free hand and covered his mouth for a moment, as if he had a secret that was extremely naughty but which he longed to tell her. She could almost hear the indrawn breaths at the table nearby.

'Paul! For heaven's sake, tell me! Is it to do with the car?'

'Yes. In a way . . .' He uncovered his face but he was still grinning; he looked elated, highly amused and almost disbelieving. 'But it's pretty wild. I can hardly credit it myself, but somehow I know that it's the absolute truth. Don't ask me why.'

'Paul!'

'You might be shocked.'

'I'm warning you!'

'You might be disgusted.'

'Let me be the judge of that. Now talk! Immediately!'

'OK,' he said, lifting her hand to his lips, giving her knuckle a kiss, then releasing her. She could feel the eyes of the three girls almost boring into her skin. 'But this is very weird. It's like finding one short reel of a film. I can remember this one . . . sort of . . . episode with total clarity. But nothing before it, and nothing after it. Most peculiar.'

Claudia held back from prompting him again, and waited, almost bursting with curiosity, while he took a drink of mineral water.

Then he began to speak, his deep voice very soft and intimate.

'I went on holiday in the car. With a friend. It must have been quite some time ago, because we were both fairly young. And we were very broke.' He hesitated, his blue eyes full of a faraway dreaminess. 'The Jag was so fragile it's a wonder it got us anywhere at all. And the cottage we stayed in was a hovel. But it didn't matter . . .' The dreamy look became fond and reminiscent. It touched Claudia deeply because it was the first time she had seen it. 'We were just so relieved to get out of the city, we were almost hysterical.'

Questions seethed in Claudia's throat, desperate to spring forth from her lips, but she held back, already excited, and more than a little jealous.

'The weather was terrible, and the first night there was a raging thunderstorm.' He flashed Claudia a quick significant smile, as if to underline the continuing portentous nature of such *sturm und drang* in his life. 'We were both scared to death, especially as someone in the local pub had told us there was a homicidal poacher on the loose in the area at night. We'd started off in separate bedrooms. There had never been anything between us until then . . .' Here it comes, thought Claudia, wishing once again that she could have wine. 'But when the storm hit its peak, Vivian came creeping into my room, and snuck into bed with me.'

Claudia couldn't help herself. There just had to be a 'Vivienne', didn't there? 'What was she like? I suppose she was very pretty.'

'More striking than pretty, I'd say,' said Paul, his voice rather indistinct. When Claudia looked at him more closely, she could see he was fighting hard not to laugh. 'He was six foot four, his hair was already beginning to recede, and he was the thinnest man I've ever seen. But yes, you could say Vivian was good looking.'

'A man!'

'Yes, a man,' said Paul, shrugging a little. 'Vivian, not Vivienne.' He enunciated each of the two names quite distinctly. 'I did warn you that you might be shocked.'

Reaching for her water, and drinking almost without thought, Claudia did a swift recalibration of the attitude she had been forming about Paul and his past 'liaisons'. Was she shocked? Was she repelled? Was she even jealous now she knew Vivian was masculine?

The answers were: not really; not at all; a little but not quite as much, somehow.

'Wow!' she murmured, then tried to look unconcerned as the waitress approached their table.

Paul appeared highly amused while their food was being served. It was apparent that the waitress, a buxom woman clearly the wrong side of 50, but not at all bothered by it, had taken a shine to him, and something of a performance was made with napkins, tongs and serving dishes, and exhortations that he should fill his plate with a little more pasta. Despite her impatience,

Claudia couldn't help smiling too, and as the waitress left, she flashed her a conspiratorial look. Claudia felt like saying, 'Don't worry, my dear, I will!'

After the first few mouthfuls were consumed and pronounced excellent, Claudia fixed Paul with a very firm look.

'Right. You and Vivian. Let's hear it!' she said crisply, making a firm little gesture with her fork.

Paul glanced quickly around him, but the three avid girls had just left – perhaps reluctantly? – and there were no other diners sitting within earshot. 'Where was I?' he enquired urbanely, as if they had been discussing the weather or some social inoccuity.

'You were in bed with your friend. Stop prevaricating!'

'That's just what I told myself then,' murmured Paul, conveying a small chunk of pasta to his mouth and chewing it thoughtfully. 'I knew what I wanted, and what he wanted – even though I don't think either of us had known it until that night – but there's a big difference between knowing and doing.'

Claudia felt the urge to clomp her fork down on the table and reach across and shake Paul into telling her what she now realised she was almost frantic to hear. And as if sensing her wishes, he went on without further delay.

'All he had on was a thin, cotton shirt, and even though it was fairly dark, I'd seen his cock as he got into bed. I realised that he'd probably wanted me to see him, and that's why he hadn't worn underpants. Anyway, the thunder crashed again just then, and one thing led to another – ' He paused and grinned ' – until we were in each other's arms, hugging each other. And we both had the hard-on to end all hard-ons.'

Helpless, Claudia found herself seeing them. Paul, as fabulous and as vulnerable as he was now, but a little younger. And the mysterious Vivian she seemed to picture as an actor she had rather admired in films and on television: a tall, louche and somewhat idiosyncratic-looking individual. As Paul had described, he was

126

extremely slender and his black hair was slightly thinning.

She pictured their lean male limbs entwining, both of them a little unsure of their caresses, even though their penises were urgently risen and straining towards each other. Would they kiss on the lips? she wondered, then almost as if he had heard her, Paul answered that question.

'The weirdest thing, at first, was kissing a man on the mouth,' he said, running a finger across his lower lip as if he could still feel the pressure of Vivian's mouth upon his. 'His tongue felt huge, like a marauding animal. I wasn't sure I liked it at first, but then I did, and I was kissing him back and pushing my tongue into his mouth.' He steepled his fingers in front of him for a moment, then picked up his fork again and immediately put it down. 'It felt more erotic, to be kissing him, in a way, than to feel him wiggling his hips and rubbing his cock up against mine.'

Claudia was entranced. It was almost as if she were perched on the end of the very bed with them, like some invisible, voyeuristic sprite, enjoying their tentative pleasure with just the same fear and surprise they were feeling. She wanted to bombard him with questions, but both his memory and the illusion were too fragile.

'He felt quite cold,' said Paul, pushing his food around his plate, hunger clearly forgotten in the face of other appetites. 'He must have been hovering on the landing for ages, screwing up enough courage to come in. It made me feel sort of tender towards him. He was more scared than I was. Once I'd got started the whole thing felt right to me. I seemed to know just what to do.'

The way you do with me, thought Claudia, feeling a moist and very familiar intimate trembling. The moment Paul had committed himself to lovemaking, he seemed to find it easy to take over, to take control. Bed, or its equivalent, was a natural habitat for him, and sex an inborn accomplishment. He was a wonder, a phenom-

127

enon. She felt in awe of him, and she blessed whatever force had brought him to her.

'I stroked his legs and his back, to get him warm first, then finally, he seemed to get impatient and frenzied, and he begged me, almost like a child, to touch his cock. I got the impression that if we didn't start then, he'd jump out of bed and run a mile.'

Lost in recollection, he halted for a moment, rearranged his pasta a little and sipped his water. Claudia got the impression that he too wished they were drinking wine – or at least one of his beloved cups of tea.

'It was weird to touch a penis that wasn't my own,' he said finally, 'but not unpleasant.' He looked up at her, his eyes spirited and a touch of colour brightening his high cheekbones. 'Oh no, not unpleasant at all.'

'What was it like?' asked Claudia, then almost instantaneously she clapped her hand across her lips, profoundly alarmed that she had asked such a question. She felt her own cheeks flame far pinker than Paul's.

'Like the rest of him,' replied Paul, with a chuckle. 'Thin, but rather lengthy. Easy to get your fingers around –' He held up one hand, thumb and first finger an 'O' ' – but needing one helluva long stroke to get the best from it!'

Claudia spluttered and giggled and had to take a long drink of mineral water to settle herself. 'You're wicked,' she said, setting her glass down and shaking her head. There was a touch of bravado to him now that reminded her very vividly of Beatrice; a kind of joy in life and sex that was outrageously appealing.

'It was true though!' he protested, taking a mouthful of pasta, then making much of savouring it and dabbing his mouth with his napkin. 'I can very clearly remember it making my wrist ache. It was a good thing for me that he came very quickly or I'm sure I would have ended up with cramp.'

'You poor thing,' she said in mock sympathy.

'Yes! Quite right. There he was spurting his way to

paradise . . . and I was left high and dry with a beast of an erection.' Paul told her this in a conversational, almost casual voice, but with one brief, flicking glance downward he belied the unconcern of his tone.

You're hard now, too, aren't you, you sexy bastard, she thought, imagining that 'beast of an erection' and how it would be pushing his pale trousers out of line. A whole wealth of scenarios assailed her mindscape, but one in particular took a hold, to entertain her.

The old cliché, so familiar from racy novels and movies: man gets hard-on; woman drops table napkin; man nearly has apoplexy trying to look unperturbed and order dessert, while woman manipulates his penis with her lips and tongue.

Oh yes! thought Claudia, her mouth watering at the illusory flavour of her lover's manhood and that of his fresh emission. She had touched his cock, handled it meticulously and lingeringly, and felt it lodged deep inside her body, but so far she hadn't treated herself to sucking it. That was a delight that still lay ahead of her – along with many others, she happily expected.

'Oh dear, how terrible,' she said drolly, feeling aroused by his plight, both then and now. 'What did you do about it?'

'Well, first I waited until Vivian got his breath back. I think the enormity of what had happened had rather taken the wind out of his sails. But when he'd stopped sobbing and creating and telling me he loved me, I sort of reminded him that the proceedings weren't quite over.'

'How?'

'By encouraging him to turn over, then massaging myself against his bottom.'

Between her thighs, Claudia felt the deep, raw pulse of acute desire. Oh God, oh God, had Paul actually fucked Vivian? The idea was so intense, so compelling, so delicious and so powerful that she knew if she clenched her vulva right now she would probably come like an express train and cry out.

And she would still have to know what happened.

'I didn't,' said Paul quietly, and for one horrifying moment, Claudia was convinced that she had asked her question out loud, in a public dining area which – though sparsely populated – was not entirely empty of fellow diners. She felt her jaw drop, and her tongue cleave to the roof of her mouth.

'What's the matter?' Paul asked, his brow pleating as he stared at her, obviously perplexed by her inability to speak.

'I – ' she began, still mentally floundering.

'It's all right,' he said reassuringly, 'you didn't actually ask me, but I could see you were dying to.' He looked from right to left. 'Don't worry, our naughty little secrets are still safe.'

'I don't know what you're talking about!' she snapped. How could he really be so perceptive, with a mind that was temporarily maimed?

'But you do want to know, don't you?'

'Yes! All right! I do! Tell me what happened!' She had let him get the upper hand again.

'Well, I know I didn't have him . . .' His voice petered out, and he frowned slightly again. Was the clarity of his recollection fading? Or was this part of the act – to make this blow-by-blow multi-dimensional account of Vivian's surrender seem less suspicious coming from a supposed amnesiac.

'We weren't . . . you know . . . "equipped" to go the whole hog. It's rather difficult, in some ways, to be both completely spontaneous and also considerate.'

'I suppose it is,' observed Claudia, feeling a shiver of luscious revulsion run up her back. With difficulty, she quashed a tantalising thread of conjecture. Images of condoms and lubricants; wild, sweaty sex; humping and groaning. Strong stuff to contemplate when they were supposed to be eating lunch.

'What we did was the nearest equivalent,' said Paul, his expression, Claudia thought, becoming deliberately coy.

130

'Which is?'

'I pressed my body against his back, and rocked my cock to and fro between his thighs.' His lean face became serious and contemplative. 'Which is just as good, in a way, if you're warm and close.'

Yes, I think it might be at that, mused Claudia, wishing for that warmth and closeness as she studied her barely touched food. Oh, to be there in that bed with Paul now, lying like spoons, his fine stiff erection between her thighs. She wouldn't mind at all that he wasn't inside her – just as long as he reached around and stroked her clitoris.

The inner scene was gentle now, but still Claudia had lost her appetite. She didn't want her immaculately prepared pasta with its clever, aromatic sauce; she wanted Paul, his marvellous body, and his strong, young penis. That *après*-lunch tryst she had idly thought of earlier became a sudden, almost painful temptation. She wondered if the Mogander Arms had a vacant room. They could say that one of them had been taken ill and needed to lie down. It wasn't a million miles away from the truth.

She imagined being with Paul in some big old-fashioned bed, all goosedown, well-darned sheets and a saggy mattress. First they would fuck quickly and passionately, slaking the keen edge of their lust before settling down to a long, summer's afternoon of leisurely lovemaking. While he told her more tall tales of his young manly escapades with Vivian, she would let him come not only between her thighs, but all over her body, wheresoever took his fancy. Across her belly, over her breasts, on her throat and face. She could almost see him kneeling over her, his prick rampant in his hand as he worked it with quick, deft strokes, then, crying out, anointed her . . .

One look at Paul's face told her he was having the same dream, or one very like it. His smooth cheeks were flushed, and he too had hardly tasted his pasta. His posture was awkward as if he were sitting with some discomfort.

'Paul. I wonder if – ' she began, seeing the familiar fire light in his eyes, and him almost leap from his seat as if he had only been waiting for the slightest word from her. She smiled back at him, knowing she didn't really have to say much more.

But as she reached behind her for her bag, hanging over her chair, her watch's accusing dial caught her attention.

` 1.45.

It was already 1.45pm, and they still had several miles to drive before they reached the hospital, and Beatrice.

'It would make us late, wouldn't it?' said Paul softly, folding his napkin and laying it methodically across his side plate.

Claudia fingered the strap of her watch for a moment, wishing she hadn't put the damn thing on so they could have forgotten time and taken that room without worrying.

'I'm afraid so,' she said with a shrug, then swung her bag on to her lap and reached inside to extract her credit card.

But as she drew out the powerful slip of plastic, she found herself smiling.

'There'll be another time,' she told her watching lover as she flexed her Mastercard contemplatively, 'and another hotel. I'll make it up to you. Don't worry, we'll have our stolen afternoon.'

Chapter Ten

Memento Mori, Memento Vivere

'So, has he remembered anything else yet?' asked Beatrice as they sat in the obscenely luxurious visitors' waiting room of the Ainsley Private Hospital.

I ought to tell her, thought Claudia, stifling a smile. Someone like Beatrice would really appreciate hearing about Paul and Vivian, and she wouldn't think it at all abnormal either. For a few seconds, Claudia actually considered describing what Paul had recounted to her, but almost as quickly she shelved the idea. She had no right to spread abroad his private recollections of his past.

'Just little bits and pieces,' she said diplomatically. 'Incidental things. Everyday likes and dislikes. Nothing about his identity or his life history.'

'It'll come,' said Beatrice reassuringly, her sensate nature clearly reasserting itself as she took Claudia's hand. 'Don't you worry. The small memories are a good sign. It shows that the actual mechanism of memory is functional.'

Paul was currently undergoing his examination and tests. The consultant had asked Claudia a few informal questions herself prior to whisking Paul off for the main part of the procedure, but it had been clear, then, that her continued presence was not required.

Claudia had not known whether to be unhappy or relieved by this. She felt responsible for Paul, and worried about him, but when all was said and done, she wasn't his mother, his wife, his sister or any kind of close relation. Only she and he – and Beatrice, and probably Melody! – had any knowledge of the degree of intimacy they were sharing. To all intents and purposes, she was barely even an acquaintance of Paul's; just someone who had taken him in as an act of good citizenship.

'I hate to say this, but have you considered going to the police in case there's a missing persons' report out about him?'

Beatrice's sudden question wasn't exactly unexpected. The spectre of her own self-centred behaviour kept rising up before Claudia and accusing her. Going to the police was the logical and screamingly obvious thing to do, and yet she couldn't bring herself to do it. And as Paul himself hadn't mentioned the idea, and had been actively reluctant to see even a doctor, there had been even less incentive to do anything 'official'. Beatrice had assured her that everything that happened here at the Ainsley was so confidential it was as good as off the record, but Claudia supposed that sooner or later Paul's presence in her home would come to the attention of someone other than her minute circle of friends.

'Yes,' she said eventually, 'yes, I have thought about it. Quite a lot actually . . .' She plucked at the cream fabric of her dress and then smoothed it out again, feeling nervous in more ways than one. 'And I know I should, for his sake.' She looked up into Beatrice's warm green eyes, seeking understanding, and feeling almost certain she would find it. 'But not for a day or two yet. I . . . I – ' She had to admit the truth. 'I want to keep him to myself for a little while! I feel so good while he's around. I feel alive again. I care for him and I think I deserve him!' She gave Beatrice a wry little smile, encouraged by the look of total comprehension – and affirmation – on the doctor's beautiful face. 'When he remembers who he is, he'll have a life to go back to. And there'll be a woman in that life – a wife or a girlfriend – and he won't want me any more. I want to hang on to him for bit, while I'm the only female he's got to turn to!'

All at once she was enclosed in Beatrice's hugging arms, and the doctor was rocking her, half to encourage her and half in what felt like jubilation.

'Bravo!' cried Beatrice, retreating a little but clasping Claudia by the shoulders. She looked excited and suddenly rather young. 'You know that's what I would do myself, don't you? I wouldn't dream of doing anything else.' She grinned – devilishly, Claudia thought. 'I know a lot of people wouldn't consider it the right or even the moral thing to do. But I – ' she released Claudia, then struck herself for emphasis ' – think it's the only thing to do. Not just for you, but for Paul too. He needs kindness right now, and nurturing, but he needs an ego boost just as much.' She gave Claudia a sly, sideways look that spoke volumes. 'Which is most definitely what you're giving him.' She leant closer again, as if to speak confidentially, even though they were the only two people in the room. 'With you he can feel like a *man*, rather than just a little lost boy caught in a mire of bureaucracy!'

'If you say so,' said Claudia, relieved in one way but disturbed in another. Being embraced by Beatrice stirred up another of the new issues which the last couple of days had raised. Even in her marginally more sober 'working' garb – a grey pinstripe trouser suit overlaid by the traditional, and for Claudia, now very evocative white coat – the doctor was an arresting and subversively desirable figure. The fact that she wore wire-rimmed spectacles and had her hair in a serious but elaborately coiled style only seemed to add to the power of her allure. For a fleeting second, Claudia seemed to see compensations presenting themselves; ways of alleviating her suffering when Paul 'remembered himself' and left.

'I do say so!' reiterated Beatrice cheerfully, with a

twinkle in her eyes. 'And that's my opinion as a physician *and* a woman.'

Claudia wasn't sure what to say next, but the trilling of a phone forestalled making the effort. She felt a sudden chill of fear, knowing it would be news of Paul's results.

'Yes?' said Beatrice, on picking up the phone. 'I see. OK, we'll be right with you.' The sound of the receiver being clicked on to the cradle was discouragingly final.

Claudia was unable to speak now. Deep foreboding gripped her, an anxiety that made all their talk of sex as therapy seem flippant.

'Come on,' said Beatrice gently, taking her by the hand again and urging her up. 'David wants to see us.' She reached out and chafed Claudia's cheek. 'Don't look so tragic. There won't be a thing to worry about!'

And, thank God, Beatrice had been right, by and large, thought Claudia as she and Paul drove back towards Rosewell through the mellow peace of the gathering summer evening. All his tests and investigations – including the imaging of his brain by the MRI scanner – had shown that there was no discernible physical injury. The only thing to worry about now was why, if all was well, he still couldn't remember.

As he was quiet for the moment, and looking out of the window, Claudia stole the swiftest of glances at him.

Well, if you are faking it, boy, you've done damn well to seem so convincing all through this. The consultant – Colville – had clearly taken Paul completely at face value, and presumably a man of his experience and qualifications would have been able to spot a bogus amnesiac with far more facility than she herself would. Despite the inconclusive results, it appeared that Paul's problem was perfectly genuine, and Colville's prescription, just like Beatrice's, was 'give it time'. Another appointment had been made at the Ainsley for next week, when further treatment would be reviewed, but for now, all they could do was wait and see while Paul rested and took life easy.

It would be interesting, Claudia mused, unable to contain a smile, to know whether the nice but very gentlemanly Mr Colville would consider what had transpired between Paul and herself in the last less than 48 hours as 'taking life easy'.

But was all that activity now taking its toll? she wondered, glancing at Paul again and seeing a deeply thoughtful expression on his long, pale face.

'Are you OK?' she asked, after she had negotiated the roundabout and they were heading towards the outskirts of the village. 'You're not worried about the results of the tests, are you? Colville said everything was fine. It's only a matter of time before you start remembering more and more.'

'It's not the tests. Not really,' he replied. Claudia had her eyes on the road, but she sensed him turn to her. She almost felt the heat of his pulse-quickening smile. 'I was thinking about the things I have managed to remember . . . Why on earth should I be able to recall making love with Vivian, but nothing else?' He tapped his finger on the upholstery beside him. 'You don't think that means I'm gay, do you?'

Claudia wanted to chuckle, but refrained. He sounded so earnest, but this wasn't a laughing matter. 'Well, you can't be a . . . how shall I say this? You're obviously not a "dedicated" homosexual, or you wouldn't want to make love to me, would you?' She paused, then went on, feeling risky. 'Unless, of course, you've discovered a way of faking it?'

'No. No way,' he said a little gruffly. 'What I feel for you is real. The response is real. How can you doubt that?'

Oh no, I've upset him! thought Claudia, feeling a pang of unhappiness. 'I don't doubt it,' she said, intently. 'I'm sorry, I was just being stupid . . . This is a very strange situation we're in. You must be very confused, and I can't help thinking I'm taking advantage of you.'

'Never!' he cried, his voice filled with sudden passion. 'I don't know what would have happened to me if I hadn't found you. I owe you everything.' He laughed softly, and Claudia felt her string-tight nerves relax. 'And I just can't believe my luck. I'm sure not every amnesiac down-and-out gets taken in by a woman who just happens to be intelligent, beautiful and a fabulous lay into the bargain.'

'Well, thank you,' said Claudia, thrilled more than she cared to admit by the epithet 'a fabulous lay'. 'But don't you think that rather puts paid to any ideas that you might be purely gay? If you can recognise "a fabulous lay" when you lay one, you must have had at least some experience of making love to women.'

'That's true,' he said thoughtfully. 'It's just that I can't remember any *individual* women. I just have an instinctive memory of the act, and the feelings, and the want and the need for them . . . but no specifics. When I try to conjure up faces and bodies, the only face and body I see are yours.'

Moved now, Claudia concentrated on her driving. She was a little afraid of the young man who sat beside her. He was remarkable and what she felt for him might well be far too much, and a good deal too soon. As they approached the Rosewell cemetery, she had a sudden need for a familiar, stabilising influence.

'Do you mind if we stop here?' she asked, easing the Jag to a halt in the small parking lay-by. 'I – I haven't dropped by for a while, and I think I need to.'

'Do you need to be alone?' said Paul as she made to get out of the car. He laid his hand very lightly on her arm.

'No . . . No, I don't think so.' she said, 'Actually, I'd like your company. We won't stay long. I just want to "touch base", I suppose you'd call it.'

Paul simply nodded, and slid out of the car as she did.

You do understand, don't you, Gerry? she queried silently as she looked down at the simple inscription cut in the polished black granite. Gerald Christopher Marwood. Beloved husband of Claudia. Rest in peace.

I don't love you any less, she told him, then felt suddenly better, seeming to see again the face and the smile she still so missed. Gerald's encouraging, roguish grin that had appeared to her when she had first made love to Paul. A tiny cool breeze, the precursor of night, made her shiver – but inside she felt warm and reassured.

'Are you OK?' asked Paul, from close beside her. She sensed him hesitate, then felt his strong arm slide around her.

'Fine,' she said, leaning against him, making her body speak as much as her voice. 'I think he'd approve of you. He liked adventures. He was faithful while we were married, I'm certain of that, but he'd had some wild times before we met. He used to tell me about them sometimes – ' she paused, and gave Paul a slanting glance from beneath her lashes – 'and I'm almost sure he and Beatrice Quine were once an item.'

'And now she's after you,' said Paul.

'If you say so,' observed Claudia, almost sure of what he had just said too.

'I do,' he proclaimed, full of male assurance. 'I've only seen you together relatively briefly, but it's patently obvious she's desperately hot for you!'

'You're crazy!' said Claudia, laughing.

'Nope, not crazy,' he replied, smiling back at her. 'Temporarily a bit addled, yes. But still fully in command of my powers of perception. Especially my powers of sexual perception.' He pulled her closer, not yet allowing his genitals to press against her, she noticed, yet still acquainting her somehow with his growing sense of interest.

Should I really be feeling this here, of all places? Claudia asked herself, having to hold back from the urge to reach down and touch him. She experienced not guilt exactly, but a strong impression of old-fashioned naughtiness – something she also knew Gerald would have heartily approved of.

'Shall we get home?' she suggested, brushing against him with more concentration, only to be rewarded by the kick of his waiting erection.

'We could,' he said, his voice low and silky, 'but if Gerald was in favour of adventures, wouldn't he like you to have plenty of them?'

'Not here, surely?' gasped Claudia, half outraged, half sorely tempted. She was aware of the strange, almost alchemic bond between the presence of death and the sex urge, but she just couldn't bring herself to indulge in some wild, teenage feat of sacrilege. A part of her wanted it, but the greater part knew that this was something she really was too old for. And anyway, even though the graveyard was deserted now, it was still quite light and anyone might come by.

As if hearing her deliberations, Paul pointed to the far end of the well-watered, emerald-turfed enclosure, where a kissing gate interrupted the stone wall. 'Where does that lead to?'

'The fields, some woods, the river,' she replied, feeling a hot, low frisson of anticipation.

'The same river that passes by the bottom of your garden?'

'Yes. The Little Ber.'

'Let's go for a walk,' he said, grabbing her hand and urging her along. 'It's a glorious evening. It seems a shame to waste it.'

'I thought you said you weren't crazy?' said Claudia, laughing as they negotiated the gate and found themselves on a narrow muddy path beyond. Both her strappy sandals and Paul's light shoes were instantly caked. As a response, he pulled her behind a tree and kissed her, his hands roaming lewdly over her body, even though they weren't quite out of sight. She tried to persist, but he only groped her harder. When she felt him popping open the lower buttons that held the front of her dress together, she shook herself free and tried to close it again.

'Paul! Please! Someone'll see us!'

He ignored her, planted his lips on hers, and thrust his hand up her disordered skirt with determination. As his tongue possessed her mouth, he touched her panties, pushing the thin fabric of their gusset between her labia.

Despite the threat of imminent discovery and the prospect of more village tongues wagging about her than had ever flapped for Beatrice, Claudia found herself responding to him instantly. The soft membranes he was caressing through the narrow slip of silk and cotton were heavily engorged in the space of a heartbeat and beginning to drip. And to make matters worse, she realised she needed to urinate. The knife-sharp jolt of confusing sensations made her jump and wriggle.

'Please don't!' she begged, twisting her head to one side, but unable to prevent him from fingering her.

'Why not?' he enquired, then kissed her neck in the particularly wild way he was good at. Between her legs, he didn't miss a single beat.

'Be – because we're still in plain sight. And I need to pee!' she sobbed. 'Oh please, Paul! Please stop!'

'Let's get out of sight then,' he said, his voice not unkind, but firm. He cupped her vulva lightly and quickly, then withdrew his hand. 'This way,' he urged, leading her further down the path towards the woods, the fields and the river.

Down the merry road to muck and ruin, thought Claudia, half running, in delicious discomfort, behind him. The churned soil still clung in lumps to her narrow, dainty sandals, but she didn't care one jot about them, she realised. She wasn't even bothered either, as she glanced down, that the pale trouser bottoms of Gerald's stylish summer suit were becoming just as plastered as Paul strode on, oblivious.

Skirting the woods, they struggled through a small break in a bramble hedge – Claudia felt protruding stragglers catching and tugging at her dress – then across

a ditch and over a stile and into the corner of an empty
fallow field that bordered the Little Ber.

'But Paul!' Claudia hissed, as he pulled her to him
once more, and began to kiss her face and throat and feel
her bottom.

'I want you,' he said, almost as if he hadn't heard her.
His voice was raw, intent, and a little unfeeling. His very
focus on his own desire was irrationally stirring. Against
all her natural inclinations, Claudia felt a strong urge to
be just taken and used, her needs and her uncomfortable
state ignored.

It's me who's going crazy, she thought, grinding her
pelvis against Paul's even though it plagued her.

'I thought you needed to pee?' he enquired, not letting
hold of her and still pressing her body against him.

'I think I need you more,' she gasped, knowing it was
true as she relished perverse sensations. Her swollen
bladder only exacerbated her mounting pleasure.

Paul didn't speak, but instead pushed her down to the
rough, miry ground, sinking awkwardly beside her as
he did so. Kneeling face to face, they kissed again,
messily in more ways than one, open mouths wet against
each other's faces as their light-coloured clothing, and
Claudia's bare shins, became quickly smeared with dirt.

You're wonderful! she thought deliriously, as her lover
pulled open the top buttons of her dress, wrenched
down her silk bra, and bared her breasts so he could cup
and stroke and fondle them. After a moment, she felt the
gritty sensation of earth between her skin and his fingers,
then looked down and saw her rosy flesh smudged with
streaks of mud.

Somehow, the very presence of the dirt on her body
was as exciting as the caress that was applying it. 'Oh
God!' she cried, throwing back her head and arching her
shoulders. She felt Paul's teeth nip the offered cord of
her neck, then travel down her chest and bosom, inflict-
ing the tiniest of mock bites as they did. Mad as it
seemed, the smeared dirt was as much a turn-on for him
as it was for her.

And still as they rocked and wrestled, her bladder tormented her, as if crying out for a pressure that was both desired and feared. 'Fuck me, Paul,' she moaned, as he sucked hard on the peak of her breast, and she was driven to jam her own hand to her crotch. 'Fuck me *now*,' she ordered, jerking her hips at the low infernal ache.

'Say please!' he hissed, then worked his jaw to roll her nipple between his teeth. 'Say please,' he repeated, his voice low with wicked laughter, 'or I won't do it and you'll have to do it yourself.'

The idea of masturbating for him, here in the mud and grass, with both her dress and her body filthy, was so piquant that she nearly had an instant climax. She imagined squatting, her knees apart, rubbing her herself and letting loose her water simultaneously, and felt her body throb in dangerous empathy.

'Say please,' growled Paul, one hand still at her breast, while the other he curved lightly round her throat.

'Please! Oh please!' she gasped. Paul would never hurt her, that she knew as sure as she could know anything about him, but the pantomime of coercion was delicious. In the furrow between her legs, her sex pulsed involuntarily, and she felt a tiny trickle of urine dampen her pants. 'Oh please,' she begged again, reaching down blindly, on automatic, to clasp Paul's groin.

For a few seconds he allowed her to hold him, to knead him slightly, then he shook her off and grabbed her hands in his. 'Turn around,' he said, his voice abrupt yet strangely young-sounding, as if he were a youth trying to be the man, with his girlfriend, for the very first time. He squeezed her fingers quick and hard, then released them.

'Oh yes ... Oh yes ...' breathed Claudia, recognising a request – albeit clumsy – for exactly what she wanted. Hitching up her dress, she shuffled around to face away from Paul, still on her knees. The ungainly movements jolted her bladder and she whimpered.

'That's right,' she heard him mutter, and as she pulled her dress even further up, bunching it halfway up her back, around her midriff, she felt him dragging off her panties, just as heedlessly. Hampered by her own efforts, she almost went face down in the field, but Paul caught her, slinging one arm around her waist, while he wrestled with her knickers with his hand.

What the hell am I doing? she thought for perhaps the twentieth time since she had opened her door to the lost, bedraggled stranger. I'm in a field, with my backside in the air, waiting to be serviced. And I don't care! Out of the corner of her eye, she saw her pants flip away towards the middle of the field, and she laughed in pure, hysterical elation.

Beginning to laugh himself, Paul took hold of her buttocks and palpated them energetically, circling the firm moons of flesh as if they were dough and he was a masterchef at work. 'Gorgeous!' he said, bending over to kiss her back as his fingers and thumbs dug in. He was almost hurting her, but Claudia wanted more of it. She dished her back and pushed her bottom into his hands.

'You have a sensational arse, Mrs Marwood,' he said softly, moving forward to rub his still-clothed crotch against the object of veneration. Leaning still further forward, he murmured in her ear – a lewd suggestion – then squeezed her even harder as if he were forcing her to answer him.

'Oh Paul ... I don't know ... I don't know,' panted Claudia, horrified, yet yearning too. She wanted what he suggested, she realised to her astonishment, but not here, in all this mud and haste and awkwardness. 'Not here.'

'Somewhere else then?' he queried, his voice like a breath of fire. 'Another time? Back at the house. Will you let me?'

'Yes!'

'You're an angel too, Mrs Marwood!' he replied, the fire turned to instant jubilation. After a second, she felt his lips against her anus. 'Take that on account.' He kissed her again, then drew back, his breathing short and ragged. 'And in the meantime, I'm going to fuck you, here in this field, until you howl!' Claudia felt him retreat, and sensed him tackling the obstacle of his clothes.

Until I wet myself, she thought, rotating her hips and feeling the weight of liquid rock heavily against the root of her clitoris. Can I do this? Can I take this? she asked herself, shaking her pelvis experimentally, then gasping at the harsh sensation that created. A trickle of urine snaked its way down her thigh.

What choice do I have? she told herself, feeling almost smug at the extremity of what she herself had invited. From the corner of her eye, she saw male clothing fly out into the field: first shoes, then trousers and underwear, but nothing else.

What must we look like? thought Claudia, laughing when Paul's penis nudged her sex, as if knocking for entrance. She was bare-bottomed, her dress gaping, her bra awry, her breasts swinging free as she crouched in the scrubby field waiting to be used; Paul was perfectly well dressed above the waist, and lewd and naked below. They were a pair of rustic libertines in the grips of a mighty passion, the sophisticated gloss of earlier in the day a thing of the past.

'What are you giggling at?' Paul demanded, pushing firmly against the entrance to her vagina. He had tried to sound fierce, but Claudia could hear him laughing again too. Especially when her body yielded, and he slid inside, curving over her. 'Minx! What's so funny? I'll give you something to laugh at!'

Claudia did laugh, but it was partly a shriek too. Without wasting any time, Paul launched himself into a series of short, shallow jabs, which, though she sensed they were an attempt at consideration, only made things worse for her full, beleaguered bladder. Each one was a shaft of silvered pleasure-pain; each one shot her nearer to her climax. She laughed louder as the sensations ramped and ramped.

'Right! I'll show you, Mrs Marwood,' cried Paul, kneeling up again but not withdrawing. She felt his left

145

hand grip her hip so he could get a better purchase, and his right go over, in and under. With the confidence of pure authority, he jiggled her clitoris.

'You bastard!' she cried, her voice the very howl he had predicted, just as an instant, jerking orgasm wracked her body like a wavefront, and to her intense delight, she could no longer hold her water. 'You bastard,' she cooed, as it gushed and dribbled from her, drenching both Paul's hand and the muddy earth on which they knelt.

'Incredible,' he whispered, massaging her with her own fluid, his body shaping to her back. His penis was still iron where it nestled deep inside her, and his warm breath and his wayward curls were tickling his neck. 'You beautiful, incredible woman . . .' He seemed elated by the fact he had made her piss.

Claudia felt beyond speech. The power of her climax and the exhilaration of such a complete release of tension had knocked the wind out of her. If Paul hadn't have been hugging her around the waist she would have fallen flat on her face, and lain there gasping in the mud beneath him. It hardly seemed possible that she would ever be able to come again, but as she thought that, her vagina rippled with promise.

'Oh yeah,' murmured Paul, in response.

As if his voice had strengthened her, Claudia stirred from her damp, glowing lethargy and swayed against him. Bracing her spine, she pushed herself backwards against him, spearing herself deliciously on the prow of his rigidity. Deep inside, behind her clitoris, she felt a pressure on her G spot, and this time, with her bladder empty, it was only bliss. Without her own volition, her vagina clenched and she came again.

This time she did pitch forward, on to her elbows, taking Paul along for the ride, juddering inside her. She didn't manage to make him howl, but his ragged cry was happy. His arms tightened around her body as he climaxed.

'Jesus! Aren't we a mess!' exclaimed Claudia, a little

146

while later. In the pleasant haze of afterglow, they had rearranged themselves somehow, and she was lying with her head on Paul's shoulder. What she could see, looking down their bodies, was a loose, abandoned tangle of blushing flesh and light-coloured clothing, and it was difficult to work out which was muddiest.

'I suppose we are,' he said, his voice lazy and philosophical, 'but neither of us knew we were going to end up rolling about in a field when we got dressed this morning, did we?'

'True!' said Claudia, sitting up and pulling half-heartedly at her bodice and her skirt. 'In fact, I'd go so far as to say it was probably the last thing I would have predicted.'

'Seems a shame to cover it all up,' observed Paul laconically, letting his hand brush suggestively over her mud-smeared breast.

'Well, I wouldn't normally bother,' replied Claudia, lifting the hand away from her and giving it a quick kiss, 'but there are some people who might be a teeny bit offended if I walked through the graveyard like this. Boring of them, I know, but there you are.'

'I bet your husband wouldn't mind.'

'No, I'm sure he wouldn't, but men of his breadth of imagination are few and far between, especially in the country.' She turned around and winked at Paul. 'Present company excepted, of course.'

Paul inclined his head, gracefully accepting her compliment. 'Why don't we go home then? That way we can do exactly what we like without outraging anybody.' He leapt to his feet, seemingly unabashed by the swing of his naked penis, then extended his hand and helped Claudia up too.

After several minutes spent buttoning up and zipping up, and brushing down and rubbing, they didn't look any less dirty but at least their bodies were covered.

'If we meet anybody, we went for a walk. I slipped down the river bank. You had to scramble down and help me up. Right?' said Claudia, as they negotiated the kissing gate on their way back to the car.

'Or you could say I slipped and you helped *me* up,' suggested Paul. 'I'm sure most people who know you wouldn't think you clumsy enough to slip down a bank,' he added gallantly.

'Maybe. Maybe not,' replied Claudia with a shrug and a grin, 'but if we hurry, we might get to the car without being spotted.'

Luck was with them; or perhaps, Claudia thought, it was the good offices of Pan, or Dionysus, or some local god of sexy, rustic revels. Either way, they got to the car without incident, and drove home unnoticed through the gathering pink-skyed twilight. Every now and again, one of them would chuckle and flash a look at the other's ruined clothing.

It was only when they reached Perry House, and Claudia swung the car into the driveway, that anything at all untoward occurred.

A small, red and rather feminine car sat on the gravel in front of the house, and a light was already glowing in the sitting room.

'You've got a visitor,' said Paul, and when Claudia glanced at him, she saw that his pale face bore a look of slight alarm.

'*We've* got a visitor,' said Claudia, touching his face and reassuring him. 'That's Melody's car and I'm sure she'll be happy to see us both.'

Chapter Eleven

Another House Guest

'Have you left him?' Claudia asked Melody as she topped up her friend's tot of brandy.

'Well, yes, sort of,' the young woman answered cautiously. 'The trouble is that he doesn't actually know it yet.'

'Oh Melody!'

'I know! I know! I should have faced up to him, told him calmly and all that, but I just couldn't ... He's gone too far this time. He's done something I just can't forgive him for.'

'Did he hurt you?' Fury flared in Claudia's chest. Oh no, he hadn't started hitting her now, had he, as well as criticising her every opinion and action?

'No! Oh no, not that!' replied Melody quickly, her pretty face brightening. 'Nothing like that. I can't do anything right for him, and he treats me like an imbecile, but he's never hit me or anything.' She laid her dainty hand reassuringly on Claudia's arm. It looked very pale against the deep-piled, royal-blue towelling. Her finger-nails were painted rose pink. 'He's a psychological thug, not a physical one.'

'Even that's bad enough,' commented Claudia, thinking how much Melody must have loved her husband in the first place to have put up with so much insensitivity and so many put-downs. The young woman was frowning now, though, and Claudia wondered what it was that Richard Truebridge had done to her.

'What is it?' she asked. 'What is it he's done?'

Melody sighed, and straightened the cuffs of her casual cotton top as if she still had on one of her chic, yuppified suits. It was strange to see her in jeans tonight, and Claudia thought how well they suited her fresh young figure. What a shame Richard had forbidden her to wear them.

'Look, I will tell you,' the younger woman said earnestly, withdrawing her hand and retrieving her brandy glass. 'But can we wait a little while? It's unpleasant. It'll spoil things. I feel so relieved to be here, I just want to revel in it for a bit.'

'Good! You revel . . . There's no rush,' said Claudia, smiling but feeling agitated inside somehow. It was strangely exciting to imagine Melody relaxing and being herself at last, returning to the carefree coltish juvenile she had been when they had first met, yet at the same time retaining the mature form of a grown woman.

Melody abandoned her brandy again, and pushed her hand through her hair, clearly worried again. 'If I was half the friend to you that you are to me, I would have gone to a hotel.'

So taken was Claudia by yet another change in Melody – the loose, natural, un-blow-dried condition of her hair – that it took a second or two to take in what the girl had said.

'What on earth do you mean, Mel?' she demanded.

'I shouldn't be here, messing things up for you and Paul!' Melody exclaimed. 'You need to be alone together, not looking after me. *Both* of you, looking after me.'

'That's bollocks, Mel!' rejoined Claudia, and felt relieved when Melody laughed too.

It was true that both she and Paul had rallied round when they had entered the house and found Melody sitting tight-lipped and alone in the sitting room. Aware of the disgusting state of her dress, yet reluctant to leave her friend in obvious distress, Claudia had felt torn between compassion and embarrassment. She had been about to forget her foibles and sensibilities, and hope that Melody wouldn't notice the earth and grass and even more suspect stains on her clothing, when Paul had whispered discreetly in her ear.

'You get a quick shower. I'll get Melody a cup of tea or a drink or something.'

'Would you?' Claudia had murmured gratefully. 'That would be brilliant. Give her a glass of brandy for now . . . And we'll all have a cup of tea together later.'

Claudia's shower had been the quickest she had ever taken, despite the fact that the mud seemed to have inveigled its way on to the most unlikely portions of her skin. From the look of her, it appeared as if she and Paul had wallowed in the stuff like a brace of mating hippos – which wasn't all that far from the truth, if you discounted the physical dimensions.

Her haste in showering had been due to genuine concern over Melody, and much the same in relation to Paul. He was fine in her own presence, and he had clearly been comfortable enough at the hospital and with Beatrice; but was it fair to leave two emotionally wounded individuals – who had previously spoken barely a dozen words to each other – to make smalltalk in a highly charged atmosphere?

As it turned out, though, Paul and Melody were chatting away like long-standing soulmates when she returned to the sitting room. Paul was describing the miracles of the MRI procedure, and Melody, with a magnificently healthy person's academic but intense interest in all things medical, was listening closely, her face rapt, yet looking more contented.

When he had completed his account of his trials and tribulations – or lack of them – at the hospital, Paul tactfully excused himself and left the two women to talk.

'And you're not messing anything up for me, Mel,' Claudia continued, reasoning with the younger woman. 'Not by any means.'

'And *that* really is bollocks, Claud!' replied Melody, grinning. 'It was obvious yesterday that there was something going on between you ... And now? Well ... What on earth had you been doing to get so muddy?' Melody's fine grey eyes narrowed, suggesting that she would brook no deception. 'And don't say just walking. Nobody could get in that sort of state simply on a nature ramble. Not that they'd go rambling in the first place dressed in those outfits.'

'But it's true. We did go for a walk. I slipped on the river bank and Paul had to save me.'

'Claudia!'

'Oh, all right!'

'Well then?'

'We did go for a walk, in one of the river meadows, but somehow we ended up doing other things too ... Celebrating the glories of nature in a more hands-on sort of way. The Song of the Earth and all that ... You know.'

'Wow!'

Claudia half expected Melody to whistle, but instead the young woman said, 'I wish I'd've been there to see that.'

'Really?' observed Claudia, feeling thoroughly off-balance for a second at the thought of Melody being there to watch herself and Paul fucking. The idea inspired a disturbing rush of lust.

Melody blushed, her fair skin colouring a delicate shade of peony. 'I didn't mean that – ' she stopped, seeming to ponder. 'No, that's a lie. I *do* mean it! I can't imagine seeing anything more seductive.' Her blush deepened, as if trying to make sense of conflicting urges and emotions. How well Claudia herself knew that feeling. 'I hope you don't mind me thinking that,' she continued, frowning. 'I mean, if you find it offensive, I'll just shut up and we can forget I ever said it.' In obvious confusion, she plucked at the arm of the sofa, as if trying to pull out a non-existent loose thread.

Claudia sensed a pivotal moment looming; a great

leap into something to which Beatrice had already pointed the way.

Why did I never see this before? she thought, looking at her dear friend, whom she had known since Melody's girlhood. They had always been close, and more so recently, during times when they had both needed comfort. But that comfort had never transcended the realm of what was considered to be normal and conventional. At times it had seemed almost a mother/daughter relationship; at others, it had felt like more sisterly attachment, despite their differing ages.

So why had their bond suddenly started changing? What she felt when she looked at Melody was like nothing she had experienced towards the girl before. Melody excited her now – in the way that Beatrice had done, only with an even stronger pull, which she supposed was due to their shared history.

She realised that Melody was awaiting a response. 'No need to forget it, Mel,' she said. 'I don't think I'd mind being watched . . . Well, at least not by you. I don't know what Paul would feel about it, but something tells me he wouldn't mind at all.'

Melody smiled, gnawed her shell-pink lower lip, and appeared to digest these responses.

'I – ' she began.

Go on! Go on! urged Claudia silently. Melody was right on the brink of her own great leap.

But the younger woman couldn't speak. She seemed unable to articulate the emotions that were vivid on her face. You can feel it, though, can't you? thought Claudia, knowing that she was so absolutely right that she could have staked her very life on the knowledge.

It was deadlock. They were both facing the same experience for the first time. Someone would have to push. Or pull. One of them would have to take the other's hand and lead her over the precipice.

'Mel,' Claudia said gently, reaching for her companion's hand and bringing it to her lips to kiss. 'It's all right,' she whispered, mouthing the lines of fate which criss-crossed Melody's soft palm. 'I feel the same way. Don't worry . . . There's nothing at all wrong with what's happening.'

'No, I suppose there isn't . . .' Melody's voice was a little shaky; in fact, her whole body was shaking. Claudia could feel the trembling against her tongue as she kissed her again.

'Oh, thank God! Thank God!' cried Melody suddenly, and Claudia felt the girl's hand brush her hair. For a moment, Melody's slim fingers ruffled Claudia's short, softly shaggy tresses, then they changed their tack, and cupped her jaw, making her lift her face so they could look into one another's eyes.

Melody's own face was almost luminous. 'Oh God,' she whispered, once again, 'you're so lovely, Claud. I only wish I knew what to do about it.'

'I wish I did too,' said Claudia fervently, 'but don't worry, I think it's something we can make up as we go along.' Without further hesitation, she kissed her friend passionately on the lips for the first time ever.

It was like kissing a man, yet entirely different. Tasting Melody's soft lips and her sweet, faintly brandy-scented breath made Claudia realise that there was a great distinction between the genders in the way a mouth felt. Melody's lips had a velvety, almost plush texture, and what lay beyond them was deliciously yielding without being weak and submissive. She accepted the kiss, and for several moments, her mouth was mild and passive beneath Claudia's. Then, just as instantaneously as the kiss had begun, Melody seemed to wake from a slumber and kiss Claudia back. Her tongue felt like a small, living dart; her lips became strong and demanding.

For as much as two minutes, they did not part; each exploring the other's mouth with just her own mouth. Finally, they almost fell apart, both panting with exertion.

'I think I've wanted to do that for a very long time,' said Claudia, taking Melody's hand in hers again, then squeezing it. 'I didn't *know* that I wanted to do it, but the desire must've been there, underneath, for ages.'

'Same here,' Melody said, rubbing a finger across her lips where Claudia had kissed her – as if there might be some tangible residue of the ardent contact that had taken place there. After a second or two, she raised her hand before her face and studied her fingertips, still searching, it seemed, for Claudia's spoor. 'I've had a crush on you as long as I've known you, didn't you realise?' she finished, sounding sure of herself yet still a little befuddled by what they were both admitting.

'No, not really,' said Claudia quietly, her fingers twisting at the tie of her robe then, of their own volition it seemed, loosening it. 'I must be as thick as a brick.' The tie fell open, and with a slight movement of her shoulders, she managed to edge open the front of the robe, partially exposing her breasts to Melody's suddenly avid gaze 'Or just find it difficult to believe that someone could have a crush on me.'

Melody's slender fingers twitched, and Claudia imagined that they were aching to reach out and touch what was on offer. Her heart pounding, Claudia took her friend's hand in hers, then drew it to her naked breast and held it there.

'I – I had ... or should I say *have*, a crush on you because you're intelligent and kind and generous.' Melody paused and gave the breast within her fingers a gentle, almost tentative squeeze. 'And because you're beautiful. The most beautiful woman I've ever seen.'

Claudia wanted to deny that last statement, say something self-deprecating, but the feel of Melody's fingers against her skin was addling her senses. She tried to accept her dear friend's praise with good grace but it was difficult. In the end she settled for a compromise.

'Thank you,' she said simply, 'but don't you think I'm beginning to get a little frayed around the edges?'

Still gently caressing, Melody seemed to have her own inner debate, but eventually she said, 'OK, so you've got

155

one or two tiny lines, but they're the good sort. Signs of character and wisdom.'

'Flattery will get you everywhere,' murmured Claudia, aware of Melody's hand with every last nerve cell in her body. And some more than others. 'If I was wearing knickers, I'd swear that you were using sweet words to get into them.'

Melody's flushed cheeks became even pinker, like a full-blooded rose. 'I think that, unconsciously, that's exactly what I *am* doing.'

They kissed again, more slowly this time, and with circumspection. Melody's hand slid down Claudia's body, making its way to as yet unexplored territory. Claudia felt her friend's fingertips brush against the hair of her pubis, once, twice, skirting the very perimeter of that sweetest and tenderest of zones.

'What do I do next?' whispered Melody, her lips exploring Claudia's jawline while her still fingers seemed to wait for permission, or direction, or both. 'Shall I stroke you? Is that what you'd like?'

Claudia had never been with a woman, unless she counted yesterday's very near miss with Beatrice. Was there a particular way to proceed? she thought, smiling inside. A protocol over who does what to who, and who gets it first?

'Yes, I would like that,' she replied, striking out boldly for what she knew she wanted, regardless of any accepted *modus operandi*. Flipping her robe fully open, she parted her thighs, feeling thankful that her regime of regular exercise was keeping the cellulite at bay. It seemed even more important that she be as perfect as she could be for Melody than it did for Paul somehow, which was irrational, as she and the younger woman had seen each other in swimsuits and bikinis often enough. She hadn't worried one jot about Melody's judgement of her body until now.

Very tentatively, Melody began to explore further, moving down into the intimate division. Claudia couldn't help but moan as the girl's middle finger settled neatly on her clitoris.

'Yes! Oh Mel, that's just right!' she croaked as Melody began to describe a circling action, at first slow, then faster and faster and faster. The familiar sensations built up at a speed she would not have thought possible, and within seconds she was clutching Melody's shoulders and bouncing about with pleasure. Pitching back her head, she growled out loud as the orgasm took her and shook her.

'Thanks,' she gasped, when she could think properly again. 'That was beautiful, Mel. Just right. It couldn't have been better if I'd given you written instructions.' She laughed, and so did Melody. There was a note of happy triumph in the younger woman's chuckle.

'Now it's your turn,' Claudia told Melody, and was just about to make some inroads into the clothing that she wore, when the sound of clumping footsteps on the stairs, and an arpeggio of seriously tuneless whistling interrupted her concentration.

'Men! Wouldn't you just know it!' Claudia hissed, as Melody shot back away from her on the sofa and she herself struggled frantically with her robe.

'Well, at least he had the good manners to warn us,' consoled Melody in a low voice, as the strangely heavy and tardy footsteps could be heard approaching via the -all.

Well, yes, he did, thought Claudia, who had already taken good note of Paul's light and athletic way of moving. If he was making such a racket as he approached them in the sitting room, there was no doubt whatsoever that he meant to. Which meant he was being uncannily tactful and sensitive over allowing them time to finish their *post mortem* analysis of Melody's marriage – or he had somehow expected them to be making love!

Claudia would have fretted slightly over this last supposition if she hadn't had all such thoughts dashed from her mind when he finally appeared in the doorway.

'That's better!' he announced, rubbing his hand

through his still-wet hair. He was dressed with perfect decorum in a pair of jeans and a light-blue sweater, but he looked as stunning and angelic as when he was naked.

'Would you like some brandy, Paul?' Claudia asked, double checking, as she got to her feet, that her robe was secured. Paul's flickering eyes told her he had noted the action, and his small grin seemed to suggest he knew why she had made it, too.

'Yes,' he said, hesitating, then going on. 'I would quite like some, but I'm still a bit dubious about the effects of alcohol on my scrambled brain cells.'

'What about a brandy and ginger?' suggested Melody, looking a little shy. 'Light on the brandy, heavy on the ginger ale. I'm sure that won't do you too much harm.'

'Sounds great!' said Paul, apparently happy with the compromise.

Claudia poured them all drinks, keeping the measures either small or well diluted. The atmosphere in the room was volatile enough without anyone getting tipsy.

'So, how are you feeling now?' asked Paul of Melody when they were all seated again, he to the young woman's right, in an armchair, and Claudia beside her, to her left, on the sofa.

Claudia was just about to point out what a strange thing that was to ask, when they had already had a talk during her shower, when she caught a flash of understanding pass between her two companions. What else had they discussed in her absence, other than his vague remembrance of his mishap and his experience at the hospital? Melody's tiny smile, and the very ghost of a nod, seemed to suggest an entirely different agenda. When the girl answered, her eyes bright and warm, Claudia's suspicions were amplified even more. She had visions of Melody confessing her lesbian desires to Paul and asking for his counsel. And she had no doubt what his advice would be. Go for it; don't hold back; she's ready.

'A lot better,' said Melody. 'Everything's becoming

more clear to me now. I'd say that I wish I'd thought of making changes in my life much earlier, but there's no point looking back.' She sat tall in her chair; her back straight, her carriage confident, and her breasts pressed forward. She raised her glass. 'Here's to the future, and trying new things, and getting what I want out of life!'

'Hear, hear!' said Claudia, feeling a little shaken but excited by Melody's toast.

'Amen to that,' added Paul softly, his eyes meeting Claudia's momentarily. It almost seemed – she could swear it – that he winked.

'I ought to make up another bedroom,' she said, feeling very, very nervous. 'Paul's in the one you usually use . . .' She was very aware that she was stepping into a minefield of implication here. Who slept where, and with whom, was suddenly a very complex set of variables.

'I'll move out,' proclaimed Paul immediately. 'After all, I don't have any belongings to move. All I possess is what I stood up in when I arrived. And my jacket, waistcoat and trousers are at the cleaners, and my unmentionables, I presume, are in the wash.'

Melody giggled, and Claudia enjoyed the happy, carefree sound. Perhaps things didn't have to be so complex after all. Maybe they could just make it up as they went along.

'I wouldn't dream of dislodging you, Paul,' said the young woman, giving him a creamy, flirtatious little smile, which was something else Claudia hadn't seen in ages. 'I'll have the little yellow bedroom, Claud. All I need is some bedlinen and I'll be fine.'

'Are you sure?' said Claudia and Paul in unison, and then they were all laughing as if the three of them had known each other for decades.

'Quite!' replied Melody eventually, then she paused, as if making a decision. 'Claudia, there's something I need to do. Tonight. And I'll need some help.' She tipped her head on one side, put up a hand, and pushed her fingers through her pale-blonde locks. 'You'll probably think I'm being very silly and impatient and hasty, but – '

She reached down into her totebag, which was on the floor beside the sofa '– I need to do this as soon as possible.' She brought out a box, which Claudia saw contained a well-known brand of hair tint, in a deep shade of brown. 'This was all Richard's idea!' She touched her hair again, then held up the box of colorant with a flourish. 'This is the real me . . . Or at least close enough until my natural colour grows through. I'll need a hand to make sure I get it on evenly . . .' She looked winningly at Claudia, her grey eyes large.

'Of course,' said Claudia, feeling strangely elated at the thought, 'but we'd better start soon so it can be done and dried before bedtime.' To her embarrassment, she felt herself blushing again – at the exhilarating connotations of that last, normally innocuous word.

Paul stood up as she and Melody did. 'While you see to the transformation, perhaps I could prepare us all some supper?' he suggested.

Claudia turned to him, feeling a little taken aback. 'Do you know how to?' She looked more closely at him, trying to detect any hint that he might have wrong-footed himself, then felt guilty at her lingering traces of doubt. 'Can you remember ever cooking before?'

Paul grinned, clearly unfazed. 'Not specifically, but I quite fancy having a go!'

Claudia realised her face must have registered momentary alarm.

'Don't worry!' he said, laughing rather teasingly. 'I might not be firing on all cylinders at the moment, but I'm quite confident I can open a packet of something frozen and master the finer nuances of microwaving . . . That is, if you don't mind something simple and "convenience"?'

'Well, I'm starving,' said Melody cheerfully. 'I'll eat anything! A plate of toast, even, if it all seems too complicated. Just as long as I'm able to get rid of this!' She touched her blonde tresses again dismissively.

Claudia looked questioningly at Paul. Could he really produce them a meal? She was intrigued, and found the idea vaguely sexy. 'Go ahead, then,' she said, nodding to him. 'Who knows, you might even be a chef!'

He appeared to consider the notion. 'I quite fancy the idea, to be honest,' he said thoughtfully, as they all trooped out into the hall, and he headed for the kitchen.

At the top of the stairs, Claudia paused, then leant over the banister and called out, 'In case you need it, there's a fire extinguisher hanging just under the fitted unit to the left of the cooker!'

She could just hear Paul laughing, and his exclamation. 'Cheeky witch!'

In Claudia's bathroom, she and Melody stood facing each other. Claudia felt like a shy girl on her first day at school, and without her make-up and her tailored clothes, Melody almost looked like one.

'What do we do now?' Claudia asked, looking at Melody and feeling confusion blended into her desire. Paul had inadvertently broken the flow of events back there in the sitting room – even though she suspected it was the last thing he would have wanted to do – and a little of her sexual confidence had dissipated. She knew she owed Melody an orgasm now, but to pitch suddenly back into lovemaking seemed too calculated.

'I don't know,' replied Melody. The young woman's face, Claudia suspected, was a mirror of her own. Melody obviously felt the sense of dislocation too.

It's down to you, Claudia told herself. You're supposed to be the grown-up here. Just take charge. 'Perhaps we should do your hair first,' she said, giving Melody an encouraging smile, 'then just see what happens.'

Melody returned the smile, her eyes filled with relief and an affection that was almost dazzling.

I just hope I can make you happy, Mel, thought Claudia as they set about their task, but her misgivings about their relationship soon faded in the face of her qualms about the radical change in Melody's hair colour.

'Are you sure about this?' she asked, blending a substance that looked like treacle mixed with coal tar. Even using her oldest towels swathed around Melody's shoulders, the stuff was bound to go everywhere, in particular on her pale T-shirt and jeans. 'We could go into town tomorrow and let Perluigi do it. He'll go mad anyway when you next go for a cut.'

'No ... Please ... Let's try,' said Melody firmly. 'I want to change as soon as possible.'

'Of course,' said Claudia, recognising a reflection of her own decisiveness a moment ago, 'but maybe you ought to strip to your bra and pants, then you won't spoil your clothes.'

Melody gave her a very level look and Claudia burst out laughing. 'No! It's a legitimate request, I promise you!' she exclaimed righteously, all the time knowing how much she wanted her friend to take her clothes off.

'Perhaps you should slip your clothes off too?' suggested Melody pertly, already unzipping her jeans.

'But this is all I have on!' protested Claudia, even though the thought of being nude for a second new lover in the space of days was deeply thrilling – and also deeply scary.

'It's a gorgeous robe. You shouldn't spoil it.'

'Then at least let me make a sarong out of one of these?' Claudia gestured to the heap of towels they had assembled for their mission.

Melody laughed, but shrugged and nodded towards the towels.

Affecting an insouciance she didn't feel, Claudia let the robe slide off and reached for a towel, being careful not to appear to be in a hurry. She didn't look at Melody during the process, but sensed her friend's grey eyes cruising her body with close attention. She's seen you in bikinis and in changing rooms, Claudia, she reminded herself. There's not much difference.

But there was a difference; an immense, yawning chasm between those situations and this one. Neither one of them had looked at the other before and lusted. Which Claudia did, seeing Melody in a sweet bra and pants set of ivory broderie anglais. It took a huge effort to apply herself to the tinting process.

After much laughing and splashing and lathering, and a constant battle against blobs of colour on the bathroom fittings, they eventually found themselves at the final rinsing stage. Throughout the whole procedure, it had been impossible not to touch each other accidentally, and for Claudia each contact had been fiery. Her whole body was in pandemonium. If she didn't embrace the younger woman soon, or be embraced herself by Melody, she felt as if she was going to scream and fly apart into pieces.

'Look,' she said tightly, 'we're both covered in splashes and drips of this gruesome brown lather. Why don't we rinse the whole lot off in the shower?' She paused, caught Melody by her arm and put the entire wealth of her feelings into a gentle squeeze. 'Together,' she finished, very softly.

'And quickly,' said Melody, biting her lip with nerves, yet clearly impatient. As she spoke, she put up a hand to catch a drip that was running down the side of her neck towards her bosom.

It was now or never. It had to be now. Claudia was almost breathless with impatience, but also aware that she owed a debt of pleasure to Melody. The girl had touched her exquisitely and brought her to orgasm with a sapphic skill that could only be pure instinct, and now it was her own turn to go boldly down that path. And what was very strange was, she suddenly knew it would be oh so easy.

Unwinding her towel, she drew her companion towards the shower.

Chapter Twelve
Creating a Stranger

Rinsing out the dye was like washing away another Melody. And another Claudia.

Or perhaps it was just the flushing of one particular set of inhibitions; the same inhibitions that had already been destabilised by Beatrice. The beautiful doctor had opened the floodgates but it was Melody and Claudia who now stood in the passionate stream.

'Tip your head back and let me massage away the lather,' instructed Claudia, relieved to have something to concentrate on first. Standing behind Melody was perhaps a little easier, for the moment, as her high young breasts and the dark triangle of her pubis were hidden. Not that her back view didn't have its attractions: her delicate shoulders; the in-and-out flare of her small waist and neatly defined hips; the gorgeous ripe peach-shape of her bottom. Claudia was tempted to trace this girlish silhouette with her fingers instead of getting on with the task they had appointed themselves, which was the eradication of the surplus hair dye. Constraining her urges, she set to work.

Using her fingers and thumbs, and a firm but gentle action, she helped the water do its work in Melody's hair. The runnels of brown colour turned gradually lighter and lighter, turning from mahogany, through to chestnut, to lightest tan. After about five minutes of continuous rinsing the flow ran clear.

'That's it.' She dropped her hands to Melody's shoulders and placed a kiss on the back of her neck on the pretext of sniffing for the dye's scent. 'All gone. You can't even smell it any more . . .' Her grip slid down Melody's upper arms to the crook of her elbows, and as she was about to move lower, the young woman made a soft sound of impatience. Taking Claudia's hands in hers, Melody placed them squarely on her own breasts.

'You're so lovely, Mel,' said Claudia, reinforcing her voice to be heard clearly in the torrent that tippled down over their two entwined bodies. 'I've always thought that. Even when I was unable to imagine doing anything about it.' Circling her hips, she massaged the girl's buttocks with her pubis.

Melody spoke more quietly but with a clarity that was still audible above the shower. 'And I've always wanted you,' she said, a little uncertain at first but soon gathering momentum. 'I thought I was ill, or mad, to begin with. Then I started to realise it was OK for me to have such feelings, but I was still upset because I didn't think you'd have them. I was convinced you'd be disgusted if you found out.'

'Never that,' said Claudia, flexing her fingers and glorying in the pert resilience of the flesh she was caressing. Her own breasts – now pressed close to the silky-wet expanse of Melody's back – had resisted time splendidly, but did not have quite the same upthrust, youthful arrogance. 'I might have been surprised, I admit, but I know I would soon have got used to the idea.'

'Oh God, why was I so silly?' Melody berated herself. Her dark head drooped. 'I should have told you! We could have been together sooner.'

Claudia forbore to mention that she had been married, but Melody then – obviously – recalled the fact herself.

'What on earth am I talking about?' she demanded, her usually harmonious voice cracking. 'You were mar-

Portia Da Costa

ried. How could I have expected you to be unfaithful to
Gerald? You loved him!' She shook in Claudia's hold.
'And now I'm expecting you to be unfaithful to Paul, for
me ... He said it was all right, but he could just have
been being nice, couldn't he?'

Hah! I thought so! Claudia didn't exclaim out loud,
but the confirmation of her earlier suspicions was intox-
icating. 'That must have been a fascinating conversation
you shared while I was taking my first shower,' she
observed, then leant around a little to take the tender
lobe of Melody's ear between her teeth. She nibbled very
lightly and the younger woman gasped.

'I – I'm sorry, I never meant to talk about you that
way ... It all just came out. I don't know what got into
me. Paul is so easy to talk to. He seemed to understand.'

'Oh, he does,' Claudia said, moving more strongly
against Melody now, feeling little spikes of sensation as
she pressed her opened vulva against the resistance of
the girl's rounded, toned-up bottom cheek. 'He understands things I never would have dreamed of. What he
lacks in memory, he more than makes up for in imagination.' She felt her clitoris jump at the deliciousness of
the friction – and her own memories of Paul, that were
quite intact. 'He was the one who first put the idea of
"us" – you and me, that is – in my mind.'

'But – '

'Melody, Melody, Melody ... Don't worry,' soothed
Claudia, trying to think of the girl in her arms rather
than the tiny knot of flesh between her own legs that
quivered and pulsed. 'Since Paul arrived, I've opened
up to a lot of new ideas. New horizons. It sounds a bit
hackneyed, I know, but I can see more ways of being
together than being with just one man. Or woman – '

She paused because she had to. An almost spontaneous orgasm flamed through her sex and her belly,
defying the moisture that teemed down all around them.
She gasped and her knees buckled, but she didn't fall.
Even through her pleasure, she felt Melody stiffen her
spine and brace their bodies.

166

'As I was saying,' she began, when she could speak once more, 'if you're happy with this, I'm happy with it ... And I think Paul is too.' She stopped talking and started laughing, because Melody was giggling too.

'You're sensational, Claud, you know that, don't you?' the younger woman said through her mirth. 'I never realised it was possible to have an orgasm then resume a conversation, just like that.' She seemed to think a moment, then spoke again, sounding just a little chastened. 'I didn't realise it was possible to have an orgasm so easily ... I've not had all that many with Richard.'

'His fault, not yours, sweetheart,' said Claudia automatically, not knowing how she knew this, but knowing it all the same. Intuition told her that when things were right Melody would soar quickly to the pinnacle.

And I'm going to make them right for you this very minute, my dearest, she silently told the young woman who trembled against her. With a murmur of pacification, she slid her hand down Melody's belly.

The hair Claudia encountered was soft and very fine in texture, and felt quite different to her own pubic thatch. It astonished her that there could be such a variance, and she felt her imagination open up to the diversity and possibilities of women. It would be just as exciting with each new one – the basic sameness to herself in anatomy was just a landscape that might include a wealth of idiosyncrasy.

What would Beatrice feel like down there? Would her pubic mane be as tempestuous and as red as the hair on her head? Would it be abundant, wispy, or even clipped?

But Beatrice wasn't here now, Claudia reminded herself, and Melody was. With another calming mutter, she ventured further, delving through the soft, wet hair in search of treasure.

Melody whimpered and began to wriggle her bottom, and once again, Claudia encountered her individuality. The sylph-like young woman had pudenda that were luscious and well developed. Melody's clitoris was bigger, Claudia realised, than her own, and the spongy inner lips were longer and more plump. Her slippery sex was a flower in bloom and it lured the fingers to explore.

Using the sensitive pad of her middle finger, Claudia began to voyage her lover's vulva; cruising Melody's labia, on and down to her vaginal portal, her perineum and her anus, and back up again to the swollen jewel at the heart of her pleasure.

But Melody was tense. Claudia intuited that the young woman was enjoying herself, feeling all the delightful sensations that she should be doing, yet there was still a lingering obstacle in her psyche.

'What is it, Mel?' she asked, letting her hand grow still. 'We can stop if you don't like this. I don't want to force you or upset you.'

'You're not upsetting me,' said Melody, her sigh just audible within the downpour. 'It's not you . . . It's me. I like what you're doing. I *love* it!' She placed her hand over Claudia's for emphasis. 'But don't feel you have to carry on if I'm a bit of a turn-off to you.' Her voice faltered, and Claudia guessed she was crying, adding salty tears to the water that sluiced her face.

She gave the younger woman a hug – a hard bear hug – while still maintaining contact with her juicy, tempting quim.

'What are you talking about, sweetheart?' she demanded. 'You don't turn me off, you turn me on!' Trying her best to swivel her hips in a matching rhythm to that of her fingers, she only prayed that her words and actions conveyed her emotion. 'You excite me just as much as any man's ever done!'

'Really? You're not just saying that?'

'Why should I? We've always been honest with each other before. Why should I lie now?'

'I – I don't know . . .' Melody was still unsure. At least, her mind and her voice were. Her body was finding its own way. Her hips were beginning to weave in time to Claudia's. 'It's just something Richard said. Something about me. You know, me "down there".'

That bastard! Claudia wanted to screech. She had an

idea of the type of thing that Richard Truebridge might
have said; the sort of insensitive, closed-minded remark
that came from the mouth of a man who liked to think
he knew everything about sex, but really knew nothing.
She would have liked to castigate him furiously for
hurting Melody on such an intimate level, but she
refrained from venting her anger in derogatory and most
likely profane terms. After all, there was probably a part
of Melody that still loved him.

'What did he say?' she asked as gently as she could,
still caressing the very flesh at the centre of their
discourse.

'That I was . . . that I was too big. Too coarse,' said
Melody, in a series of breathy gasps. Claudia's distraction was obviously working, because the young woman
didn't sound focused on her so-called problem at all.

'You're gorgeous,' said Claudia, meaning it. The feel
of Melody's sex against her fingers was conjuring up all
sorts of urges inside her. Urges to do things; urges to
have things done to her. She wanted to stroke and stroke
and stroke the girl; to understand everything about her
intimate shape and texture. Her ins and outs. Her fluids.
Her resilience. Her responses. She wanted to know what
another woman's orgasm felt like against her; to experience the minute, passionate dance of Melody's lush
membranes. To feel that plump clitoris jump; to hear
Melody cry out with each pulse.

Always orally fixated, Claudia knew now that she
would soon have to lick her friend; to put her on the
receiving end of all the delicious procedures that she
herself had always found so blissful. The nibbling; the
flicking; the sucking. The long, hard sucking that made
her legs kick, her belly lurch and her throat and vocal
chords eject a wild cry.

In a strange aside, she suddenly found something else
to look forward to. The taste and texture of Paul in her
mouth; his cock and its silky, salty essence.

Later, slut, she told herself, laughing inside and relishing the sumptuous banquet she had assembled, in her

house, for her own delectation. A feast of two lovers, two strangers; one that she had found and one that, in a mystic way, she was almost creating for herself. She was transforming Melody from friend into lover, just as surely as she had made a brunette out of a blonde.

'I love your quim, Melody,' she said, her flickering fingers reinforcing her words. 'I don't have much to compare it with, but to me it feels like a lovely, succulent flower. Perfect to touch and fondle; to play with and enjoy.' Using her whole body as a guide, she shifted Melody's position so that the young woman's buttocks were against her thigh, split around it to stretch her anus. It was one of her own intense pleasures to be soundly fingered while having her bottom stimulated too. She was absolutely certain it would work just as well for Melody.

'And this,' she said, pushing forward with her leg to increase the pressure as she took hold of Melody's clitoris between her finger and thumb, 'is just amazing. Beautiful. Like a pearl; a plump little berry. I can't leave it alone.' She rolled the tiny organ and Melody half laughed, half groaned. 'Now we've started, I won't be able to give up, you know,' she continued, warming to her theme. 'Whenever we're together, I'll be wanting you . . . I'll just be dying to get my hand in your pants and play with your clittie.' Melody chuckled, then gulped. Her pelvis started gyrating. Claudia hung on.

'Just think,' she said, pinching very lightly and feeling the flesh against her fingerpads flutter and beat. Melody made an uncouth, choking sound. 'We might be out shopping and I'll have to whisk you into a ladies somewhere and masturbate you! Because I can't stop thinking how hot and wet and tempting you are between your legs. It'll be the only thing on my mind. Your quim. All the time we're looking at clothes, I'll be imagining how swollen you are . . . How puffed up your sex-lips are . . . How hard your clitoris is . . . What it feels like; what it does when I do *this*!' She squeezed, and Melody wailed, her vulva pulsating.

How strange, thought Claudia, I never thought I would experience my own orgasm from the outside. Completely from the outside. How wonderful, too. How fulfilling, yet also how frustrating. Stimulating Melody had had a reciprocal effect on her own body, invoking the need but not providing resolution. Her sex felt a mile wide, congested and uncomfortable.

But she had to concentrate, for the moment, on her companion. Melody was half collapsing in her arms, gasping and muttering. Claudia could swear she heard the words 'I love you' muttered under Melody's breath, but it was difficult to be sure in the pelting streams of water.

'Are you all right, Mel?' enquired Claudia cautiously, still supporting the younger woman, though feeling her try to stand up and pull herself together.

Melody eased herself free, lifted her face to the flow of the shower for a moment and sluiced back her trans-formed hair; then she turned around, her face glistening and radiant.

'Oh Claud, I'm more than all right!' she cried, throwing her arms around Claudia and almost sending the pair of them sliding and flying. 'I feel incredible, thanks to you. I haven't come like that in months! Years! Ever! Oh, thank you, thank you, thank you!' Still lauding her, she kissed Claudia on the lips.

It was a long kiss, a messy kiss, and it stoked the fires that were already well raging in Claudia. She wanted Melody; wanted her desperately to do something that would release a growing pressure. Her quim ached. She was wetter than the shower could ever make her. She would have to come, and come soon, or she would scream.

'I wonder if I'm a real lesbian, and I've never really been into men at all, but just thought I was?' mused Melody, breaking the kiss and resting her dark head on Claudia's shoulder.

'I don't know, my sweet,' said Claudia, tensing up with the need to control herself. Melody's feelings, and

the moment, were still friable. 'Can you still see yourself
in bed with a man? Can you imagine being touched by a
man and getting excited?'

I can, thought Claudia as Melody seemed to ponder
these questions. If it were Paul here now I would want
him just as much as I want you, Mel. She imagined
bending over in the shower and being taken crudely
from behind, just as she had been taken, earlier in the
day, in the meadow.

But what if he wanted more? Something different?
What if he insisted on her making good her promise and
allowing him to bugger her?

Claudia's whole body shook with the power of that
vision, with a sensation of yielding that seemed to melt
the pit of her belly and make her sex and her anus tingle.
God! Oh, how she wanted that now! Her whole being
wanted Paul to be with her now, so she could bend
before him, holding apart her own buttocks so he could
possess her nether entrance. Unable to control herself,
she moaned into Melody's slick, mahogany-dark hair.

Now it was Melody's turn to make solicitous enquir-
ies. 'What is it, Claud?' she murmured, cradling the back
of Claudia's head. 'Is something the matter?'

'No,' said Claudia, gathering herself and pulling a
little way away from Melody so they could look into one
another's eyes. 'Just thoughts . . .'

'What thoughts?' asked Melody, her grey eyes bright
and wicked. 'Thoughts about me?'

Claudia's heart sank. She thought again of her friend's
lingering emotional fragility. How could she say she had
been fantasising about Paul? But then again, lies and
deception were bound to be more damaging.

'When I told you to start thinking about men, I
couldn't help myself. I started thinking about them too.
Or should I say, I started thinking about one man in
particular.'

Melody chuckled. 'I don't need a million guesses to
work out which one,' she said, pulling Claudia closer

again, 'and if it makes you feel any better ... well ... I was thinking about the same one!'

'And did you find yourself wanting to make love with him?' asked Claudia slowly, sliding her wet belly against Melody's. Would she feel jealous, she wondered, if the answer was yes?

Melody seemed to have acquired the same mind-reading powers as the man they were discussing, because she said, 'Would it hurt you if I said I did desire him? I'd do anything rather than upset you, Claud, you know that. If you'd rather I didn't ... um ... *want* him, I'll put him completely out of my mind, I promise you.'

'You don't have to do that, you silly!' said Claudia, without even having to think. She knew she could allow thoughts and fantasies of her own into her heart and see images of Paul and Melody together quite painlessly. The only problem was they only increased her arousal – a state of tumescence that was already a plaguing torment.

'I *want* you to think about Paul!' she said, smiling at Melody, and at the same time pressing their two pubises closer. 'In fact, I want you to do far more than think about him.' She gave her friend a slow, lascivious wink. 'With his libido the way it is, there'll be more than enough of him to go around! We could even go three in a bed if you want to. I'm sure our friend "The Stranger" won't mind.'

' "The Stranger"?'

'That's a sort of secret pet name I've been using for him ... in my thoughts,' Claudia admitted, and in the next instant she darted forward and kissed Melody hard.

'Are those the same thoughts you were having a few moments ago?' asked Melody, gasping for breath as Claudia finally broke the kiss.

Claudia nodded.

'Phooargh!' growled the younger woman. 'I've never done anything so wild before, but I can't imagine anything more blissful than making love with you *and* with

Paul. It'd be just perfection!' She smothered Claudia's face and jawline with a dozen or so inaccurate kisses.

'Well, then,' said Claudia, cupping Melody's bottom and caressing it roughly, 'we'll have to make sure that we all have the opportunity to ... er ... try out that perfection, won't we?'

'I can hardly wait,' crooned Melody, stroking Claudia's buttocks in return. 'I don't know what's come over me, Claud,' the younger woman went on, her voice exultant but dreamy as she shimmied her faultless body against the form that Claudia knew wasn't quite so immaculate. 'Before today, I used to think even just stuff like oral sex was a bit daring. And now look at me!'

'You're wonderful, Mel. A sensualist just waiting to blossom.' Claudia was gasping with desire now; she couldn't think straight. The idea of release, of the explosive rush of orgasm, seemed to barrel towards her through the aether like a comet. She embraced her beautiful friend, trying to communicate her need via their contiguous wet skin.

'Mel,' she went on huskily, 'about oral sex. How do you feel about it now? Does it still seem daring?' She put her hands on Melody's shoulders, then bore down with an almost infinitesimal pressure. At the same time she let her eyes flick downward for an instant.

Revelation dawned immediately in Melody's eyes, and she laughed, low and almost demonically. 'It still does seem daring,' she said, and Claudia felt a quick kiss pressed fervently to the hollow where her neck met her shoulder, 'but somehow today "daring" is just what I need.'

Then, with the utmost of grace, Melody sank slowly to her knees.

'Am I imagining things, or can I smell chicken?'

Claudia dropped the towel she had been drying her hair with on to her shoulders and sniffed the air in response to Melody's remark.

'You're right. I can smell it too. Paul must be getting

ambitious and cooking the pack of breasts and thighs I had in the fridge.'

Melody giggled, and Claudia smiled fondly at such a sweet and carefree sound. It was good to hear and see her friend so happy, even if it was a bit of a shock to look across at a brunette now.

'*Chicken* breasts and thighs,' she pointed out, getting up and walking across to where Melody was sitting, titivating her new, dark, reddish-brown hair. 'This looks wonderful,' she said, leaning over and dropping a kiss among the glossy, vibrant waves, 'but it's been such a long time since I saw you dark and wavy. It's going to take a little while to get used to the new you. You're as much a stranger to me now as Paul is.' She rubbed her cheek against the top of Melody's head, then let her hand slide down her companion's shoulder and settle on her breast, squeezing the soft orb very gently through the thin fabric of the burgundy cheesecloth shirt she was wearing.

'Not too much of a stranger,' said Melody, stretching into the caress like a contented cat.

'No, not really,' replied Claudia, experiencing a slight, aroused stir, even though Melody had satisfied her beautifully only a little while ago. She could still feel the softness of those lovely shell-pink lips as her friend had kissed her and nibbled her delicately between her legs. 'It's just that . . . well . . . there's a whole new dimension to you now. We're still friends, but it's like I've been given an extra bonus I'd never expected to receive.' She rubbed Melody's nipple and felt it become plump and erect again in a flash.

Melody laid down her comb, swivelled around on the stool, and reached up to pull Claudia's mouth to hers, pushing with her tongue to obtain immediate access. They wrestled a moment, bodies and mouths, hands and hair, then reluctantly, and with some amusement, Claudia pulled away.

'What about the dinner?' she said, tapping Melody playfully on the nose. 'Poor old Paul's been slaving over a hot stove while we've been up here enjoying ourselves. The least we can do is show up and eat what he's cooked.'

'I'd rather eat you,' said Melody, running her tongue graphically over her lips and making Claudia feel close to swooning with remembrance of their frolics in the shower. The younger woman had proved to be just as adept at providing cunnilingus as she had been eager, some minutes later, to receive it. Both women had ended up waterlogged by the time they had finally climbed shakily from the stall.

'Maybe later,' said Claudia, in a casual attempt to placate her latest lover. She supposed she should be worrying about the possible permutations which might now arise between the three of them: Melody, Paul and herself. But there seemed no way she could stir herself to be concerned about the situation. It was a lottery, really, from now on. A adventure of chance, companion-ship and carnality. There were three of them in the game and it was just a case of letting the cards fall exactly how they may. And she had a strong instinct that the others would feel much the same as she did.

'Yes, maybe,' said Melody mildly, as if confirming Claudia's thoughts. 'I'm hungry anyway.' She grinned again, the mirth lighting up her pretty face and making it exceptional. '*Really* hungry, I mean. And whatever Paul's doing to that chicken, it smells fabulous!'

'I agree!' Claudia said, taking a last glimpse in the mirror to check her look. 'Let's eat!'

'You look amazing!' said Melody, her voice warm. 'There's no need to worry.'

Claudia *felt* amazing, and though she sometimes thought she overrated her own belief in the idea that she looked far younger than a forty-something should, tonight she was convinced she could be ageless. Her hair, her eyes and her face all shone with fulfilment, and even her body seemed to possess a sly, discreet lustre; a kind of glow that enhanced what she was wearing. 'Do you think this is OK?' she enquired, still needing a trace of reassurance. She smoothed down the cotton of her fuscia Capri pants to make them sit a little better around her thighs, then twitched the hem of her matching, sleeveless top.

'Ravishing!' pronounced Melody. 'And I don't think I look too bad myself, either. What do you think?'

'You know what I think, you vain little madam!' cried Claudia, swinging around to grab Melody's bottom and give one cheek a little squeeze. The younger woman was wearing a pair of trim, denim cut-offs with her cheese-cloth shirt, and their tightness seemed to constantly invite the hand. Claudia wondered if they would invite Paul's hand too. If she couldn't get through the evening without goosing Melody two or three times, she thought it unlikely that Paul would be able to resist either.

'Come on,' she said, taking Melody by the hand, 'let's get downstairs and join Paul before I'm forced to rip your clothes of and whisk you off to bed!'

'Dear God!' exclaimed Paul, letting the pan he was holding drop down on to the stove top with a clatter. Luckily for him, nothing spilled.

Claudia smiled, heartened that she didn't feel too jealous of the way he was staring at Melody. I had a big hand in this miracle, she told herself silently. The way he's admiring her is as much a vote of praise for me as it is for her.

'What an amazing job you've done,' he said, abandoning the stove and moving towards them. He took both their hands, and Claudia knew that once again, her instincts had been right. 'You've worked wonders!' He smiled at Melody, then at her. 'It's like seeing the same person, yet someone completely different.'

He speaks as if he's known us both for years, thought Claudia in wonder. He has the authority, yet I don't know quite how or why. I just know that what he says sounds utterly right.

It puzzled her, but as she looked from one smooth, beautiful face to another, she became aware of an even greater conundrum. Now that Melody had dark hair, she bore an uncanny resemblance to Paul. It wasn't a likeness in a grand sense – his features were too masculine, and hers too womanly – but there was a nuance of the same intriguing mystery about them both; a sexual allure that was as strong in some ways as it was delicate and subtle in others. And to have the two of them in her house, both wanting to be with her, made her heart pound, her head spin and her body tingle.

An *embarras de richesse*, she thought, looking from one to another and wondering if they were aware themselves of their elusive similarity. She saw Melody smile shyly at Paul, and something faint yet intriguing flicker in his eyes, and she had a feeling that at least he had recognised the strange affinity. He returned Melody's smile, then swung his face around and gave Claudia one just as warming.

'You seem to have a knack for this, Mrs Marwood,' he said softly, giving her a kiss on the cheek while still holding Melody's hand. 'You're a transformer. You've changed two of us for the better.' He looked her in the eyes, asked a silent question, and she gave him her silent answer. Without a moment's hesitation, he kissed Melody gently too.

Not one of them said anything for a second or two, but surprisingly, the atmosphere didn't seem awkward. Paul had effortlessly assessed the situation and set the mood.

Claudia wondered what on earth was going to happen next, but perhaps fortuitously, there came the spitting sound of grilling chicken from the cooker.

'Agh! Duty calls,' said Paul, squeezing both their hands briefly but fiercely, then turning his attention to his culinary endeavours. 'Perhaps you two ladies could organise the drinks while I finish up here?' he suggested from over his shoulder, while expertly prodding and turning the meat.

Cheek! thought Claudia. Anyone would think you lived here, young man! 'Certainly,' she said crisply, suppressing her snort of amusement. 'I think we'll bring up something a bit special from the wine cellar. This does seem to be something of a unique occasion.'

And then some, she added silently, leading Melody in the direction of the cellar stairs.

Chapter Thirteen

Secrets and Lies – and Stars

*A*fter a slight, abortive, erotic fumble and a lot of giggling, and having selected a very good bottle of Australian Chardonnay, Claudia and Melody returned to the kitchen.

'Wow, what a splendid table!' the younger woman exclaimed, admiring Paul's handiwork when they walked in.

Claudia had to agree. He had set the long, deal table in the kitchen with the everyday cutlery, but he had used a tablecloth and dressed up the display with a pair of terracotta-ware candlesticks, which Claudia always liked to use to light cosy, evening meals in the kitchen. The napkins, which matched the cloth, he had folded into very passable attempts at waterlilies.

'Well, on this evidence, you're either the *maître d'hôtel* at a very superior restaurant, or you're an interior decorator,' remarked Claudia. 'Which do you think it is?'

'I'm still betting on chef,' he replied lightly, 'but we'll soon see. Would you like to sit down and I'll dish up the first course.'

'Wow! There's more than one?' enquired Melody, sliding on to a chair. It seemed natural to Claudia that she and the younger woman should sit facing each other, with Paul at the head of the table, presiding.

Their starters were a couple of crispy, aromatic crostini apiece, and once again, Claudia was mightily impressed. She recognised the component ingredients as the most simple of items, culled from her own well-stocked store cupboard, but somehow Paul had added a strangely inspired touch to them. Which was a miracle, really, because the fact that he had prepared them at all beat most men she had ever known hands-down. She could see Melody looking just as shaken as she was by their companion's unexpected skills. It was unlikely that Richard Truebridge even knew where the kitchen in his house was – although now, Claudia thought with some satisfaction, he would bloody well have to find it!

Their next course was plain grilled chicken, but served with a salad full of imagination and colour. As well as the mixed leaves she had expected, Claudia saw and tasted slivers of sun-dried tomato, herbs harvested from the pots that stood on her windowsill and Parmiaggano Reggiano shaved fresh from the block, not to mention the croutons he must have made himself because she kept no such thing pre-prepared in her pantry.

'Amazing!' she said, forking up the last mouthful, then chewing it with Sybaritic pleasure. 'Where on earth did you learn to cook like that?' Suddenly, realising what she had said, she apologised. 'Sorry, you probably don't know, do you?' Lifting the bottle, she topped up all their glasses, with the wine which might have been created especially to complement the amalgamated flavours of the salad and the chicken.

'I'm afraid not,' said Paul, his brow crumpling for a moment, 'and I have tried . . . I hoped something would come to me as I worked, but nothing did. I can remember what to do instinctively, but I've no idea how I acquired the knowledge in the first place.'

'Don't worry about it,' said Melody cheerily. 'The end result is scrumptious, and I'm sure the whys and wherefores will come back to you before long. I just know it!'

'Thank you,' said Paul, smiling and reaching out to pat her hand. 'I hope you're right.' He gave them an apologetic look. 'I'm afraid there isn't any dessert as such. The culinary memory bank seemed to crash where pudding was concerned.'

'I don't think I could eat any anyway,' said Claudia. 'You've done us proud, Paul. I'm tempted to be selfish and hope your memory doesn't come back too soon. Then you can stay around here and be my cook.' She felt a heat rising up her throat and cheeks that had nothing to do with good food and wine. 'Among other things.'

Melody chuckled, and Paul had the grace to blush a little too.

'What have we got ourselves into here?' said Claudia, glancing from one of them to the other, and feeling grateful for the gentle, mellowing qualities of the wine. She didn't feel tipsy at all, but the delicious Chardonnay had nicely smoothed the awkward edges from the situation. Her predominant emotion was anticipation, not anxiety. 'Let's go out on to the patio and watch the stars a while,' she said, rising from her seat and taking her glass. With the others following suit, she was just about to lead the way out when she noticed that the notepad she kept handy for jotting down kitchen reminders and the titles of pieces of music that came on the radio while she was cooking was lying open on the counter, and that the upper page was filled with a jumble of unfamiliar writing. When she picked it up and started to read, she was first touched, then very quickly, deeply puzzled.

At the top of the sheet was a list of cookery ingredients, obviously the ones which Paul had used up, and which now needed replacing. But halfway down, the pencil seemed to do a hop and a skip, as if Paul had been struck by some kind of revelation in mid-thought, and had grasped the new concept and run with it before it escaped from his shattered memory.

The only thing Claudia could liken the fast and almost shorthand-looking squiggles to was the long-forgotten remnants of her grammar school algebra studies. And having been better at humanities than at sciences, the fragments she could decipher meant nothing at all in the world to her – it was just a morass of letters and figures; of add, plus and integer signs; of figures and letters squared, and to various powers. The whole thing had a decidedly unfinished look to it, but Claudia couldn't be sure of that. She would have better understood a tablet of hieroglyphics.

'Paul . . . What's this?' She held out the pad to him.

'Brainstorm,' he replied, looking uncomfortable. His face was like a shuttered room all of a sudden and she wasn't sure if he was scared or resentful.

'Of what?' she persisted, her own fears and doubts bobbing up to the surface. What was he up to?

'I don't know,' he said, taking the pad from her and studying his own work. 'It was like the cookery. It just came to me, out of the blue, and it seemed important to put it down before it went away again. It beats me what it is, but it felt natural to be writing it, and at the time, I really felt as if I knew what I was doing. But it's meaningless now.'

'Phew!' said Melody, looking over Claudia's shoulder. 'You're obviously a very, very clever man . . . at something.'

Claudia forbore to comment. She didn't want to think about the possible ramifications of these arcane symbols, and for a moment she felt resentment too. She didn't want to be reminded of the essentially temporary nature of Paul's presence in her home.

'Come on!' she said briskly. 'Those stars are waiting.'

The influence of the ancient heavens was pacific; and either they or the wine or the youth and beauty of her two companions managed to banish her misgivings in a very short space of time. It was a clear night, with only the thinnest of crescent moons, and the residual scraps of a different scientific discipline came back to her as she stared up into the velvety darkness at the scintillating pinpoints of light. They were all so far away, these astral phenomena which were as huge and majestic as the noonday sun in reality, and in many many cases far more so. Yet another instance of something lovely, yet secretive and mysterious.

Throwing back his head too, Paul raised his hand, fingers pale and tapered as they seemed to reach for the distant stars.

'Ursa Major,' he said, his voice very distinct and disturbingly scholarly in the night's stillness. 'The best-known constellation.' Claudia peered at him and saw him narrow his eyes, as if zeroing in on individual light sources, 'And the stars are . . . Alkaid, Mizar, Alioth, Delta Ursa Majoris, Phecda, Merak, Dubhe . . .'

'Paul,' said Claudia, softly, 'where's all this coming from?'

'I know them. I just know them,' he said, sounding full of wonder, 'but I'm sure I didn't know them the other night.'

'Your memory must be returning,' said Melody. Claudia sensed the younger woman sliding her arm through Paul's free one, and almost laughed at her own tiny plume of jealousy. She couldn't take Paul's other arm as he was pointing out more stars.

'You could be right,' he said, after he had run through one or two more constellations.

'Yes, yes! I must be!' Melody was warming to her theme. 'First it was the recipes, then the complicated maths, and now the names of the stars. Your life's gradually coming back to you, I'm sure of it!'

'It's certainly a good sign that you're beginning to remember things,' said Claudia, keeping her voice more circumspect.

In the darkness, she sensed him look at her sharply, and could almost hear his thought: You still don't absolutely believe me, do you? He lowered his arm, and she could feel his scrutiny intensify, as if he were challenging her to cling to him as Melody was doing. She resisted.

'Yes, it is,' he said levelly, 'but I think I've been lucky too, in where I've ended up. And with whom.'

'I haven't done anything special,' Claudia returned,

feeling as she spoke that she was merely being argumentative. She *had* done something special. How many women, taking an amnesiac total stranger into their house, would also take him into their bed?

Paul didn't reply, but as she risked a sly sideways glance at him, light from the house revealed amusement in the dramatic, shadowed planes of his face. He continued in silence for a few moments, looking back at her, then spoke again:

'I doubt if I would have regained as much of myself, as quickly as this, if I had been shunted from police station to hospital to hostel ... Or whatever it is that usually happens to people in my situation.'

'If you'd gone to the police, they could well have traced your identity by now,' Claudia pointed out.

'True,' said Paul, 'but then I would have been pitched back into my life before I was ready for it. I thought I explained that to you.'

As if sensing a vortex of antagonism building up, Melody suddenly pitched in. 'She's always like this, Paul. She's the kindest, most giving person I know, yet she has a pathological resistance to being properly thanked for that kindness.'

'Oh please,' murmured Claudia, 'I think I'm going to throw up.' Nevertheless, she felt gratified.

'Then perhaps she should be *made* to accept thanks,' said Paul, his voice suddenly alight with something that made the pit of Claudia's belly quiver. She had heard that silky, puckish tone before. 'She deserves a recompense for her services to us lost souls, doesn't she, Melody? I think that it's only right if *we* make sure she receives it. What do you think?'

What was he up to?

Claudia knew she hardly had to ask that question; her heart and her loins already knew where he was heading. But was Melody ready for this? Was she picking up on Paul's implications?

'I agree. Oh, how I agree,' purred Melody, sliding around so that she and Paul were bracketing Claudia.

Of course she knows what he's up to, thought Claudia, recalling Melody's exquisite empathy in sensing her own fears and hopes. The basic moral unworthiness of Richard Truebridge was the younger woman's only blind spot.

'Thank you, Claud,' Melody whispered, pressing her lips to Claudia's shoulder. 'Thank you for taking me in too. I would have been lost if I hadn't been able to come to you.'

Oh dear, thought Claudia, feeling Paul's mouth against her other shoulder, the contact as co-ordinated as if he and Melody were in a mind-meld. As he kissed her, his long hands settled on her waist, taking hold of her, then turning her to face Melody.

In the starlight, the younger woman was an enigma, unknown with her dark and lovely hair. 'Claudia, Claudia, Claudia,' she whispered, placing her gentle hands on either side of Claudia's face and bringing it to her own to kiss her properly. As their mouths met, Claudia felt Paul's lips press down on the nape of her neck.

'Oh please . . .' murmured Claudia when her mouth was freed. She wasn't sure she could cope. Either one of these two, separately, had the power to play havoc with her senses; there was no knowing what they might achieve together. She shuddered finely as Melody breathed against her ear.

'Don't be afraid,' the girl whispered, totally confident now, as if the presence of Paul had braced her somehow.

'No, don't be scared,' he said, his mouth very close to Claudia's other ear. 'Let us take care of you this time. Give something back for all you've given to us.'

'I don't want your gratitude!' protested Claudia weakly, feeling every fibre of her sex and body contradict her. She *did* want it. She wanted it very much, because she was enraptured by the way they would express it.

'Then take pleasure simply because *we* want to give it!' said Paul, more forcefully this time. He and Melody were creating their own momentum, and Claudia knew that she could not resist them, even if she had been foolish enough to want to.

Too swept away to answer, Claudia replied by relaxing back against him. She felt his erection butt against her, seeking her heat through her thin cotton trousers, but she knew that this interlude was not about his satisfaction for now; or about Melody's, even though the girl's sweet, hard nipples were rubbing Claudia's own as their two torsos moved together in a slow, tender dance.

Graceful hands – Paul's – slid forward over her thighs and set up a tantalising rhythm of stroking, while a second pair inveigled their way between his body and Claudia's, curving delicately to cup the rounds of her buttocks. No-one touched her crotch, but something told her this was deliberate. They were only at the very beginning of the process.

Her mouth was possessed, Melody's lips becoming mobile and rapacious, and at her back Paul swooped down and kissed her too, ravishing the hollow of soft flesh where her neck met her shoulder with an enthusiasm she vaguely realised would leave a mark. She tried to object, but Melody's tongue subdued hers and kept her silent.

Between them, they rocked her pelvis to and fro, using teamwork to keep her moving and keep her wanting. Claudia was desperate to participate, to be as active and as assertive as they were being, but even so her arms hung limply at her sides. She felt out of control, yet at the same time strangely dominant. There was a part of her that seemed to be floating above it all, surveying the scene and subliminally directing the action.

You're what I want, you two, she thought, in a dream, visualising her bare flesh being touched and feeling, in response, someone unfasten her Capri pants. As both pairs of hands had moved she did not know who it was. The same hands, or perhaps the other set, drew the cotton trousers down to her knees, then peeled down her G-string to follow them. Then they sandwiched her

between them once again, accentuating her uncovered-
ness with the feel of their still-clothed bodies. Melody's
slim but flexible hands took a firm hold on her nude
buttocks; and at the same time Paul reached around and
cupped her mons pubis. Her mouth was still deliciously
stopped my Melody's tongue.

Claudia opened her eyes. Up close, she could see the
highlights and shadings of Melody's familiar yet unfamiliar face, and the lush dark crescents of her lowered
lashes. But when she focused over the girl's shoulder
and looked upward, she could once more see the stars.
They were further than she could comprehend, and so
unknown, yet no stranger, in a way, than what was
going on, down here, on terra firma. As Paul's fingers
divided her labia, she almost choked.

The sensation of him stroking her was like coming
home somehow. He was meant to handle her thus; his
fingertip was where it should be, moving in exactly the
cadence that suited her. And that Melody was kneading
her bottom at the same time only increased the finesse of
the experience. After just a moment, she grunted savagely, her climax intense.

'You two!' she hissed lovingly, coming back to her
senses and realising they had been supporting her
weight between them. 'Have you no respect for your
elders?' Shimmying herself free of their hold, she reached
down to pull up her G-string and her Capri pants, then
was thwarted when Melody sank to the ground, kissed
the triangle of Claudia's pubic hair, then rose again,
putting the disarranged clothing to rights as she did so.

'There, is that better, old thing?' the younger woman
said pertly, fastening the last button.

Claudia narrowed her eyes and smirked. Then, giving
no warning, she grabbed Melody and kissed her soundly
on the mouth, this time making the girl yield to *her*
tongue. 'Old thing?' she queried, pushing the gasping,
bruised-mouthed Melody away from her.

'I'm sorry,' said the girl cheerfully, rubbing her fingers

across her lips, 'I meant old in wisdom, not in spirit or beauty.'

'I should think so,' replied Claudia roundly, sensing the close attention of Paul behind her. She thought he might grab her again, so she turned quickly towards him. 'Let's take this inside,' she said, more as an order than a request. 'I want more of you.' She looked from one to the other, enchanted again by the rare, intangible likeness between them. 'Both of you. Come on!' In control now, she smiled and walked away, perfectly sure that they would follow without question.

In the hall, her facade of poise wavered a moment when the phone trilled right beside her and made her jump. She was just about to reach for it, then changed her mind and let the answerphone click in.

She was even more surprised by the smooth, light voice of one of her late husband's business partners, Tristan Van Dissell, who had sexual designs on her, if Melody was to be believed.

'Hello, Claudia, it's Triss. I'll be surprised if you're not in, so if you're call screening, please do pick up.'

He sounded confident – more confident than most people did on an answerphone – but at the heart of things, Claudia did detect a trace of doubt; an unsurety in himself and his purpose. She supposed that the events of the last few days must have sensitised her somehow, because she was certain she would never have picked up on such a subtle nuance a couple of weeks ago.

'I've been meaning to ring you for some time, but I didn't want to rush things,' Tristan went on. 'There're some business things we need to discuss, and Richard has deputised me to raise them, fortunately . . . But I'd like it to be a social thing for us too. I thought a nice dinner somewhere, a few drinks, get the business out of the way, then get to know each other a little better. I don't think it's too soon, do you?' He paused and made a small, cough-like sound that betrayed his nervousness. 'Anyway, Claudia, please think about it. You know my number. *Ciao*!'

'I told you,' said Melody, but something sour in her tone made Claudia look at her friend more closely.

'Yes, you said he fancied me, but there's something else, isn't there?' Melody was biting her lips. The worried runaway had replaced the confident temptress who had performed beneath the stars.

'He and Richard are up to something,' Melody said tightly. 'They're trying to cheat you somehow. I heard them talking about it on the phone . . . I think the plan is for Tristan to sweet-talk you into something, perhaps put you off the scent with a bit of romance. And things.'

'Things?' Claudia and Paul chorused. She would have laughed but Melody looked too serious.

'I don't know the exact details,' the younger woman went on, her demeanour more and more uncomfortable by the second, 'and I do know that Tristan does genuinely fancy you, but the two of them are cooking up something between them.' Her head came up, and suddenly she looked more steely. 'And I can prove it, I think. Or at least someone who understands maths and accounting can. There were some disks and papers in Richard's office, and I've made copies and brought them with me. He thinks I'm just a stupid bit of fluff without a thought in my head, but he'll have another think coming if we can expose what he and Triss are up to!' She was defiant now, and some of her earlier, new-born persona had returned. Quite a lot of it, in fact. 'I could kill him just for plotting to damage you, Claud,' she said, her beautiful face set in lines of determination and passion. Claudia felt her body stir and flare.

'Are you going to ring him?' Paul asked neutrally, although Claudia, on turning, saw something in his body language that suggested tension. Was he jealous of another man? It certainly didn't bother him that she might be involved with a member of her own sex, but even the remarkable 'Stranger' might be prone to the deeply ingrained caveman mentality that haunted even the finest of men.

'Not tonight,' she said, then reached out and laid her

hands on both his chest and Melody's sweet, firm breast. 'Let him cool his heels. Let him wonder a bit. We've got a more important kind of business to attend to, remember?'

'Of course,' said Paul, his thick lashes flashing downward for a second.

Melody said nothing, but her flesh shook under Claudia's fingers.

'Come on!' urged Claudia, again leading them towards the destination they all yearned for – her bedroom. 'Tomorrow morning, we'll make a plan. We'll work together.'

But it seemed, a few minutes later, that Paul and Melody were already working together. Having excused herself a moment to visit the bathroom, Claudia returned to the bedroom and found the two of them grinning complicitly. And when she advanced into the room, she saw Paul nod as if giving Melody a signal. In answer, the young woman approached Claudia with a slight, enigmatic smile upon her face.

'What are you two up to?' asked Claudia when Melody reached her and slid her arms around her. She wasn't really worried about what her two lovers might do to her, but it seemed the proper form to at least resist a little.

Melody didn't favour Claudia with a reply, but simply kissed her lewdly and powerfully, using her tongue again as she had in the garden. Somewhere in the background she heard Paul's murmur of approval.

With her mouth deliciously opened and Melody's hands once more on her bottom, Claudia suddenly felt herself being half pushed and half pulled backward, towards her own bed. Paul was guiding and Melody was propelling. When the mattress hit the back of her knees, Claudia flopped down.

'Take off your clothes, Claudia,' instructed Paul quietly when Melody had retreated a little way.

Something wild churned deep in Claudia's stomach. She felt an immediate rush of wetness to her sex and knew it was an instinctive reaction to Paul's unforced and understated dominance. In his own milieu, whatever that was, she was certain he was a master, a powerful force, a person of consequence and authority; he might not know who or what that person was yet, but the primal cues had been restored to his personality. He was used to being looked up to, and he expected it.

Not speaking, she reached behind her and unbuttoned her simple cotton top, her throat and ears blushing the same hot colour as the fabric when the flimsy bra she wore beneath it was revealed. A wisp of cherry-coloured lace and underwiring, it virtually screamed out that she had been expecting sex tonight. It was rather tight, and when she unclasped it, her breasts spilled out like two ripe fruits. Standing just beside her, Melody took the garment from her hands, and without a word, reached across and stroked her nipples.

Claudia felt strung tight with intense erotic tension. She hardly dared look at her two companions but she was acutely aware that they were watching every detail of every move she made. Unfastening her Capri pants, she first kicked off her sandals then slid the pants down, uncovering the G-string that she had already lowered once that night, a cherry-pink notion that matched the saucy bra. She was very conscious, as she slipped it off, that it was soaking.

'Lie back now,' urged Paul, coming closer to her and leaning over her as she complied. His blue eyes flashed kingfisher with arousal. 'Put your arms back. Hold the bed rail. Now part your legs.'

Claudia had a fair idea what was coming, especially when she felt Melody reach under the pillow and then saw her pull out a handful of silky scarves. She recognised all her best ones, bought to tone with her favourite formal outfits.

'I – I don't know about this,' she said, sensing that they still expected a token protest.

'Neither do we,' said Melody, setting to with the

scarves, 'but for my part, I'm having a great time making it up as I go along.'

And what about you, Stranger? asked Claudia silently as her hands were tied with an efficiency that suggested Melody had natural talents they had both been unaware of. Paul was still watching her steadily, only his lambent eyes betraying the substance of his passion.

Had he indulged in games like this before? Tied them up and taunted them for their pleasure and his? Something in his calm demeanour suggested that such activity was familiar.

I'll get you back for this, she thought almost dreamily as her legs were drawn further apart then secured, giving her no opportunity to disguise the slickness of her vulva. She felt as if a thousand pairs of eyes were staring at the glossy juices that had gathered in – and were in danger of overflowing from – her overheated furrow. It seemed difficult to credit that there were only two people in the room besides herself.

Closing her eyes, she revelled in the sensation of being fastened. It gave her a strange kind of sovereignty, somehow. It released her from responsibility and the burden of keeping a rein on her own reactions. Bound like this she was free to thrash and scream and howl.

As if she had voiced this thought aloud, Paul looked at her, his beautiful eyes narrowed. Taking swift, light steps, he crossed the room to where Melody stood and whispered in her ear. Her face lit up with a grin of perfect devilment, and she glanced across at Claudia and giggled.

'Oh, Paul, what a perfectly disgraceful idea. I love it!' she said, still looking at Claudia, her eyes full of wicked promise.

'Well, jump to it then,' said Paul briskly, running his hand down Melody's smooth, bare thigh where it emerged from her nearly rudimentary shorts.

'Delighted,' she said, her dainty fingers instantly at work on the shorts' zip.

Oh, what is she doing? thought Claudia, in a panic of

luscious anticipation. Several sublimely rude suggestions sprung to mind and she didn't really know which one of them she longed for – or feared – the most.

In the blink of an eye, Melody's denim shorts were on the floor, and she was stepping out of her black satin knickers with the long-legged grace of a supermodel. Leaving herself half naked, she handed the panties to Paul.

'Perfect,' he said succinctly, and from where she lay, Claudia could see that Melody's underwear was just as lust-stained as hers had been. Watching him as he wadded the delicate garment into a little bundle, it dawned on her exactly what he was going to use them for – and though the thought shocked her, she felt a fresh burst of desire that was close to painful.

'Open up,' he said, gently stroking her face with his free hand while holding the fragrant knickers close to her mouth. 'Don't be frightened,' he whispered in her ear. 'It's just part of the game. If you really don't like it, I can take them out.'

How completely he understands me, thought Claudia, in awe of him as he very carefully inserted Melody's panties in her mouth. He knows I want adventure but that it's new to me.

The taste of Melody's quim was salty, almost marine, yet still had a strangely fresh and almost honeyed quality. She was like a wine from a premier vintage; superbly complex and lingering on the tongue. Her aroma stirred the need in Claudia's own flesh.

Oh God, I want her, or I want him, so much! she bewailed in silent ecstasy. And I can't tell them. I can't instruct; I can't command. I must wait until they deign to grant me pleasure.

She began to stir in her bonds, the very fact of her confinement as stimulating as an hour of intimate caressing. Her sex throbbed and dripped, and she could feel herself becoming hopelessly engorged and uncomfortable. She didn't want to move. She didn't want to betray the extreme degree of her need to her companions, but there seemed to be no way of containing her energetic wigglings.

'Patience, my sweet Claudia, patience,' murmured Paul, lying down beside her and freeing his swollen cock from the fly of his jeans. She almost fainted with frustrated lust when he pressed its fat, wet tip against her thigh. 'You'll soon feel better,' he said, rubbing his member to and fro on the bare, sensitive surface of her skin. His silky pre-come seemed to scald like liquid fire.

'Oh yes, my dearest,' said Melody, moving in close herself then lifting the hem of her floaty top and knotting it securely at her waist. With her lower body entirely naked, she settled against Claudia's flank, on the opposite side to Paul, and for a moment did nothing else but suck slowly and lasciviously on her own middle finger. 'Soon we'll all feel better,' she continued, sliding the wetted digit from between her lips then placing it with a blind yet delicate accuracy into the lovely groove that nestled between her legs.

What about *me*? Claudia longed to scream at them. Paul was as good as humping her thigh for his own selfish pleasure and Melody was unashamedly masturbating. And all the time, her own quim lay aching, stretched and weeping.

Please! What about me? she raged silently, as first one then the other of her lovers came to a climax. What about me? What about me! What about me?

But as she closed her eyes and tossed her head, and her hips and thighs jerked with frustration, she felt those same heartless lovers begin to soothe her. A hand caressed her breast and another stroked her belly, and after a second a single finger found her clitoris . . .

Howling inside her mind, Claudia had the first of a score of orgasms.

Chapter Fourteen
Tristan in Trouble

I wonder if you can imagine how I spent last night? thought Claudia, surveying her handsome young dinner companion.

Tristan Van Dissell was as alluring as Paul in his own way, she supposed, but somehow she now preferred lovers with dark hair rather than those who were blond like herself. Studying Tristan's carefully styled flaxen locks while he scrutinised the wine list as if his life depended on it, she couldn't help but see Paul's wild, curly mane – black with sweat as he brought her yet again to orgasm. Or Melody's hair – born-again brunette and in the sweetest of disorder – as the girl crouched between her thighs and licked her quim.

Oh, it had been a mad, bad night, and Claudia could still feel twinges in her limbs where she had fought her bonds and an overwhelming might of pleasure. That either of her lovers, especially Melody, could be capable of such high-art devilment had come as a shock to her, but she had learnt, while tied to her bed, that it was foolish to prejudge anyone when it came to the excesses of the flesh. Even just thinking about what they had done to her almost made her come.

'Are you enjoying yourself?' asked Tristan brightly after ordering a rare wine, she suspected, solely to impress her. 'I knew you'd like it here. It's got a certain *savoir faire*, don't you think? I'm convinced it's a valuable addition to our holdings.'

'*Our* holdings?' queried Claudia. She gave him a long, measured look and thought how scared of her he seemed. He was up to no good, even though he didn't know she was aware of it, and his nerves were making him babble and spoil his usual suavity. She sensed that under normal circumstances he would have been the epitome of cosmopolitan cool in this setting which he himself had suggested; a Michelin-starred restaurant attached to a major hotel. It was an establishment in which Gerald had often expressed interest.

'You know what I mean,' he said, reaching over to place his hand over hers. 'I'm so concerned about the continued success of Gerald's businesses, *and* I feel so close to you, that I do tend to get a bit possessive.'

'And does Richard also feel possessive?' she said, becoming aware that Tristan's palms were warm and that he was sweating slightly. The poor boy really was in trouble.

'Er ... yes, I think so,' he faltered, fiddling with his wine glass. 'But not quite in the same way as me.' Pausing, he appeared to take a metaphorical deep breath and regain his poise somewhat. He favoured Claudia with his wide, youthful smile. 'I like to think my interest is a little more personal than his.'

'And he's married, of course,' observed Claudia, narrowing her eyes at him. She wondered if Tristan would say anything about the absence of Melody from the Truebridge marital home. He must know of it, she decided, as he and Richard would have had to co-ordinate their efforts.

This sally seemed to nonplus Tristan again, and in the ensuing silence, Claudia took a sip of the wine and considered the preceding 24 hours.

After the orgiastic extremes of their night together, she now trusted both Paul and Melody completely. And with her stranger, this trust transcended even the possibility that he was not quite what he seemed and that he might be concealing his identity. A deep, almost primal feeling told her that even if he had initially set out to deceive her, he was now no longer bent on that course. She was convinced he was concerned about her welfare.

And not just her sexual welfare. He seemed to be looking out for her financial interests too.

You think you can hoodwink me with your slick moves, don't you, Tristan? she asked silently of the aspiring smooth operator who sat before her. You and Richard think that because I'm not exactly Mastermind where money is concerned, you can hide whatever you please in an over-complex balance sheet.

Well, think again!

Giving Tristan an amenable 'I'm having a lovely time' smile to keep *him* entirely in the dark, she thought back again to the discovery, this morning, of the near-miraculous extent of Paul's remarkable facility for figures.

'This is pretty difficult for me ... I think,' her lover had said pensively, studying the documents Melody had purloined from her husband's office and the print-outs they had just run off on Gerald's now little-used computer. 'I have a feeling that financial calculations aren't actually my strong point.'

Nevertheless, while she and Melody had struggled with the data on the computer screen, finding it virtually impossible to decipher, much less spot any cleverly embedded anomalies, Paul had worked silently and at furious speed, using only a notepad, a pencil and his brain.

From time to time during their labours, she had looked across at him, fascinated by his complete absorption in what he was doing. She had never seen a face so calm and composed; in fact, he appeared more serene while poring over her late husband's – and now *her* financial status than he had at any time so far. His face wore a relaxed, almost post-orgasmic expression that she found utterly desirable.

Was he one of those men who did sums in his head to

avoid coming too soon? she thought gleefully. There was a certain piquancy in imagining that fine mind operating on some high, arcane level while the body that housed it squirmed and bucked in frantic sexual congress.

Just as she thought this, Paul looked up suddenly and smiled knowingly at her. Had he read her mind, as he often seemed to do? It appeared not.

'I've found something,' he said, leafing back several pages through his pad. 'In fact, I've found quite a few things.'

'Here. Here and here,' he pointed out as he joined Claudia and Melody at the computer screen, comparing what they saw there with what he had uncovered.

Not that she had entirely understood what had been done, or how, Claudia realised now, coming back to the present and the rather apprehensive-looking Tristan. But Paul had promised to document the deceptions for her in a form that could be presented to an independent financial auditor. She had a powerful lever available to her now, if she chose to employ it. At the very least, the business reputations of both Richard Truebridge and Tristan Van Dissell would be annihilated, and if she pressed the matter, they could very well face serious charges.

'About the proposed new acquisitions,' began Tristan, making Claudia smile with his earnestness. How blissfully unaware he was of impending doom – or the hold she would soon have over him, should she decide to give him the second chance that so tempted her. Of the two of them, Richard Truebridge was the venal one; instinct told her Tristan was merely misguided.

'Let's not talk business tonight, Triss,' she said, cutting him off when he seemed about to launch into another complicated pitch for his proposals. 'It's a long time since I've been out to dinner, and I want to enjoy myself. I want some fun!' she declared. 'We both know that Gerald wouldn't have wanted me to become a dried-up old widow on his account.'

A bit blatant, Claudia, she told herself, relishing the

flare of hope in Tristan's hazel eyes. But what the hell! Melody's claims about Tristan's interest in her were obviously quite true. The fact that he desired her was written very plainly in the light flush that lay across his cheekbones. And he was probably hard inside his underpants. She gave him a slow, silky smile at the thought of that.

'You're right, Claudia. Of course you are,' he replied, impressing her with the return of his self-possession. 'What do you say we forget the wine and I order us champagne instead? We could drink a toast, then, to fun . . . and perhaps a non-business relationship?'

'What say we forget the dinner altogether and see if this hotel has a decent room going begging?'

Tristan's jaw dropped and he stared at her open mouthed, showing his even white teeth to advantage. He obviously hadn't expected her to be two steps ahead of him.

'Well, a – actually,' he began, his schoolboy stammer sounding strangely appealing, 'I did take the liberty of booking a suite for us.' Brilliant colour flooded up towards his golden hairline. Claudia could almost taste the chagrin he felt at appearing so gauche before her. 'Only so that we could talk in private, if we needed to,' he insisted, and she wondered whether he had really believed she might buy such a tacky line.

She gave him an arch look, as if to say, 'How quaint', then rose from her seat, without warning, and picked up her evening bag.

For a moment, Tristan's eyes seemed to pop with horror. Clearly, he was afraid that he had slipped up and that she was affronted by his assumption that she would want to go to bed with him. Claudia extended the torture by keeping her face perfectly straight, showing neither warmth nor displeasure, and simply smoothing her skirt in a gesture that gave no indication of whether she was leaving or staying.

Tristan stood up too. He seemed about to say something, then changed his mind.

Claudia laughed inside. She had managed to regress
him to his childhood. She held the pause just a little bit
longer, then turned on her heel, glancing over her
shoulder at him. 'Well, if we're going to acquire this
hotel, Tristan, it does seem a good idea to check out the
accommodation.' Without further consultation she set
out across the restaurant, sensing a satisfying degree of
interest from other diners – principally the male ones.
She had no doubt whatsoever that Tristan was following
her, shadowing her steps like a devoted but chastened
puppy.

In the lobby, too, Claudia's female radar discreetly
picked up admiring glances. She was pleased to get them
as she had made a deliberate effort to dazzle tonight;
using every bit of her skill with clothes and style and
make-up to create an image that would take Tristan by
surprise.

The little black dress. What an understated description
for a garment that could make such an impact. Claudia
had paid more for her 'little black' than many women
would spend on clothes in a year, but the superior cut
and panache of it were well worth the ludicrous expense.
Tastefully snug on the bodice, its little cuff sleeves were
just enough off the shoulder to be seductive without
being overt, and its slightly flared skirt was flirtatious
without being embarrassingly girlish. With a perfectly
gauged just-on-the-knee length, and worn with slender
black suede court shoes that were high, but not awkward, it made her look and feel every inch an enchant-
ress. A neat, single-row diamond necklet – a gift from
Gerald – was the fine top note to her shimmer of allure.

And she had seen unequivocal evidence of the accuracy of her assessment in Paul's eyes, which had been
almost feral with desire when she had left him. She
didn't think he was jealous as such – at least, that was
what he had told her – but she had no doubt he would
have liked to fuck her while she was wearing this dress.

Thinking of Paul, as she rode up in the mirror-lined
lift with Tristan, forced her to indulge in a tiny smile of

satisfaction. The existence of her stranger was only adding to Tristan's confusion.

She had deliberately invited Tristan in when he had arrived to collect her, and just as deliberately she had made sure that Paul was conspicuously in evidence during that time – loafing on the settee, barefoot and with a glass of wine to hand, listening to a Schubert sonata as if he had lived in the house for years. It had been obvious then, and it still was now, that Tristan was almost bursting to know who the unknown visitor in Claudia's home was, but to further off-balance him she had given no explanations. As they approached the suite, she could almost hear his inner questions.

She also wondered if he suspected that Melody was staying with her too. It was certainly unlikely that Tristan was unaware that Richard Truebridge's wife had left him, but Claudia felt it prudent that Melody's whereabouts should remain a secret. The girl had been sequestered in her bedroom during Tristan's flying visit.

The suite was unsurprisingly sumptuous; almost clichéd in its ambience of provocation. Although thoroughly relishing its unmistakably sultry atmosphere, Claudia had to laugh at her companion being so obvious.

Tristan looked alarmed. 'Is something wrong?' he said, pouring some of the champagne that had just arrived for them and spilling a little of it on the polished silver tray.

'Well, it's not exactly subtle, is it?' Claudia received her glass from him and took a swallow of the delicious dry wine with unalloyed pleasure. 'If we were going to *talk* – ' she emphasised the word heavily ' – I would have thought a suite with a conference room, or at least a sitting room, would have been better.'

Tristan gulped down his wine and moved quickly towards her. 'I think we both want to do far more than talk.' Trying to regain the high ground, he slid his arms around her, but even still holding her glass, she was able to lightly elude him.

Just like a spring lamb, old thing, she told herself, pouring a dash more champagne into her glass and giving Tristan what she hoped was her most enigmatic look.

Whatever facade of self-confidence Tristan had built up for himself now began to crumble. He looked unnerved, pink-faced and at a loss. 'What is it?' he demanded. 'Is it him? The guy with the scruffy hair? The one with his feet up on your sofa, drinking Gerald's wine?'

'My wine,' said Claudia softly. 'And Paul's presence in my house has no relevance to my presence here.'

'But who the hell is he? He can't be someone you've met through Gerald.' Tristan was moving towards her again, but he was still unsure and hesitant. A look of frustration began to form on his charming face.

'No, Paul is a more recent friend. Someone who I met a short while ago, who needed somewhere to stay. I've got plenty of room. I took him in. End of story.'

It was a preposterously lean explanation, but she had no intention of elucidating. She too was beginning to feel frustrated – but not quite in the same way as Tristan.

'But – '

'If you don't stop prying into matters that don't concern you, I shall leave immediately.' She made her voice sharp and peremptory, even though she knew it was a gamble. Tristan might not be quite as besotted with her as Melody claimed.

But her gamble paid off. Tristan dropped his head and looked contrite. 'I'm sorry,' he said. 'It's none of my business.' Inside her boned bodice, Claudia felt her nipples tingle and harden.

'No, it isn't,' she said, schooling her voice very carefully, even though her body was almost singing now and her quim was growing moist. 'You and I have other business to transact, I believe?' She regarded him levelly, standing tall in her 'fuck me' shoes. I'm a goddess, she thought; in the full flush of my prime yet all-conqueringly young.

Tristan swallowed, his face and his body language exhibiting fear and burgeoning excitement in equal measures. At his groin there was a clearly discernible bulge.

'But I thought – '

'Thought what?' she questioned, making it her turn to close in on him. Tristan, erect yet terrified, backed off.

'I don't know,' he mumbled. 'I don't know.'

'And I suppose you don't know exactly how Richard Truebridge is planning to defraud me either?'

Still backing, Tristan flopped inelegantly on to the bed, his face a stricken picture of guilt and hunger. He opened his mouth, Claudia presumed, to utter some sort of denial, then shut it again. She sensed that at heart he didn't want to cheat her and that he had never really wanted to. The truth was that Truebridge seemed to have a knack for bamboozling people who should have known better than to have dealings with him.

'It's impossible to deny,' said Claudia more gently, sitting down beside him. 'I have an analysis of the latest set of figures and projections.' She reached out, touched his hot cheek, and drew her nails lightly down it. 'I think we both know that we could stop the whole thing right now, and let everyone off unscathed . . .' She caught his lower lip with her little finger and pressed down. A muscle flicked and spasmed beneath his cheekbone. 'Or it could proceed further – and the consequences will be dire.' Her own threat pleased her as she perceived that it might work on many levels.

'I'm sorry,' said Tristan, his fingers clenching. To Claudia's amusement, she saw his cock twitch in his pants. His imperilled state only seemed to fire his lust more. She was also impressed by his lack of denial. 'What can I do to make it up to you?' he went on, sounding more composed now his deception was over. 'I'll do anything, if you'll only forgive me.' He stiffened his spine and seemed to pull himself together even more. 'Look, let me work solely for you. Just on a nominal salary. Let me prove that I can be of some use to you. That I can be loyal.'

'Oh, I don't think the salary has to be too nominal,'

she said, after a long hiatus in which she had looked into his eyes as unwaveringly as she could. 'But I do have other expectations of you, Triss.'

'Anything! Name them!' He was smiling again, edging towards her.

Claudia put out her hand and pressed it against his chest, making him keep his distance. Her mental star rising, she continued to hold his look. 'Do I need to?' she said, lowering her lashes for just an instant.

To Tristan's credit, he seemed to understand her. He stilled where he sat, waiting quiescently for instructions.

'Unzip your trousers and get your penis out,' Claudia instructed him quietly. 'I'd like to see if this is going to be worth my while.'

Eyes downcast, Tristan immediately unbuckled his narrow, lizard-skin belt, then made short work of unfastening his trousers. Easing open the flies of both his trousers and boxer shorts, he exposed to her a prodigiously hard erection.

Oh yes, this will serve me very well, mused Claudia, faintly surprised by the dispassionate nature of her own thinking. This was the penis she would enjoy when Paul was gone, as go he surely would when his past history was restored to him. She would still need a man to satisfy the fires the stranger had stirred in her; a man she found amenable and attractive, who would be there for her not just because of his obligations but also because he genuinely wanted her.

I'm not just a lesbian, thought Claudia, watching a drop of pre-come form at the tip of Tristan's prick. I have Melody, and perhaps Beatrice too, to enjoy myself with, but they aren't everything I need, I know that.

One of the things they couldn't provide her with was just inches from her fingertips. She could handle him now, if she wanted to; delight in the toy which his perfidy had more or less rendered her possession. But for the moment, she chose not to. There were more devious ways to bind him to her use.

'Masturbate for me, Tristan,' she said, keeping her

voice velvety. He was her creature now; there was no need to shout at him. 'Show me what you do when you're alone. When you're thinking of a woman you desire, but you can't be with her.' She laid her hand on his thigh, near his bare penis and his own trembling hand, hoping he could read her unspoken implication. That dream woman of his had better damn well be her!

Tristan looked at her, offering up one last plea for his self-respect, but she shook her head ever so slightly. He flexed his fingers then laid them on his flesh.

Not quite the elegant savage that Paul is, thought Claudia, observing Tristan's fist making short, energetic strokes. She wondered if he was trying to get it all over with as soon as possible in order to keep his shaming to a minimum, and she made a small 'tsk'ing sound of disapproval.

'You're not competing against anybody, Triss,' she reminded him coolly. 'Try and be a little more . . . more "artistic", if you can.'

Tristan ran his tongue around his lips, rather in the manner of a small boy concentrating fiercely, and the rhythm of his rubbing became less frantic. Shuffling slightly on the bed, he adjusted the position of his balls, presumably, then closed his eyes as if to make his efforts a little more Zen.

'That's better,' breathed Claudia, beginning to be enchanted by him. She had always suspected that Tristan had possibilities.

'Lie back,' she urged him, pushing on his shoulders as he continued to manipulate his manhood. 'That's it,' she said, as he settled on his back. His long slim legs, in their marvellous tailoring, were still stretched out.

'Better!' she praised him. 'Much better!'

He was handling himself far more delicately now, holding his glans between finger and thumb and massaging more than pushing and pulling. The precise movement highlighted his excellent dimensions.

'Much, *much* better,' she said, wetting the tip of one

finger and touching the long, tense shaft. Tristan gasped and bared his teeth but didn't falter.

Well done! she praised him silently, sliding her finger very lightly up and down him, then letting it slip, down and under, to search out his balls. Again, Tristan drew breath and seemed about to protest, but held the line, still circling his thumb around the tip of his penis. Claudia cupped his testicles and he whispered, 'Oh God!'

All this is mine to command now, thought Claudia, almost laughing aloud at her own whimsy. Through an error of judgement, Tristan had given her the mastery of his genitals. She found herself dreaming about ordering him to wear some kind of harness on himself, and to have it on always, to remind himself of his folly and just who it was to whom he now owed total allegiance.

As she fingered his perineum, he bucked on the bed, his hand rising with his cock as his hips jerked. His penis looked very red, painfully stiff and rampantly inflamed. She sensed that at any second he was likely to ejaculate. Withdrawing her own hand, she spoke to him firmly.

'Enough now. Lie back. Hands at your sides.'

'But – '

She quelled him with a quick, hard kiss, pressing her crotch to his hip as she half twisted over him. It was time for him to hold steady while she raced ahead. Withdrawing, she whispered, 'Close your eyes,' and his long, surprisingly dark lashes flickered down.

Scooting just a little way away on the bed, Claudia lay back herself and opened her legs beneath the pretty froth of her petticoats, which were of net to give bounce to her mildly coquettish skirt. Then, moistening the same finger that had traversed the length of Tristan, she reached down inside her panties and found her clitoris.

'What are you doing?' croaked Tristan, sounding desperate.

'Hush! Never you mind!' replied Claudia, doing her best to keep her voice even while she delicately flicked at the very nexus of her pleasure. Turning to the side, she saw an expression of extreme strain and yearning excitement on Tristan's face, and it was that as much as her fingers that made her come.

Clamping her jaw against her cries and closing her legs around her hand, Claudia strove with every muscle not to react to the waves of feeling. She wanted, in every fibre, to thrash about and revel in gorgeous sensations, but to do that would be to reveal too much to Tristan. Instead she contained the bliss within herself.

It took her what felt like an eternity to regain her equilibrium, and even as she sat up she felt the after-shocks of climax. The expression on Tristan's face was yet more tense – almost a look of agony – and she had an inkling he was fully aware of what had happened. His cock was even stiffer than before, if that were possible.

But this is only the beginning, my boy, she thought fondly as she slid to her feet, beside the bed, and slipped her knickers off.

Over the next hour or so, she made sure that Tristan Van Dissell went both to heaven and to hell. While he struggled to stay immobile without the assistance of the bonds she had enjoyed so much in her dealings with Paul and Melody, Claudia utilised his fine male body quite shamelessly.

'If you come before I want you to, Triss, I've a good mind to start legal proceedings against you,' she teased, squatting over him, his penis lodged deep inside her. A tear rolled down his cheek as her inner muscles squeezed him.

But he did impress her. In his own way, Tristan had excellent qualifications as a lover. He was strong, he was good looking, and he took good care of his body; and though lacking the untamed mystique and the obvious intelligence of her foundling Paul, now that he was completely in her thrall, Tristan did everything that was humanly possible in his efforts to placate her. The degree of his sexual self-mastery was prodigious, and despite her tormenting him, he managed not to climax before

her order – which was a minor miracle, given the ferocity
with which she rode him.

And even when he was spent, he was more than
willing with lips and tongue, licking and sucking her to
the pinnacle again and again. Claudia could think of no
purer way to express the natural superiority of woman
than to sit ecstatically upon the face of a sweet young
man.

When she was ready to leave him, she had wrung him
out like a well-worn wash leather. He lay on the bed, his
legs akimbo, quite devoid of all strength, while she
outlined her final instructions – practicalities that
seemed mundane after the madness they had just been
sharing.

'If you can do all that for me, Triss ... well, we'll
certainly have dinner again.'

His groan was muffled, an expression of fatigue, but
she hadn't the slightest doubt that he had heard and
understood her. On her behalf, he would put a spanner
in the works of Mr Richard Truebridge.

Claudia felt like laughing as she rode home in a taxi.
What could have been a dreadful problem and a terrible
insult to her late husband's memory had been contained
before it had even really begun. And not only that, she
had acquired yet another in a string of younger lovers.

'You would be proud of me, Gerald, my love,' she
murmured, shuffling in the seat of the taxi, trying to
keep the thickness of her skirts underneath her because
when she had last seen her panties they had been
wrapped in a bundle round Tristan's rising penis.

And the sweetest icing on this scrumptious cake was
the fact, unbelievable as it seemed, that she felt not the
slightest trace of guilt – on anyone's account.

She wondered if she would have felt like this when
she had been married to Gerald, but the situation had
not arisen. All her major internal changes had taken
place with the advent of Paul into her life. He had
activated her, somehow; opened her up to events, possi-

bilities and people in a way in which she doubted he understood himself.

Yes, she thought, feeling a quiver of reborn desire in spite of all that she had just put Tristan through. Her beautiful stranger had a great deal to answer for – and she could only hope that when he was gone, his power to change her would not go with him.

Chapter Fifteen
Invitations

'*B*eatrice Quine rang. She wants you and Paul to go to a fancy-dress party . . . She thinks it might help him remember who he is.'

At first, Claudia couldn't think of a notion less likely to help Paul regain his memory. The high-spirited tra-la-la of a masquerade party would be both tiring and confusing; the very last thing he needed during recuperation.

But then again, had he not been in fancy dress when he had turned up on her doorstep? Maybe this shindig of Beatrice's would act as a trigger? Hurl him backward, past his trauma, to last time he had dressed up in his Edwardian outfit? It certainly didn't do to underestimate the professional wisdom of Beatrice Quine, reflected Claudia with a smile.

'Does she now?' she said, observing Melody, who seemed to have waited up for her, and who looked enchanting in a wrap of striped cream satin. 'And what did Paul say about the idea?'

'Well, not much really.' Melody twisted a strand of her dark hair between her fingers, her face a classic portrait of evasion. Claudia wondered what had been going on at the time of the phone call, and discovered that just as she hadn't felt guilty about her own conduct

211

tonight, neither did she feel jealous of anything that Paul and Melody might have done. After all, she had whispered to him, before she left, 'Be kind to Melody.'

Deciding not to press the matter, she said, 'Where is Paul now, by the way?'

'He came over all sleepy all of a sudden,' replied Melody, still vague. 'He says that that's what tends to happen to him. He went to bed about an hour ago. He couldn't keep his eyes open.' It was the silk robe's turn to be pulled and twisted this time.

Claudia felt her heart turn over with compassion. Melody had endured too much with her pig of a husband to be consumed with guilt and remorse now. Especially when Claudia herself felt so blame-free.

'It's all right, you know,' she said, gently touching her friend-lover's face. 'I don't mind in the slightest. I was a bit of a bad girl with Tristan, too. So you've nothing to reproach yourself for.'

Melody's instant smile was brilliant with relief. She let out a held breath, and her sweet, rounded breasts shifted intriguingly beneath the silk of her wrap. Claudia almost sighed, feeling a renewed twist of interest. It was quite alarming to feel desire again so quickly; it was less than an hour since she had been debauching herself with Tristan.

'How bad?' enquired Melody.

'Oh, absolutely terrible! Abominable!' Claudia answered with a flourish. 'I'll tell you all about it while I get out of this lot – ' she indicated her *soignée* dress and her high heels and stockings ' – and then you can tell me what you did to Paul.'

'Um ... What he did to me, really,' said Melody, keeping her voice low as she followed Claudia up the stairs.

Is she looking up my dress? thought Claudia, when she reached the landing. It must be quite a sight with lacy stockings, narrow suspenders – and no knickers.

'Mmm ... Excellent,' she murmured, turning to give Melody her most conspiratorial grin.

Melody's face was rosy; it seemed likely that she had been looking.

Once in the bedroom, Claudia kicked off her high-heeled shoes. They had been surprisingly comfortable and had a certain power which had done the trick with Tristan, but after several hours in them, she had certainly had enough. It was delicious to feel the carpet against her toes, and to get the best of it she quickly shed her stockings, noticing a sleazy-looking ladder in the process which made her smile. Had Tristan spoilt her stocking with his teeth? she wondered. That was something he might come to regret when next they met.

'Unzip me, would you, please?' she asked, despite the fact that her dress was quite easy to unfasten. She was suddenly hungry to have Melody's hands upon her.

Slowly, oh so slowly, the young woman slid down the zipper, then caught the dress as it too slithered down, its lining coasting smoothly on the black satin basque Claudia wore beneath it to create a sleek, svelte line. Before the frock reached her feet, Claudia felt soft lips caressing her bare shoulder.

'You're so beautiful, Claud,' Melody murmured, her breath hot. 'I've always thought so. I just wonder why I didn't realise quite *how* I felt it.'

'Thank you,' said Claudia, simply, enjoying the peachy contact of her young lover's mouth. When Melody withdrew, she stepped out of the dress and let it be whisked away and laid across a chair.

The younger woman laughed. 'Oh Claud, where on earth are your pants?'

Claudia chuckled too. 'Wrapped around Tristan Van Dissell's dick the last time I saw them.'

'You are bad, aren't you?' said Melody with a happy sigh.

Claudia nodded, intensely aware of the nakedness of her pubis. She rather liked the piquancy of having half of her body covered and the other part quite naked, but she was also conscious of the constriction of the pretty little corset. 'Come on, girl, make yourself useful! Unfasten this for me too,' she said briskly.

'I wish you'd keep it on. You look so gorgeous in it!'

'Maybe I do,' said Claudia with a shrug, 'but it's a bit much for my undisciplined old body after all these hours.'

'You have a perfect body,' said Melody, obediently applying herself to the hooks and eyes. Claudia could almost feel her friend's gaze burning her nude buttocks where they swelled from beneath the basque. For a moment, desire almost made her dizzy, especially when Melody manipulated the lower hooks and sank to her knees, her face just inches from the globes of Claudia's bottom. As the basque fell away, Melody brushed her cheek against Claudia's nether one; the fleeting gesture as much affectionate as sexual.

'And you smell of sex,' Melody continued, rising to her feet again, then sliding her hands around Claudia's waist and down across her belly.

Claudia caught Melody's hands in her own. 'I do. Very much so. Which is why I need a wash or a shower before this goes any further.'

Melody made a small impatient sound which seemed to indicate she didn't really care about that, but satisfying as her encounter with Tristan had been, Claudia did care that she still had his odour and his aura upon her. Melody was too fresh to be tainted in that way.

'And first,' said Claudia firmly, turning and touching her fingers to her own face, and to her make-up which had endured surprisingly well, 'I need to get this lot off. It's been a long time since I wore this much warpaint, and it's beginning to feel a little like a mask.'

'Let me help you,' said Melody, skipping across to the dressing table and returning with cleansing lotion, cotton wool and a box of tissues. Setting them out on the bed, she reached for Claudia's hand to draw her down to sit on the counterpane.

'Don't I need a robe?' suggested Claudia, about to comply.

'Are you cold?'

'Not in the slightest.'

'Well then?'

'OK,' said Claudia, brushing her fingers through her hair to push it back from her face.

There was something extraordinarily intimate about having her face cleansed and pampered by another person; a special, almost more than sexual closeness that was only highlighted by her vulncrable, naked state. Melody's actions were super-light as she applied the lotion.

'You were going to tell me about Tristan,' Melody reminded her friend, her fingers making tiny circles along her jaw. 'Do you think you frightened him sufficiently? I'd like to think that all Richard's plans and schemes will be over now.'

The sensation of being massaged, however chastely, was blissful, and Claudia was tempted to purr rather than answer. 'Well, I don't know about frightening him,' she said, rolling her shoulders in appreciation, 'but I think it's highly unlikely that I'll have any trouble from him on the financial front from now on.' She smiled slowly, and Melody's fingers rode the muscles of her face. 'Or on any front, really.'

'I told you he adored you,' said Melody smugly, beginning to tissue the creamy emulsion off Claudia's face.

'Well, I don't know how he felt before tonight,' Claudia said, as the tissue skimmed delicately over her skin, 'but I think it's pretty safe to say he rather likes me now.'

'So, what was it that you did that put him in his place?' enquired Melody, clearly all ears.

Claudia considered editing her account, then decided that Melody deserved more. Even though she had never spoken as freely and explicitly in her life before – except sometimes to Gerald – Claudia outlined her latest erotic adventure to her friend in detail.

'Dear God, you're amazing,' said Melody when Claudia had finished. The girl was breathing heavily and the pupils of her eyes were dilated; if she hadn't been aroused before, she certainly was now. Claudia couldn't imagine many sights more delicious. Melody's hard nipples were pressing through the pale silk of her wrap and she was shifting uncomfortably where she sat on the counterpane.

But do I look any less of a wanton? thought Claudia, looking down at the stiffened peaks of her own breasts and the delicate sheen of perspiration that lay like a lacquer across her skin.

'Now it's your turn,' she said, shuffling back on to the bed and getting comfortable against the pillows. 'Tell me what happened with you and Paul. It's only fair.' She patted the mattress beside her and Melody shed her robe and moved into the indicated space.

Then, with a sigh of surrender, the young woman began to speak.

'It was when I was on the phone to Beatrice,' said Melody, wishing to God she could stop trembling and tell her tale with all the full-blooded spice that Claudia had just used. Claudia had done everything for her: taken her in, restored her faith in herself, even shared her lover with her – the first one Claudia had taken since her widowhood. Claudia deserved the very best; she deserved uncensored frankness.

'Well, I suppose you know how Beatrice Quine loves to chat and to draw you out?' She sensed Claudia nodding beside her. 'It turned into a long conversation. She asked me all sorts of things about myself and what's happened ... with Richard. And I found her very easy to talk to. Very comforting. Very much like you.'

She dropped her hand timidly on to Claudia's thigh and was rewarded by a small encouraging sound as she gently squeezed it. 'Anyway, the minutes were passing and passing, and I was leaning on the wall beside the hall phone, absorbed in conversation, when suddenly he was behind me and sliding his arms around me. I felt his lips on the back of my neck, then . . . then his fingers cupping my breasts through my top.'

In a house where excitement had become a way of life, feeling Paul making love to her while she was on the phone had been yet another brick in a growing edifice of pleasure. As Beatrice had enquired solicitously about her future plans, Claudia's stranger had wreaked havoc with Melody's senses.

Rolling up her T-shirt, he had completely exposed her braless breasts, then sidled slyly around the front of her to see them, giving each nipple a tiny flick to make them bounce.

'Er . . . I'm sorry, I didn't catch that,' she had said when his impish little trick had made her half choke down the phone. 'Oh, yes. I'm going to do that,' she went on, replying to Beatrice's enquiry over lawyers, and at the same time watching Paul dip down over her and take the tip of one breast into his mouth.

The suction he created with his soft, mobile lips was a sensation she could not keep control of. As Beatrice rambled on companionably about the importance of good legal representation, Melody found herself squirming against the wall, making matters worse – and much, much better – by creating a drag on her own flesh with her movements. Paul did not bite her breast but he sucked harder as if determined to maintain contact. With one hand on her bottom and the other cupping the soft orb of flesh that he was suckling, he would not allow any interruption of his efforts.

'Oh please,' murmured Melody, almost beside herself, then came sharply back to her senses when Beatrice asked if she was unwell.

'No, I'm fine . . . I'm fine!' Melody insisted, parting her legs because what was happening to her breasts was making her vulva swell and throb. 'I was just saying . . . um . . . Yes, please give me the name of this fellow you know. I know Claudia has a good lawyer, but I'm not sure if he's a specialist in divorce.'

As Paul cupped both her breasts and pushed his warm

and very faintly stubbly face between them, it occurred to Melody that Beatrice Quine, of all people – Rosewell under Berfield's most disreputable woman of the world – must surely have an inkling by now that something was up. Melody knew she was panting, and that Beatrice, at the other end of the line, must be able to hear it, but it was almost impossible to control her own breathing. The only thing to do was to find a polite way to ring off so Paul could have his way entirely, but just then the doctor seemed to find new conversation – launching off on to a fresh but related tack.

The bitch! She knows! thought Melody, wondering hysterically if just the same thing would have happened if Claudia had answered the phone. There had been a strange light in her friend's eyes when she had mentioned the notorious and beautiful doctor. What had gone on between them when Beatrice had visited Paul?

'And is there anyone new in your life?' the doctor asked, and Melody almost shouted, because at the same moment Paul abandoned her breasts, flipped up her skirt, then with a swift, shocking jerk, dragged at her panties.

'I . . . um . . . I'm not sure . . . Sort of,' said Melody shakily, amazed at herself because she was stepping out of her knickers like a docile little girl being undressed by a benevolent old nanny. Her eyes bulged when she looked down and saw that Paul was tucking her soft, cotton skirt in a bunch at her waist.

Beatrice expressed kindly scorn and Melody tried to elucidate without naming Paul – which was difficult given that the unmentionable one was on his knees, licking and nibbling at the soft skin on the insides of her thighs.

'It's a bit complicated,' Melody said faintly, feeling the marauding mouth move higher and higher.

'Enough said,' Beatrice replied, her voice full of devilment and empathy. Melody's knees were shaking, but she still had sufficient of her wits about her to be certain that the doctor was instinctively *au fait* with her situation. And not only that. She had the distinct impression that Beatrice had also guessed what was happening even as they spoke.

But even so, the doctor still seemed in the mood to gossip, and launched off enthusiastically on yet another topic. Meanwhile, almost giddy with anticipation and precursive spasms of sensation, Melody clung on to the phone and to the wall beside her for support. Paul was kissing the soft fluff at her groin now.

'You know, I'd really like to get to know more women in the village,' said Beatrice breezily. 'I already feel very close to Claudia, but I would really like to be your friend too, Melody. If you'd like that?'

'What? Oh! Oh yes,' gasped Melody, feeling deft fingertips parting her pubic bush and opening the sticky, engorged lips it protected. 'Oh, yes, Beatrice, I'd really like that,' she went on, summoning every last scrap of her self-possession as erotic oblivion began to threaten from below.

'That's wonderful,' exclaimed Beatrice.

Oh God, yes it is! thought Melody frantically, as Paul flicked the tip of her clitoris with his tongue. She had never experienced a pleasure-stroke quite as accurate; not even her own fingers spoke the language of sex so well.

Unable to stay upright any longer, Melody slid slowly and very clumsily to the floor; yet, despite all the struggling and thrashing, Paul somehow managed to stay with her. It was as if he were attached to her as a bizarre form of life support.

If he stops sucking, I'll stop breathing, Melody thought, then giggled helplessly as she sensed the approach of climax. It was rolling towards her now like a typhoon in the tropics, and when it hit, she would not survive its impact. At least not without giving away her secret.

'Are you all right?' There was sly humour in the gentle voice that asked the question, but the inquisitor was no longer the one she had been thinking about. Melody blinked away her dream of Paul's mouth, and Beatrice on the phone, and surfaced, as if she had been sleeping, to the face of Claudia.

'Melody?' Claudia persisted, and even though there was concern on the face of her friend, Melody saw the unmistakable lineaments of desire upon it too.

'Yes, I'm fine. I feel great, thanks to Paul. And to Beatrice, I suppose – ' she smiled shyly, then tentatively put her hand on Claudia's waist ' – and to you. Mostly to you.' The warm skin beneath her fingers flexed and trembled.

'Good,' replied Claudia, matching her movement, then advancing on it by pulling Melody's body to her. 'But you can tell me all about the rest of your phone call – ' she pulled more determinedly, and Melody was drawn on top of her ' – later.'

Much later, thought Melody, beginning to kiss.

Much later – in fact, a number of days later – Claudia had not managed to persuade Melody to accompany her and Paul to Beatrice's party. There was very little else that she and Paul hadn't persuaded Melody to do – and indeed very little that Melody hadn't persuaded her and Paul to do – but on the subject of socialising the younger woman was adamant.

'There's nothing I can say that'll change her mind,' Claudia told Paul as she studied his refurbished 'Edwardian' outfit, freshly cleaned and pressed upon her bed. She was supervising his preparations as well as her own, just in case, like Melody, he too decided to wriggle out of going to the party. For while he recognised its value, his enthusiasm was ambivalent.

'I'm beginning to wish I could change *your* mind,' he said from where he sat before the mirror, looking thoughtful. He was trying to bring a modicum of order to his freshly washed hair, and not doing too good a job of it, even with the help of some ridiculously expensive designer pomade that Claudia had bought for him the day before.

Claudia fingered an imaginary wrinkle in the grey satin cravat. 'If you're unhappy about the idea, I'll phone Beatrice and tell her we're not coming. She'll understand.' She glanced across at him and watched him running his narrow fingers through his wild hair in an attempt to tame it. Any thought of hurting him made horror twist inside her.

'Don't take any notice of me,' he said, and giving a final primp to a lovelock which hid the last traces of his graze, he turned to her and gave her his magic smile. 'I'm just being a baby, Claud. I want to remember, I really do, but there's a selfish part of me that never wants any of it to come back.' The smile warmed and the twist of worry became a tangle of desire. 'So I can stay here indefinitely with you.'

Claudia dropped the cravat and almost ran to him. She was unable to speak; what he had just said represented a deep wish she had tried not to articulate even to herself, for fear of wanting it too much. But she could not contain the way her body responded both to him, and to the way, for the first time, he had called her 'Claud' in a tone of pure affection.

He looked so extraordinary tonight, and that was even before he had donned his dashing costume. While completing his toilette he had on a particularly favourite robe of hers that had belonged to Gerald. It was the colour of Cabernet Sauvignon, long and luxurious, with a wide quilted collar and a tasselled sash. Her husband had always called it his 'Sherlock Holmes dressing gown', and worn by Paul it seemed to impart to him a certain 'nutty young professor' charm that jived well with his uncanny mathematical abilities. The trouble with the lovely robe at the moment was that it covered up the far lovelier flesh beneath.

As she reached him, he swivelled on the stool to face her, and instinctively she sank and knelt before him.

'Oh Paul,' she managed to gasp, burying her face against the heavy, silky fabric of the robe and breathing in the male fragrance of the body it encased. A car would be coming for them shortly to take them to Beatrice's masked ball, but with all her heart, she suddenly wished that time could freeze. That Paul, with all his mystery and his arcane, locked-up knowledge, could actually still the clock and keep them here, together, for ever. Looking up at him, she almost believed he could do it. His eyes were the burning blue of a summer's afternoon sky, yet everything about him, save his lust, was unfathomable.

Without stopping to think, she parted the wings of the heavy robe and uncovered him, discovering to her delight that he had not yet put on any of his clothes; not even the designer briefs that she and Melody had chosen for him on their self-indulgent shopping spree. His long penis was uncontained – and very lively. It rose up from the nest of hair at his groin, almost bouncing in its self-determined eagerness to be touched. Only this morning, she had watched Melody take this fabulous organ into her mouth and suck it, and ever since then, Claudia realised now, she had wanted to do the same. At the moment, the pretty young woman was busy cleaning Paul's mud-caked shoes – which had somehow, among everything else, been overlooked – so now Claudia had a chance to fulfil her wish.

Slowly, she moved her face towards him, then let the very tip of his prick brush her cheek. She felt a smear of moisture being drawn across her skin and smiled inwardly, thinking that they were adding yet another chore to the list to be completed before their departure. Perhaps the expert Melody would help her re-do her make-up?

Paul made a low, almost growling sound in his throat and butted his swollen glans towards her waiting, red-painted lips. She parted them just a little way, and used her mouth to effect a tiny, detailed caress, rolling and sliding him against the edges of her teeth.

'Sweet Jesus, Claudia!' he hissed, his hips lifting from the seat. She felt him brace himself to get the best from her: one hand on the stool, for purchase; the other at the nape of her neck to guide her actions.

And my hair now, too, she thought dreamily, as she worried his frenum and his fingers gouged her scalp. When his nails dug deeper, in inadvertent cruelty, she jabbed her tongue against the very eye of his penis.

'Oh God! Oh my God!' chuntered Paul as she plagued and played with him, folding one hand around his shaft and searching out his balls with the other.

Steady, boy, don't overcook it! she thought, giving him, the lightest of sucks, then licking him again, very delicately, across the love-eye. Even so, she let a finger find his anus.

Claudia could feel Paul shaking his head now; he was *in extremis* and very close to coming. And, though she heartily desired him, she felt a strange urge to sacrifice her own pleasure on the altar of his. It would be a gift to him, her own frustration, her own discomfort, throughout the evening ahead. Every twinge and every spasm of her needy, engorged vulva would remind her of the beauty of this moment. Feeling like a holy sacrifice, she thrust her exploring finger into his body.

Paul cried out a foul profanity as he orgasmed, but in a voice that made it the sweetest of praises. His whole pelvis jerked and rose as his tribute spurted into her, then as he subsided, she felt his body shake with sobs. Letting his penis slip from her mouth, she hugged his hips.

'It's all right, sweetheart,' she murmured, her nostrils filled with the pungent yet cleanly scent of fresh, young semen. 'It's all right,' she said again, and he bent and curved over her, cradling her face against his wilting cock and his flat belly.

It seemed to be Paul's turn to be unable to speak now, but the rough fervour of his embrace said all he needed to. Holding, and being held, Claudia wanted nothing of parties, intrigues or revelations. The moment itself was enough for her; even her desire seemed strangely muted now. Simple contact was her most pressing human need.

'Claudia,' he murmured at length, and disentangling herself, she looked up into his face. He was a study in both repletion and confusion. 'I – I want to do something . . . Something for you,' he said, his demeanour unexpectedly bashful as he nodded vaguely in the direction of her groin, her womanhood.

'There's no time, and no need,' she answered gently. Then she rose and stood before him, knowing she was magnificent in the long, fitted princess petticoat which was the underpinning for her own hastily acquired costume – an Edwardian dinner gown supplied by a connection of Beatrice's. The slip was pure white, and its hem, and deeply décolleté bodice, were both trimmed with a heady froth of lace. It was so lovely, she was almost tempted to attend the party without the dress that went over it. Only the sheerness of the fabric – crêpe-de-chine – prevented her. As she was uncorseted it revealed more than it concealed.

'I'll have my moment later,' she said, reaching up to fluff her hair.

'But I want to see you come,' said Paul almost petulantly. He rose, seemingly oblivious of his open robe and his bobbing penis, and crushed her to him. Claudia tried to struggle but it was useless; his hands were everywhere at once, goosing and grabbing her through the thin, slippery stuff of her petticoat. It was only a knock at the door that curtailed his stimulating incursions.

'It's OK, Mel, come in!' Claudia cried, whirling away from him.

But to Paul, she mimed a hasty, 'The night is young!'

Chapter Sixteen
Un Ballo in Maschera

'*A*re you ready?' enquired Claudia as the car slid to a standstill.

'As I'll ever be,' answered Paul, his long face ghostly. He peered out of the tinted glass, the very picture of nerves and apprehension. The insistent lover of just an hour ago had vanished.

'Don't worry,' said Claudia as the chauffeur opened the door for her and handed her out of the Bentley limousine that Beatrice had sent to collect them. 'We don't have to stay for the duration. And remember, it's masked, anyway, so you'll always have something to hide behind if you need to.'

'You're right,' said Paul as he stepped lightly out behind her. As she turned to him, he straightened his frock coat and tugged down his waistcoat, an act which reminded her just how flattering the ensemble she had first seen him in was. The dashing, beautifully cut black velvet jacket had returned as good as new from the cleaners, and the white wing collar of his shirt and his heavy silk cravat seemed to frame a face that had come from another age. He was even more the Edwardian dandy than ever now, with at least a portion of his self-possession and identity restored. And with any luck, tonight would restore a little more to him.

'I'm being an idiot,' he went on, self-deprecatingly. 'I should be thanking my lucky stars to be out on a perfect summer's night like this –' he gestured to the vault of the heavens which was just beginning to darken to twilight azure '– with a woman as beautiful as you.' Without warning he caught her to him and kissed the deep swell of her cleavage where it was revealed by the plunge of her ruched and beaded bodice. Claudia was so surprised that she dropped the evening bag and fan that Beatrice had so thoughtfully supplied with the gown.

'You look fabulous,' Paul growled almost soundlessly against her skin, 'and I want to make you come now more than ever!'

Claudia's knees went weak as his lips nuzzled the upper slope of one breast. Her daring lover had returned to her, banishing the nervous amnesiac of a few moments ago, and she wanted to sing from both relief and fresh desire. Between her legs she felt a humid ache gather.

'Oh, way to go!' cried an admiring voice from just behind her, and when Paul lifted his face, Claudia quickly turned around.

A handsome young woman in some kind of cat-girl costume was coming down the stairs to greet them; she wore an elaborate embroidered domino mask, and a pair of fake feline ears nestled neatly in her short, black curly hair. She was accompanied, one step behind, by a tall, brawny but intelligent-looking man dressed in a fusilier's uniform from the Peninsular Wars.

'Hello, I'm Alexa, and I've been landed with greeting duties for the moment.' From a velvet pouch that hung from her belt, she produced what appeared to be a pocket computer organiser and flipped it open. 'May I take your names? We don't want any gatecrashers, do we?' Her bodyguard looked on steadily, obviously providing the muscle to keep out guests his partner vetoed.

Taking her fan and bag, which Paul had gracefully retrieved for her, Claudia felt suddenly a little agitated. She hadn't foreseen having to supply a name for Paul.

'Of course,' she said as smoothly as she was able, giving the cat-girl a smile of mock confidence. 'I'm Claudia Marwood, and I was invited by Doctor Beatrice Quine. And this is my friend Paul.' In a minor panic she glanced around at him, saw his minute shrug, then happened to noticed a stand of fine trees that lined the long gravelled way up which they had just been driven. 'Beech. Paul Beech.' Paul grinned, and it was her turn to shrug.

'Ah yes, Claudia and Paul,' said Alexa cheerily. 'Bea asked me to look out for you especially. Please come this way.' She gestured towards the brightly lit interior of the house, and her dour companion moved back to let them pass. 'No probs, Drew,' she said, giving him a nod.

Once inside an imposing hall, which had twin rows of tall marble pillars and floor-to-ceiling mirrors on every wall, Alexa handed Claudia and Paul masks from a large selection laid out on a polished gate-legged table. There seemed to be something to match every possible costume; Claudia's was of white satin, trimmed with soft, downy feathers, while Paul's was more austere in edge-stitched grey velvet.

'Beatrice is about here somewhere. You can't miss her,' said Alexa as more guests began appearing. 'She's Salome, and you know her ... You could say she's nearly wearing a costume.'

Claudia didn't really know Beatrice all that well, but she could believe she would make an exceptional Salome. As did the tall, dark Drew, apparently. He smiled knowingly as he directed them to the bar and buffet.

'Well, here we are,' said Claudia, taking the arm that Paul held gallantly out for her after they had rearranged their hairstyles and Claudia's delicate little coronet of flowers to accommodate the masks. 'Does any of this make the bells start ringing?'

At a measured pace, they walked into a large salon where drinks and food were being served in great and clearly very expensive abundance, and as they did so Paul looked around intently.

'Not really ... Yet,' he said, a little frown puckering his forehead above the mask. 'I can't say that I ever remember being at a fancy-dress party before.' He turned to her and gave her a resigned look 'But I still can't remember a great deal about what I do when I'm *not* at fancy-dress parties.'

'It'll come,' said Claudia, squeezing his arm.

Paul bent near to her and whispered, 'And so will you, Mrs Marwood. If I get half a chance.' His frown had vanished and his eyes were hot and wicked.

'Really, Mr Beech!' she said, tapping him with her fan and feigning outrage. 'You do suggest the most disgraceful things sometimes.' With her own eyes, she told him she could barely wait.

Although they knew no-one, it was surprisingly easy to circulate. Masks were a great leveller; they made everyone a stranger to everyone else.

'There must be dancing in another room,' observed Claudia, as they both sipped the light wine cup that was being served along with other, more punch-packing beverages.

Paul cocked his head a little to one side and then nodded as he caught the strains of what had sounded to Claudia like a big band. 'Well, whatever I can and can't do, I'm almost certain I'm no Fred Astaire,' he said with a little shrug.

'Oh, I don't know,' replied Claudia, sipping her cup. 'You're light on your feet, and you're very graceful for a man.' She moved a little closer. 'And we both know you've got a fabulous sense of rhythm.'

'Now you're the one that's being disgraceful, Mrs Marwood,' he murmured archly, toasting her with his drink.

Claudia gave him her most old-fashioned look, although she guessed that the mask somewhat ameliorated its effect. 'Shall we get something to eat?' she suggested, nodding to the almost Roman super-abundance of the buffet.

'Yes, that's an excellent idea,' said Paul, abandoning his glass and taking Claudia's from her. 'You need to build your strength up for what I'm going to do to you later!' Taking her elbow, he led her towards the food.

All the dishes on offer were superbly presented, and no doubt just as delicious to the taste as they were pleasing to the eye, but after Paul's last remark, Claudia's appetite had waned. She had butterflies in her midriff and a low pressure in her pelvis, and her hunger was more for him than for caviar and canapés. For appearance, though, she sampled one or two delicacies.

While she ate – very conscious of Paul at her side, eating as little as she was – she scanned the assembled party-goers with interest, with a view to locating Beatrice.

There were many wonderful costumes: some breathtakingly elaborate and obviously hired and some quite possibly home-made but put together with impressive ingenuity and flair. She saw Robin Hoods and rajahs, Native Indian braves and astronauts, but to her relief she didn't see any outfits that were quite like hers and Paul's. Nibbling a quail's egg, she turned to him to tell him so.

She got a shock to discover him watching her closely, his attention firmly focused on her mouth. Her appetite dying, she swallowed quickly and put aside her plate.

'And what are you staring at?' she demanded, although instinctively she knew what was on his mind. He was thinking of another purpose to which she had recently put her lips.

'You were superb,' he said in a low voice, then ditched his own plate, took her hand, and began to lead her towards a set of open french windows, which accessed a long, wide patio. 'I've never had a blow job quite like it,' he breathed in her ear as they stepped out into the dying evening and the quieter ambience of the gardens and a country park. There were a few guests strolling around on the patio, but far fewer than they had left feasting inside.

'Oh, so you remember having your prick sucked then?' she enquired, also *sotto voce*, feeling the same thrill in using coarse language as she felt in hearing it from Paul's lips.

'Not specific instances,' he purred, his hand settling on her hip as he led her to a balustrade which overlooked some magnificent formal topiary and beyond that, a maze, 'but I'll remember being in your mouth, darling Claudia, until the day I die.' He squeezed her through the light fabric of her gown and petticoat, the contact of his curving fingers full of promise. 'In fact, I'm determined that it's going to be the last thing I think about on my death bed.'

'That's morbid,' protested Claudia, trying to disguise the fact that his wild claim had moved her.

'No, it's good sense actually. I don't know whether I believe in the hereafter, but at least my last thoughts will be heavenly.' His pressing hand slid down and cupped her bottom; his fingertips slotting neatly into the crease.

'Claudia, I want to watch your face while I give you an orgasm,' he said quietly and distinctly as he palpated her buttock, 'and I need to see it soon or I swear I'll go quite mad.'

Claudia's head began to swim with a delicious anticipation. She wanted him to see her climax, because she wanted him to make it happen. Between her thighs, her vulva quivered, crying out to him. A moan of need and pleasure escaped her lips.

'Come on, let's go down there,' he said huskily, giving her one last rude squeeze, then half dragging her along the patio towards some steps. At the bottom of these was the first of a series of gravel paths which wound their way through the strange menagerie of carved box trees and led towards the entrance of the maze.

Within seconds they were crunching along the gravel, weaving in and out of giant birds, heraldic beasts and abstract forms. Paul was whisking her along almost too fast to allow her to stumble, and though Claudia hated to think what the gravel was doing to her satin-covered heels, when it came down to it she didn't really care. All that mattered was the imperative of desire.

Ornate electric lamps lit the maze, to allow for the evening stroller, but after a couple of turns, they found a stone bench in a secluded, dark, dead end. Paul's face was tight and intense as he struggled with her skirts, and though his hands were shaking, he had the hem up at her waist in seconds.

'Kneel on the bench,' he commanded, his usually light tones sounding deep and ragged. 'I want to see your bottom, Claudia. I want to touch your sex.'

Dropping her bag and fan, Claudia caught the hem in her own hands, then holding it in one she turned and climbed up on to the bench. With just a pair of cotton drawers between her and Paul, she felt weak and vulnerable. And more than that, she suddenly remembered certain promises and threats that had been exchanged out in a field. An agreement which hadn't yet been honoured.

This was not the suitable place and time to perform such an act, she reflected, waiting for Paul to pull down the voluminous underwear that went with her period dress. The circumstances could not have been less appropriate.

And yet she wanted it. She was a heroine from some dark romance of yesteryear, waiting for her lord and master to have his wicked way with her – to exert his divine right to commit plunder, no matter how demeaning and uncomfortable it would be.

'And you know what I want, don't you?' she murmured, dropping her voice when she heard the sound of other guests passing close but on a different path in the maze.

'Of course,' he mouthed against the back of her neck, his fingertip brushing her anus through the fine, almost voile-like fabric of her bloomers. 'So let's have these off, shall we?'

Claudia felt a thrill of fate and yearning pass through her. Paul's voice was low, pitched for her ears only, but it was strong, with a note of real dominance. He had gained control of not only her but himself. His hands were deft and sure as they drew down her underwear.

'Dish your back. Part your legs,' he said, still quiet and mindful of fellow revellers close by. 'I want to see everything you've got before I take you.'

Hampered by her mass of underskirts and the baggy drawers around her knees, Claudia nevertheless managed to obey him, shuffling her legs apart and striking an awkward, inelegant pose.

'Gorgeous,' he said, running his open hands over her thighs and her buttocks, then pressing her downward a little. Adjusting her position, Claudia felt runs pop in her gossamer silk stockings.

'God, how I want you,' he groaned, pressing his trousered crotch against the slope of her thigh, as if to acquaint her with that which she already knew, then drawing back and beginning to attack his buttoned fly. Claudia was torn by an urge to assist him with his clothing, in the manner of a true handmaiden, but she knew she must stay quite still and wait.

She didn't have to wait long. Within seconds she felt his hand between her thighs, testing her wetness and readiness. His soft laugh only confirmed what she suspected; that her quim was a well-spring of desire, a font of moisture which only overflowed yet more on agitation. She was almost ashamed at the slickness of her vulva.

'This is good, my darling Mrs Marwood,' he said, dabbling playfully in her juices and inducing the most tantalising feelings. 'A little of this – ' he took up a fingerful of the heavy viscous fluid and drew it up over her perineum, heading towards but not quite reaching his target ' – will make things more comfortable for both of us.'

You needn't be so matter of fact, you young pup, she thought, experiencing indignation and elation both at once. It didn't seem possible that she could so adore this earthy, almost ruthless side of Paul, but she did. He made her want to grovel; gyrate her bottom; invite him to bugger her. The urge was so strong it overrode her inhibitions.

'Get on with it then!' she hissed, only just managing to resist the temptation to use profanity. 'Don't just tease me with talk.' She thrust herself backward, spreading her haunches even further, despite the encumbrance of all her clothing. 'Of course, if you're not up to it . . .' She let the challenge dangle, while offering him everything.

'Bitch!' he growled with affection, then laid his hands crudely on her bottom, pulling the cheeks apart as if inspecting an animal. 'I'll show you who's up to it!' His slender thumbs dug deep into her buttocks. 'I was going to be nice to you, Mrs Marwood. Really nice. I was going to play with you first, until you had an orgasm or two, but now I think I'll just have this – ' he slid one thumb inward and brushed it lightly across her dilated anus ' – straight away. And to hell with the niceties!'

'Fuck you!' replied Claudia, but even as she spoke her sex began to jerk in a hard, spontaneous orgasm. 'Oh God, you bastard, Paul! Fuck you!'

'Oh no, fuck you, Claudia.'

The words were little more than an urgent, thrilling whisper, yet Claudia heard them with a weird echoing clarity. Her senses seemed to be functioning on a high, almost machine-like pitch while her loins were aglow with pulsing pleasure. He hadn't even taken her yet – barely even touched her – and already she was a panting slave of bliss.

And then he was anointing her, smearing both her anus and his own genitals with her copious lubrication and – to her shocked delight – his own saliva. The very primality of that action made her come again.

In the long, long moment before the onslaught began, her senses revved up yet higher, became even more detached and took a portion of her consciousness with them. She saw Paul as all the other guests must see him:

a young but distinguished stranger in his beautiful
antique clothing. The very epitome of sensitivity and
genteel, Edwardian refinement, yet given a touch of the
exotic by his grey velvet mask. He would look ascetic; a
stainless angel; untouchably pure.

If only they knew, she thought, then gasped and
almost choked as the head of his penis butted hungrily
against her bottom. She felt him grip her cheeks again,
stretch her, part her; then his glans was edging inside
her, firm and determined.

The sensations were both provoking and precarious,
and Claudia closed her mind to certain possible consequences and tried to concentrate on the voluptuousness
of the experience. And all the time, she imagined Paul as
her unspoiled hero. A heavenly, contemplative being
who would never even look at a woman with lust, much
less sodomise her in the rapidly gathering moonlight.

It seemed to take him an age to fully get into her, and
she had a sense that he was as new to the process as she
was. In a convoluted way, then, he *was* as pure as she
had imagined. They were a pair of virgins – both
engaged in a scary foray into a dark, dark land.

And yet, despite the perils, his intromission was
tender. Claudia had never felt more close to him, to his
mind, now as his penis breached her bottom. Though
she didn't know his name, she knew him. She knew he
was special; knew he was brilliant; knew he was not like
any other man she had ever encountered – even the
husband she had loved so much and even now still missed.

Then, she was coming, and against all reason she saw
the notepad in her mind, and his elaborate figures . . .

Claudia wasn't sure if she cried out herself, but she
heard Paul moan softly as he bucked and slumped
against her. Within her body, she felt his sated flesh
subside.

'Oh, Claud, that was – Oh, God, woman, it was beyond
words,' he said into her ear after a few moments, still
holding her close as he slid his penis from her. 'You're a
helluva lover, Mrs Marwood. You were incredible.'

'I'd say you were *both* pretty incredible,' intoned a quiet but familiar voice from close beside them.

'Dear God, Beatrice!'

'Doctor Quine!'

Beatrice Quine was grinning from ear to ear, and her avid eyes were darting all over the place, taking in every last condemning detail.

As she stumbled off the bench, Claudia felt her stockings rip into tatters, and she hauled at her drawers in the same ungainly movement. Beside her Paul managed a little more grace in putting himself to rights.

It was difficult to look their discoverer in the eye but Claudia was aware she had to. She saw Beatrice's features form a deeply admiring expression.

'How long have you been here, Beatrice?' she enquired, hoping that the mask would obscure some of her blush. 'Couldn't you have coughed or something to give us warning?'

'What? And miss probably the most erotic sight even at *this* party?' replied Beatrice, quite unrepentant. The doctor seemed to be showing little sign of any kind of embarrassment or self-consciousness either, which given her outfit made Claudia rather admire her in return.

Beatrice's Salome costume consisted of little more than a handful of – presumably seven – relatively small chiffon veils in shades of tan and amber that beautifully complemented the colour of her hair, which she was presently wearing loose around her shoulders. The brilliant tresses covered more flesh than her veils did, and her mask was of papier mâché but painted and lacquered to look as if it had been beaten out of gold.

'That's a stunning costume, Doctor Quine,' commented Paul with an impressive degree of sang-froid. Claudia resisted the urge to turn round and give him a 'What are you up to?' look.

'Do you really think so?' Beatrice twirled, showing them her bottom for a second instead of her breasts and lush pubic triangle. When she faced them again, she gave Paul a roguish wink. 'Then why not show your appreciation of it in the same way you just did to Claudia?'

'I'm afraid I'm not quite ... er ... up to it at the moment, Doctor Quine,' he said, sounding a little more subdued, and when Claudia did turn round she saw his face was a touch pink where it showed beneath the mask.

'Never mind,' said Beatrice brightly. 'You deserve a bit of a break after a sterling performance like that.' She paused, and Claudia wondered just how much detail the good doctor had seen. 'A buggery amongst the shrubbery,' Beatrice went on with a chuckle, confirming Claudia's worst fears as she gestured to the high hedges all around them.

Almost as if he had sensed her discomfiture, Paul's fingers suddenly closed around hers and squeezed. His mouth curved into a resigned little smile. Smiling back at him, Claudia instantly felt better and stronger.

'Do you make a habit of this kind of thing, Beatrice?' she enquired. Her own smoothness impressed her; doubly so, considering the precarious sensations that still roiled through her nether parts. 'Do you have any more treats lined up? Any more trysts you can spy on, in other nooks?' She flicked her hand towards the rest of the maze.

'Oh, I'm sure there are some ... Lots in fact,' said Beatrice, with a slow and rather teasing smile. 'But where we're going, there's no need to spy.' She made a gracious little gesture of invitation.

'And where *are* we going?' asked Claudia, not resisting the urge to follow Beatrice, even though the doctor took a turn that logically would lead deeper and deeper along the puzzle path. Still holding her hand, Paul in turn followed Claudia.

'To the party,' said Beatrice over her shoulder, somewhat cryptically.

'I thought we were already at the party,' said Paul.

'Oh no, not the *real* one,' continued the doctor, moving along swiftly in her flat, leather slave sandals. 'All that's just for show, to be honest.' She waved dismissively to the mass of guests, who were still milling in and around the beautiful house consuming vast amounts of gourmet food and fine wines, chatting about affairs they thought greatly important and dancing to a large and accomplished show band. 'It amuses Sacha to have them there, completely deaf and blind and oblivious to the night's main events.'

'Who's Sacha?' Beatrice had mentioned a 'friend' who had organised the event but it was the first time she had named this unknown entity and Claudia was immediately intrigued.

'Sacha D'Aronville,' replied the doctor. There was a tangible excitement in the way she spoke the name. 'The Comte D'Aronville, if we're going to be formal.'

'And are we to be? Formal, that is?' chipped in Paul.

Claudia could hear voices other than their own now, and the splashing of water. There was clearly a pool beyond the convoluted hedges.

'It depends on Sacha's mood,' replied Beatrice, beginning to hurry, as if she were impatient to reach her titled Frenchman. 'Things were decidedly informal when I left but he has a tendency to be volatile. Cold but volatile.' Claudia was even more fascinated than ever.

Just when the voices were getting so loud that it seemed impossible that they were not already among them, Claudia and Paul followed Beatrice round a complicated series of back-switching twists and found themselves in what could only be described as a Shangri-la in the centre of a forest. Two pools – one deep, one clearly just for wading – were separated by an ornate and explicitly erotic fountain in the form of copulating nymphs and satyrs.

All around the pool people were copulating too. Some of them were engaged in other pursuits: a few that were frankly obscene, some very likely painful, and others that were nothing short of mind-boggling.

Claudia gasped, but behind her Paul chuckled softly. 'It's a Roman orgy, Mrs Marwood,' he said squeezing her hand again. 'What a shame we're not dressed for the appropriate era.'

'It doesn't seem to matter,' observed Claudia, noting both costumes and the lack of them as they followed Beatrice right into the heart of the Saturnalia, towards a classical villa-like structure which was clearly a very deluxe type of pool house. There was more food and drink set out here, of an even higher degree of luxury than was being served at the *faux* party. A piece of delicate but intricate string music which Claudia half recognised was playing quietly in the background, but on a series of tables, a little way from the buffet, was an assembly of items she was most definitely not familiar with. Well, most of them were new to her, especially those fabricated from leather, rubber and steel.

'Let me introduce you to our host,' said Beatrice, sweeping them past the fantasia of sex toys, instruments of punishment and peculiar, uncomfortable clothing. 'Unless, of course, you'd like a drink or a chance to freshen up first?' She smirked knowingly.

The temptation of a bath, or at least a wash, after the rigours of being sodomised was almost irresistible to Claudia, but even so, she was curious about Count Sacha. She flashed a glance at Paul and he nodded as if divining her decision.

'Well, I suggest a drink with our host first, then the freshening up,' he suggested, lifting his eyebrows. 'But of course I'm at your disposal, Mrs Marwood.' His mouth curved in a little grin that made Claudia quiver all over again. For a moment, she wished they were at home, in her bathroom, with a bottle of chilled Chenin Blanc and a large loofah, but then she acknowledged there would be time for that tomorrow.

She fixed her eyes on him. 'That sounds like an excellent idea,' she said, suspecting that he would enjoy her deliberate ambiguity. She turned to Beatrice. 'We'd love to meet our host, and I for one could certainly do with a glass of wine.'

'Coming up,' said Beatrice, snagging a couple of

glasses from the tray of a passing waiter. 'Try this. I believe it's from one of Sacha's own vineyards.' It didn't seem to affect her that the young man distributing drinks was naked apart from his mask and a fearsome-looking assemblage of straps that held his cock against his belly. Perhaps the staff at Le Comte's parties were always restrained? It might be quite appropriate if the rest of the guests were as forward as Beatrice Quine was.

'This way,' said the doctor, handing them each a glass of wine then heading off again towards a nearby group of people. Holding Paul's free hand with one hand and her glass with the other, Claudia realised that somewhere along the line she had lost contact with her evening bag and fan. It also dawned on her that she didn't care a fig.

'Our host,' murmured Beatrice as they approached a tableau being played out on a brocade couch beside the pool between a naked woman and a distinguished older man.

It was immediately apparent who the Comte D'Aronville was portraying, both from his costume – eighteenth-century French – and what he was doing. He was soundly spanking the hapless wench across his lap. It seemed that one Gallic aristocrat was bent on recreating the spirit of another. Donatien Alphonse Francois, Marquis de Sade, was alive and well and apparently living, for the moment, in Oxfordshire.

And Claudia discovered that, in spite of his stern and uncompromising behaviour, she found Sacha D'Aronville instantly attractive. He was just her type – his cool, masked face showed his strength and his lithe body looked commanding in dark breeches and satin waistcoat. He wore no powdered wig, as she might have expected, but instead his thick, silver-white hair was brushed back in a faintly leonine style.

He's like Paul at his most collected and unworldly, Claudia thought, as they drew close – totally focused and almost completely apart from the mêlée around him. D'Aronville's concentration on the job – and the girl – in hand reminded Claudia of her house guest as he had worked on his calculations. It was uncanny how such detachment could arouse.

But just as she had classified the Comte D'Aronville as distant, he looked up from his task and gave her a measured but extremely inviting smile.

'Madame Marwood,' he said, showing his even white teeth while his hand and arm continued their relentless labours. 'It is a great pleasure to meet you. I would rise, but as you can see there is much yet to be done with Alexa.' In lieu of a handshake, he nodded his silvered head.

As far as she knew, Claudia had never met D'Aronville before, but she assumed Beatrice had been the one to prime their host. '*Monsieur le Comte*,' she said as graciously as she was able, given the distraction of the naked woman sprawled between them, 'may I present my friend, Mr Paul Beech . . . Who's staying with me for a while.'

The two men greeted each other. Their body language was mixed, as far as Claudia could see. D'Aronville seemed a little guarded although it was difficult to know whether or not this was his normal manner. Paul, on the other hand, was almost palpably defensive; almost as if he had sensed her own interest in the distinguished Frenchman. He was also very obviously interested in and turned on by the squirming Alexa and her bottom – which was glowing like a cherry.

D'Aronville noticed this. 'Please, my friend, enjoy the show,' he said amiably, not halting the steady raining spanks. 'Perhaps you would like to take over when my arm tires? A fresh hand can sometimes make all the difference.'

Difference to what? thought Claudia, feeling a response to the girl's plight within her own body. She had thought Alexa beautiful and lively when she had first met her, clothed in her cat costume, at the door, but now, seeing her nude and with her buttocks punished and her quim glistening, she found the dark-haired young woman to be a lure she couldn't deny.

It was difficult to know which she wanted to be: Alexa or the person chastising her. Claudia felt a strong urge to hit the girl herself, and yet equally it was the idea of having her own buttocks trounced that filled her vulva with a heated rush of yearning. She turned to Paul – suddenly wishing it were possible for them to flee the scene and have him sling her across his knee and slap her bare bottom – and discovered that he too was potently affected by what he saw. His pale, narrow face was masked not only by grey velvet but by a look of purest lust. She could almost see his long fingers twitching to go to work.

How would she feel, she wondered, if her companion accepted D'Aronville's suggestion? Would she let him spank Alexa? Or would she be bold, take her chances and live the life she now suspected her late husband had given up for her sake?

Could she bare her own buttocks and offer them up to Paul's strong hand?

Chapter Seventeen
Saturn, and After

*I*n the end, at least her chastisement had been a private affair and far less gruelling – she suspected – than Alexa's.

Claudia stirred against Paul's shoulder and he took her hand in his. They were gliding back towards home in the same luxury car that had collected them, and as she looked back over the evening's events, she was still astounded.

It had been an education watching Alexa being spanked, yet that virtuoso performance had been just an introduction. The beautiful brunette had been only the first of the Comte D'Aronville's many willing – and multi-orgasmic – victims. And again and again, Claudia had been tempted to join their ranks.

After watching Alexa *et al* receive the sweet benison of pleasure to take away the sting of their 'medicine', Claudia and Paul had been escorted away by Beatrice, as promised, to a place where they could freshen up.

The villa within the maze was purely a recreational building, a glorified summer house, but it certainly didn't suffer from a lack of facilities. In addition to a large changing and bathing area – in which a spirited extension to the festivities outside was taking place – there were a number of smaller, more intimate suites which were obviously designed to accommodate a single couple.

It was into one of these that Beatrice had ushered them, before leaving again almost immediately with a broad wink and the rejoinder, 'Have fun! Or else!'

'Do you think that meant she might spank me?' Paul had enquired, shucking off his velvet frock coat and then running his hand over the heap of thick towels that had been provided for their use.

'Quite likely,' Claudia replied, picturing the image and finding it much to her taste. There didn't seem to be anything now that she could do, have done to her or see that didn't have a sexual effect on her. She wondered idly if there was an aphrodisiac in the drinks that were being served here. Deciding it was possible, even likely, she poured them both a glass of wine from the bottle she had just found cooling in an ice bucket.

'In fact, very likely,' she amended, savouring what her palate told her was a first-class Semillon-Chardonnay blend. 'Do you think you'd enjoy it?'

Tackling his cravat, Paul seemed to ponder the question. 'I think I might,' he said cautiously, 'but if I were to be honest, I'd say that to administer a little punishment would be my first urge.' His eyes glittered hot blue from behind the mask he still wore and made Claudia remember an essential difference she had noticed between her dear stranger and the elegant Comte D'Aronville. The Frenchman's eyes were blue too, but so pale that they almost looked like chips of ice. Instinct told her they reflected a cold nature. At least Paul had a heart that was fundamentally warm and loving, despite the unsolved mystery of his background.

The bath that they shared was one of the most welcome that Claudia had ever taken. After their deranged animal coupling in the maze, she had felt grimy and decidedly 'used', even though there had been virtually no evidence of it visible to an observer. The scented foam in the king-size marble tub was luxurious beyond measure, and with a soft terry washcloth, Paul cleansed her every curve and hollow before lying back, totally pliant, and letting her perform the same task for him.

And all that stroking, touching and exploring led, inevitably, to lovemaking, a process as sweet and as utterly orthodox as what they had done in the maze had been deviant. Claudia couldn't and didn't want to decide which of the two was more exciting but at least the straight sex was a little gentler. She didn't feel her age in the slightest these days but not even the youngest and the fittest could go at it hammer and tongs all the time.

Afterwards, lying on the deeply upholstered and lavishly cushioned day bed, she drowsed in the nude while Paul got up and padded around.

'Televison!' he said suddenly, drawing her attention to a small set which stood to one side on a bureau. 'I haven't seen TV since – ' he paused, frowned and pushed his hand distractedly through his hair. 'It's a cliché but it's true. I haven't seen television since I don't know when.' Sitting down on the couch, he smiled winsomely over his shoulder.

The idea of watching television programmes made Claudia shudder, and it dawned on her why she hadn't bothered with the box herself for the last few days. Broadcasting involved news bulletins, and these might contain items on missing persons. You selfish old witch, she told herself, feeling horrified by her own hidden agenda. With a sensation of fatalism, she watched as Paul switched on the set.

The programme that was showing puzzled her. It seemed to be a drama but there was no dialogue and no narration of any kind. Not only that, the studio lighting was extremely peculiar – almost amateurish – and the content of the show was something she could not imagine that even the most liberal-minded of channels would show. And that included satellite transmissions from the Continent.

In a room not unlike the one they were currently occupying themselves, a naked man was lying on a bed, shackled at head and foot, while two women prowled around him, carrying straps of leather. From time to time they lashed him across the bottom.

It took but a moment or two for the penny to drop, and as it did Paul laughed aloud and looked around at Claudia.

'CCTV,' he said, waggling his eyebrows then returning his attention to the screen. 'And isn't that our good friend Beatrice?' he added, as one of the women moved closer into the shot.

She was wearing what looked like a leather body suit now, with strategic cut-outs at breast and crotch, but even in a black velvet domino mask and with her magnificent hair drawn back severely into a pleat, the forbidding figure in the scene was clearly Beatrice Quine. And just as Claudia recognised her friend, the doctor looked up directly towards the camera.

Was there a trace of a smile on that masked face? The merest hint of a nod, as if she knew she was being observed?

'Come here,' said Paul, gesturing that Claudia should sit beside him on the mattress. 'This looks as if it's going to be interesting.'

Claudia wasn't sure how he or indeed anyone at this perverse gathering would define 'interesting' – but suddenly she was a little afraid of what she might see. The fear wasn't that she might not like it; rather that she might like it far too much. Nevertheless, she settled before the screen at Paul's side.

Studying the tableau more closely, Claudia concentrated on the man. The monitor was transmitting the images in full colour, perhaps in too much colour, because the stripes across his buttocks were a deep, sore pink. Beatrice and her unknown friend were belabouring him relentlessly, and though he was hooded and gagged, he still made sounds of anguish.

There was no way to tell who this sorry unfortunate was, purely by observation, but some instinct told Claudia it was D'Aronville. She didn't know how she knew this, but the idea of that cold, proud creature being humbled was particularly arousing and delicious. Even as she wished herself into the picture with Beatrice and the other woman – Alexa perhaps? – Claudia felt a strong, hot response in the pit of her belly. Paul had satisfied her and yet she wanted more sex. Kissing. Caressing. Fucking. Anything. She didn't care what. Sliding her hand up his thigh, she cupped his cock.

Losing interest in the television monitor, Paul gave her a level, impassive look that would have been worthy of D'Aronville at his haughtiest.

'You'll have to pay,' he told her. His voice was as mild and emotionless as his face, but Claudia's arcane super-awareness lingered with her. She knew he was as madly turned on as she was – without even glancing at his crotch – and she knew in which coin he wanted payment.

Can I? she thought, observing his long, pale face and his possessed blue eyes. Can I give him what he wants?

Oh Claudia, did you ever have any real doubts? she asked herself, returning almost with shock to the present, and the car. Paul was adjusting his position slightly, for her greater comfort, and his shoulder felt solid and muscular where she leant on it. There was no way he had brought his full strength to bear on her . . .

The spanking he had given her had been a somewhat measured affair, although it had hurt her bottom mightily at the time. But with every stinging, smarting slap, she had been aware that what was happening was just a prelude – a spicy starter to a sweet and soothing main course – to a long and supremely exuberant copulation in which Claudia had ridden Paul to climax while he clasped her pinkened bottom. When it was over, they had both admitted they had had enough.

'I wonder who was watching us?' Paul mused aloud, and Claudia realised he was reviewing the evening just as she had been doing. To encourage him, she threaded her fingers in his. 'Certainly not Beatrice. Or our host, I suspect,' he went on, bringing her hand to his lips and kissing it briefly. 'Just think, Mrs Marwood, tonight we had some perfect stranger watching us while we fucked.'

'Or strangers,' added Claudia, drawing their two meshed hands to her own mouth and kissing Paul's knuckles. That they *had* been watched was a logical deduction; indeed, it had occurred to her subliminally at the time. She was even convinced she had tried harder to impress her audience.

Just about to snuggle down into the seat and selfishly let Paul cradle and support her, Claudia caught a glimpse of the passing view outside the window.

Good Lord, they were already in Green Giles Lane! She had felt so relaxed during the journey, in spite of their bizarre evening, that she had barely noticed the normal transit of time. It was a telling measure of how at ease she felt with Paul.

The big gates to Perry House were open and to her surprise an unfamiliar dark-coloured car – a sporty little Renault Megane coupé – was standing outside on the gravel, brilliantly illuminated in the glare of the security floodlight.

'Who the devil's that?' she muttered as she climbed out of the limousine, leaning on Paul's arm as she negotiated her wayward skirts. Paul didn't answer her but she didn't really expect him to. How could he? He couldn't remember his own name, much less who owned an unknown car.

When the chauffeur had taken his leave and accepted Claudia's thanks for such a smooth drive, she returned her attention to the dark Renault.

'Well, it certainly doesn't belong to anyone I know,' she mused as they moved towards the house. 'Unless Melody's taken it upon herself to buy a new car and have it delivered this evening.'

Paul was still silent. Feeling the hairs on the back of her neck prickle, Claudia turned to look at him. He was staring at the Renault with a raw expression of fear in his blue eyes.

'Paul?'

Still no answer.

'Paul? Do you know this car?'

He swallowed as if his mouth were dry, then seemed to come back to her from some far and difficult place.

'I don't know,' he said, his voice a little gruff and slow. 'I – I might . . .' He walked ahead of her, then circled around the car, studying it. 'I think it might be mine.'

A dozen questions clamoured in Claudia's throat, but before she could utter any of them the front door burst open and Melody came shooting down the steps clutching a beige satin wrap around herself that she had obviously flung on in haste and forgotten about.

'I wish you'd left a number or something,' the young woman cried without preamble. 'It's all been happening here. There's been something on the telly about Paul. On the news . . . And now this woman's arrived, demanding to see him!'

Melody was clearly in something of a state but even so Claudia could only think of Paul. She hardly dared look at him but she made herself, feeling her blood chill when she saw his thunderstruck face.

'Paul, what is it?' she asked him, wanting to take his hand but wondering how much longer she would have the right to. 'Is it the car? Are you remembering something?'

His mouth moved slightly but no sound came out, and in that instant, Claudia knew that he was finally reclaiming his past. Or at least some of it.

'Paul,' she said again, putting her hand on his arm, which felt unnaturally still beneath the velvet of his frock coat. 'Shall we go in and see this person who knows you?'

And still he stood like a statue, his face ivory in the harsh glare of the floodlight. Claudia felt a flare of alarm, fearing for an instant that he had fallen into some kind of shock-induced trance, then she breathed again when he shook his wild-haired head as if to bring order to an excess of thoughts.

'Yes . . . Yes, of course,' he said, infinitely slowly, 'but give me a minute . . . I need a minute to think.' Shaking his head again but not really acknowledging her, he walked across to one of the stone garden benches and sat down hesitantly like an old, old man.

Torn between several actions yet knowing instinctively that all of them were wrong, Claudia didn't move until Melody grabbed her and pulled her a little way away.

'It was on the evening news about him,' reiterated the younger woman, glancing quickly at Paul, who sat on the stone bench as motionless as if he himself were a carved extension of it. 'They showed a picture of him all done up in academic robes and a mortar board ... Apparently he's one of the country's brainiest scholars, a doctor of mathematics umpteen times over or something, and he works at Cambridge University. They even said he's a colleague of Stephen Hawking!'

A genius. A rare, rare man. I knew it even before the calculations, thought Claudia, staring at the still, hunched figure on the bench, the noble brow, furrowed with deep thought, and the tousled hair of the archetypal eccentric professor. But he's so young, she thought. So young to be so acclaimed, so special and so serious.

'What else did they say?' she asked, idly noticing that both she and Melody were shivering in the chilly night air.

'Not a lot. Just that he was missing. Last seen on the night of a big college fancy-dress bash, and his wallet and other personal effects had been found – '

A notion of sudden, crystal significance occurred to Claudia. 'What's his name then?' she asked, almost afraid to hear it, as if it would break his spell in some way.

'Paul Bowman,' replied Melody, sounding rather taken with the name despite its relative ordinariness. '*Doctor* Paul Bowman!' she went on, dressing the academic title with something of a flourish.

'And this woman?' Claudia asked dully, trying to face what she had been preparing herself for but finding it excruciatingly difficult. This would be a revelation far more affecting than his name. 'Who is she? And how did she come to turn up here? In Paul's car?'

Melody's lovely features assumed an expression of reluctance and Claudia saw her friend's arms tense where she had them hugged around herself for warmth. 'I ... um ... I think she's involved with him. His girlfriend or something.' Melody scowled then and looked unexpectedly vindictive. 'And it's all Richard's fault she's here. And Tristan's. Triss must have told Richard that you had a house guest called Paul ... Maybe they were together, crying over spilt milk or something, when the news came on. Anyway, Richard must have got in touch with the TV company or the police ... And they told this woman – who came here to get Paul.'

'This woman? Does she have a name?' asked Claudia, making every effort to keep her fears out of her voice.

'Felicity something or other. But she won't say who she is or what relation she is to Paul.' It was obvious that the fears had leaked out anyway and that kindly Melody was working cautiously around them.

'What have you told her?'

'Well, I admitted that there was someone called Paul staying with you, but I said it might not be *her* Paul . . .'

Her Paul. Claudia stiffened her spine, quashing her desire to shout and break things and say that life just wasn't fair because she had only had *her* stranger to herself for such a little time.

'Did you mention his memory loss?' she asked.

Melody looked distraught. 'Yes. And she seemed to take a very dim view of you dragging him off to a party when he's got amnesia. I told her it was therapy but somehow I don't think she sees it that way. I wouldn't have told her anything if I'd had my wits about me but it just slipped out when I was trying to put her off the scent.'

Bless Melody. She understood the situation perfectly.

'Don't worry, Mel,' said Claudia, feeling impressed by the sound of her own well-faked calm. Inside she was raging illogically against the inevitable. 'This must be what Paul's been praying for really. That someone who knew him would turn up . . . and take him back to his life.' She smiled wanly. 'He isn't a lost kitten, love. We can't *keep* him.'

Melody gave her a 'Why not?' look and Claudia shrugged. Her disappointment – and that of Melody too – hung heavily between them in the silence.

'I think we'd all better go inside now before we catch our deaths.' The risen gooseflesh on her arms matched that on Melody's. Paul would be warmer in his frock coat and trousers, she supposed, but when she looked at him closely she could see he too was shivering.

I should be helping him, she thought, propelling herself across the gravel towards the slim, deeply pensive figure on the bench. If I care at all I should welcome this; it's what's best for him.

'Paul, let's go in.' She touched his arm gently and her heart twisted in her chest when he flinched. 'It's very cold.' She hesitated, then rushed on, wondering if she had to be cruel to be kind. 'And you have to face up to things some time.' She wanted to ask him what he remembered but somehow she just couldn't bring herself to do it.

'Of course,' he said, rising from the bench like an automaton yet curiously retaining a great deal of his grace. 'Yes, you're right. We must go in.'

The word 'we' offered a shred of irrational hope but even so there was no putting the dreaded moment off. Claudia led the way into the house and thence to the sitting room, with Paul at her heels and Melody in their wake.

A dark-haired young woman sat on the sofa, flipping quickly through a magazine with a rather agitated expression on her face, and in the split second before the reader looked up, Claudia wondered why on earth the visitor hadn't come out, with Melody, to greet them. Was she trying to gain some subtle upper hand?

'Hello. I'm Claudia Marwood,' said Claudia, gathering

her nerve and smiling the smile of the perfect hostess she certainly didn't feel like.

The young woman, who was firm of eye, prim of mouth and wearing what looked like immaculate Jaeger clothing from head to toe, sprang to her feet but ignored the proffered greeting. 'Paul! My dear!' she cried, almost pushing Claudia aside in her haste to get to Paul. 'How are you feeling, my love? Do you know me? This girl – ' she gestured vaguely to Melody in the background ' – says you've lost your memory.' She took his hand in hers and squeezed it earnestly as Claudia looked on, feeling helpless.

Paul looked equally befuddled but once again Claudia saw knowledge and recognition dawn in his eyes.

'Yes,' he began hesitantly, 'I did lose my memory . . . but I think it's beginning to come back now.' He turned to Claudia and gave her a look so stricken she felt her heart turn over.

Oh, my poor stranger, thought Claudia, realising that she wasn't the only one for whom a hard time lay ahead. To reclaim the past would mean a loss for Paul as well.

'My dearest Paul, do you know me?' persisted the young woman, her refined brow furrowing. 'Come along. Sit down.' She guided him to Claudia's sofa and made him sit. 'Could someone make him some tea? I'm sure this has all been an awful shock for him.'

'I'll get it,' said Melody, and Claudia cast her a swift look of gratitude. She herself had to remain here, she decided, and get this rather dismissive newcomer to acknowledge her in her own home!

'Paul!' The young woman peered into Paul's face as if he were a shell-shocked, blank-eyed war veteran. To Claudia's horror, she proceeded to snap her fingers. 'Paul, answer me!'

In the folds of her gown, Claudia clenched her fists, wanting to do far more than click her fingers.

'Felicity?' Paul said tentatively. 'You're Felicity, aren't you?'

'Oh, thank goodness! You remember!' The young

woman sighed and her smooth young face fell into lines of determination. 'Don't you worry, my dear, everything will be all right as soon as we get out of here.' On her feet again, she took him by the shoulder.

That was enough. Claudia took a step forward and spoke up. 'Perhaps Paul would like that cup of tea before he leaves? I'm sure Melody won't be a moment.'

'And what would you know about what Paul likes?' demanded the younger woman, her eyes suddenly venomous as they fixed on Claudia. 'Who on earth are you, anyway? And what could you possibly have been thinking of, taking Paul out to a party when he's ill?'

Claudia drew herself up to her full height, taking comfort in the fact that she was slightly the taller, and deriving a sense of strength from her elegant gown and its beautiful resonances. 'As I told you before, I'm Claudia Marwood, and I offered Paul a place to stay as he didn't seem to have anywhere.' She considered offering her hand, but knowing now that it would be rejected, she saved herself the embarrassment. 'I wonder if you could tell me who you are, please?'

The young woman's eyes narrowed and she gave a thin, triumphant smile.

'I'm Felicity Neston,' she said, and the smile broadened but didn't become any more pleasant. 'And I'm Paul's fiancée.'

Claudia couldn't look at Paul but she sensed his pained eyes close.

Chapter Eighteen
Regeneration

*P*aul closing his eyes. Why did she still keep reliving that slight action, even now, several long weeks later? What had he been shutting out: was it her or was it the fact he had to lose her?

'I can't deny my whole life,' he had said, in one of the few moments that Felicity had not been clucking around him.

True, thought Claudia now, rubbing her eyes and temporarily abandoning the spreadsheet that her ever-dutiful Tristan had prepared for her. And I would never have expected you to, Paul Bowman – *Dr* Paul Bowman – so why did the tautness of your face and something in the set of your shoulders suggest that given half a chance you just might do it? That you might jettison your entire past history to stay with me?

It was silly, of course, to speculate on such notions, she told herself as she tried to refocus on Tristan's beautifully presented and perfectly accurate data. Silly and unnecessary. For heaven's sake, she had no shortage of lovers now. Younger ones, and one a little older; and they were all either gratifyingly willing or possessed of impressive sexual skills. She had Tristan, she had her beloved Melody, and she even had – as she had always expected she would – the outrageous Beatrice.

But Melody and Beatrice were women, which was an entirely different dynamic. And diverting though Tristan's slavish devotion to her was at times, and no matter how genuinely fond of her new PA she had become, it wasn't the same. Neither he nor Melody nor Beatrice could fill the niche in her heart and mind that Paul had occupied – that Paul still did occupy. It was a space peculiarly tailored to the stranger.

'Leave me alone, Doctor Bowman,' she muttered, admitting defeat and exiting from the spreadsheet program. 'You've got the lovely Felicity and I've all my friends and a brand new life. You were lovely but I really have moved on.'

And in many ways, she had. Gone was the lethargic dilettante Claudia of her time of mourning and healing. Since the advent and exit of Paul, she had been a regenerated woman. Even if she didn't exactly run Gerald's business interests yet, she now had a strong hand in them, especially since the dismissal of Richard Truebridge. She found the cut and thrust of buying and selling extraordinary sexy. The figures she had been looking at up until a moment ago, the projections for the new hotel had fired her up and made her edgy, overwarm and restless. It was only a pity that Tristan was elsewhere, at a routine City meeting, discharging his duties. She would be seeing Melody later – they were doing some decorating and remodelling at the younger woman's new cottage – and Beatrice was working – or at least that was what she had said – at her chic London practice.

'Dear God, I hope this isn't hot flushes starting,' Claudia muttered, leaving the study and the work behind. Her simple cotton shirt was suddenly sticking to her – and her jeans, which had hugged her pleasantly, felt an inch too tight. She pushed a hand through her short but shaggy fringe and found it damp.

Of course, the weather didn't help. It was a muggy, oppressive day, the hottest it had been for a week or so, even though the tide of summer was beginning to turn.

The garden needs a shower as much as I do, she thought, taking a bottle of San Pelegrino from the fridge, then she realised that at least her lawn would probably be getting its dowsing straight away. There was a rumble of thunder and drops of rain began to batter the path outside.

'Oh great! A thunderstorm to remind me of him now!' she growled, then took a swig from the bottle of water and carried it through to the sitting room, *sans* even a glass.

Flipping through her compact discs, she roundly rejected *Madama Butterfly* and put on Fauré's *Requiem*, hoping for spiritual solace. At least this was a recording she hadn't played during Paul's sojourn at Perry House so she could hear it without the disturbance of poignant memories.

At first the music seemed to have the desired effect and by the time the 'Sanctus' was playing she felt quite tranquil. But as the ethereal voices and the solo violin wove around each other, her sense of detachment was shattered in a way that could not have been more affecting. Just as the first round of 'Hosannas' pealed out, there was an answering peal of knocks from her front door.

No! Don't be stupid! It's just coincidence, she told herself sternly, rising from the sofa where she had been lying and making her way to answer the summons. If you had been listening to 'One Fine Day', yes, it might have been possible to believe you had conjured him up. But you're not. You haven't. And it isn't him.

But it was him. And just as she opened the door, the very first flash of lightning lit up the face she had told herself she did not need to see again to be happy.

Doctor Paul Bowman was not dressed as she would have expected such an august academic to be; not in the slightest. No tweed jacket; no leather elbow patches and cords; no mud-coloured pullover. What was almost as shocking as his arrival was the fact he was wearing the same black frock coat he had turned up in in the first

256

place! Although it looked a little different when teamed with jeans, lived-in running shoes and a T-shirt bearing the face of Albert Einstein.

'I kind of took a fancy to it,' said Paul, brushing his fingers down his velvet-covered sleeve but offering no particular greeting or explanation for his presence.

Claudia said nothing; could say nothing. She simply stepped back to let him into her house. Without further comment, he followed her into the sitting room.

Once there, she turned away from him to retrieve the bottle of mineral water from the floor, using the moment of respite to breathe and breathe and breathe. It was ridiculous but she was feeling lightheaded. When she faced him again, he gave her a small sheepish smile and glanced quickly at the bottle she held in her hands.

Claudia followed the look. 'I think we might need something a little more bracing than this ... At least, I will.' She stepped over to her tray of drinks, picked up the whisky decanter and waved it at him. 'Some of this? Or is tea still your favourite tipple?'

'It's all right ... Please. I'd love some whisky,' he said, swaying from one foot to the other like a schoolboy awaiting retribution for misbehaviour. 'Apparently mathematicians are quite partial to a drop of Scotch.'

'Is that a fact?' She drew forward two heavy glasses. 'Ice? Water? Soda?'

'Just as it comes, thanks,' said Paul, the words sounding brittle and depressingly forced.

Like two virgins at their first dance, they sat down again. The Salisbury Cathedral Boy Choristers sang on.

'So, how are you? Have you got your memory back yet?' said Claudia, after inwardly rejecting a selection of desperate questions, frantic pleas and declarations.

'Yes, almost completely now,' he said, studying the amber fluid he was swirling slowly in his glass. 'There're just a few bits and pieces, but more comes back to me with every day that passes.'

'And can you ... you know ... work again? Can you do what you do? Add up huge numbers and all that?'

Paul pulled a face then took a huge sip of whisky. 'Oh, I can do it all right, but I do still have some concentration problems.' He looked away and seemed to be watching the flickering red lights on the graphic equaliser.

Claudia drank a little of her own whisky. 'And is Felicity looking after you all right?' Gritting her teeth, she promised herself a gruelling run or double her usual exercises later. Anything to punish herself for giving in to such a pathetic, jealous impulse. God alone knew what she would say or do next. Tear her clothes off and leap all over him, probably. He certainly looked beautiful enough for it. His curly hair was even longer and wilder and his piercing eyes seemed bluer than ever.

'Felicity and I parted when I remembered why I left the party, then crashed her car, cracked my head and lost my memory.' Paul's voice was more natural now, more relaxed, and had far more of the soft, melodious inflection she had quickly become used to hearing when they had made love together.

'And why was that?'

'Because she had chosen that particular evening to admit she'd had a bit of a fling with someone while I was working all out on a paper.'

'What a bitch!' said Claudia, letting rip with the first thought that popped into her mind. How could that mealy-mouthed young madam possibly prefer another man to Paul? Didn't it occur to the girl that a special man needed special allowances made for him? Even as much as temporary celibacy? Then she began to laugh, thinking of Tristan, and of Melody and Beatrice.

'What's so funny?' enquired Paul. He was frowning but she could see he was dying to laugh along with her.

'Nothing really. Certainly not you.' She fingered the crystal fluting of her glass. 'No, I'm laughing at myself. For being a hypocrite. Here I am thinking evil thoughts about your Felicity, when in a lot of ways I'm just as bad a bitch myself.'

'She's not my Felicity any more,' said Paul, allowing the grin he had been suppressing to break loose. His long face seemed to light up like an angel's. 'And I like it when *you're* a bad bitch!'

'I'll consider that a compliment, shall I?' Claudia peered at him over the rim of her glass, took a last little sip, then put it down. 'Why are you here, Paul? Do you want me to help you with your concentration problems?'

'Something like that,' he said, abandoning his own glass but not yet making the move she was waiting for. 'I came here to either get you out of my system or get you back into my life. And it's entirely up to *you* which one it is.'

'Isn't that a rather heavy responsibility to lay upon my old shoulders, Doctor Bowman?' said Claudia, making fists on the sofa, beside her thighs, to prevent herself from punching the air in triumph.

'Don't be stupid, Claudia!' cried Paul, apparently reaching some kind of limit. He grabbed her by the shoulders and put his face right up to hers. 'You're younger than Felicity's ever been in her life!' Then before she could comment, he was kissing her so hard she could barely breathe.

'Is that one of these mathematical anomalies you spend your working life pondering?' she enquired breathlessly when he freed her mouth and began kissing his way enthusiastically down her throat towards her cleavage. She could already feel him pulling at her shirt buttons.

'No! It's the simple fucking truth!' he said, glancing up fiercely then tugging open her shirt while some of its buttons were still fastened. She deemed it fortunate that she wasn't wearing a bra today; otherwise she felt sure he would have half destroyed that too.

As he kissed her breast, she moaned at the lovely familiar sensation – the unique feel of his lips rolling and sucking on her nipple – but even while her loins surged reciprocally, her mind rose pure and clear, above sensation.

'Paul! There's something – Oh, God! Oh, God!' She was coming . . . So soon . . . Only the stranger could do

Portia Da Costa

that. 'There's something I have to say before . . .' The
waves of hot pleasure caught her breath and it was
difficult to speak, much less marshall her most cogent
vocabulary. 'Dear God, you bastard, there's something
you need to know!'

'And what might that be?' Paul said, then extended
his tongue to lick her other aching nipple.

She was forced to grab him by the ears to make him
look at her.

'All right! I'm listening!' he said, giving her his perfect,
beautiful, little-boy-lost-grin, and making it almost
impossible for her to concentrate. Schooling all her
willpower, though, Claudia forced herself to think, and
to further focus Paul's attention she drew the panels of
her shirt back together.

'Whatever it is you've got to tell me, I'll still want
you,' continued Paul reasonably, his eyes fixed very
pointedly on the insubstantial protection that was her
unfastened shirt. 'Couldn't we make love first, then have
a discussion?'

Claudia was so tempted, especially when he inveigled
one long finger between her shirt flaps and began working it between her jeans and her belly in search of her
navel. And it wasn't just that. There was something all
too sincere and affecting in the way he used the term
'make love' – his inflection seemed to suggest literality.
Love, not just sex.

'But what I have to say has a bearing on lovemaking,'
she said, knowing that the slight waver in her voice
betrayed she was weakening. Paul's fingertip had found
her navel now and was slowly caressing her there.

'I don't doubt it.' The finger circled on, then made a
sudden darting foray upward. With a clever flick of the
wrist, he bared her breasts again. 'Why don't we compromise?' he suggested, cupping her breast once more, the
light grip feeling as if it had been carved by a master to
fit her contours. 'Why don't you tell me what I need to
know *while* I'm making love to you?'

'I don't know if that's a very good idea,' said Claudia,

260

already fighting the urge to gasp, and to push her chest forward towards him. 'In my experience, your love-making is too distracting to permit rational thought at the same time. We don't all have the superior brain capacity that you do.'

He seemed to genuinely consider this notion. 'Your brain is fine,' he said, in all apparent seriousness, while peeling her shirt back down over her shoulders. 'I enjoy it just as much as your body, believe me.'

'Oh yeah, as if we have long conversations about equations and integers and whatever else it is you specialise in.' She tried to sound flip but somehow her breasts were brushing against the velvet of his jacket and the delicate stroke of the soft-textured cloth was almost unbearable. And as well as that, she was getting tangled in her own sleeves.

'If I was so clever, I wouldn't have let this happen!' cried Paul, ripping at her shirt cuffs and sending more buttons popping. 'A real genius would have had the simple savvy to unbutton your cuffs first before trying to take your shirt off.'

Claudia laughed, then kicked off her canvas slip-on shoes, getting rid of another obstacle before Paul encountered it. Seeing this, he began to laugh too, but it didn't distract him from grabbing her breasts again. 'Well then, what is it?' he demanded, flicking her nipples with wicked vigour, using his thumbs.

'All right then. Here it is,' answered Claudia through gritted teeth, wanting to squirm and whimper. There was only one way to even this score. Reaching for his jeans fly, without warning, she unzipped him.

'You've split up with your fiancée, and obviously you're now looking to start a relationship with me. Is that right?' she asked, fishing his penis out of his briefs and taking a firm hold of it.

Paul drew a sharp breath, said 'Yes!' and nodded furiously. To his credit, his thumbs still moved in perfect rhythm.

'And there's no-one else? No other girlfriend or

admirer? No super-intelligent young calculus groupie waiting in the wings?'

'No! Of course not!' His look of outrage was somewhat undermined by his long, broken moan of delight when she manipulated his glans between her finger and thumb. 'I want you, Claudia. There is no-one else!' His hands faltered on her breasts as she rolled his penis more strongly, then exerted pressure just below its tip to calm any untimely rushes towards orgasm.

'And that's the point, Paul,' she said, holding both his cock and, she suspected, his attention in a way that nothing else except his work could. 'I want you, Paul. But I can't be yours exclusively.' She paused, considering the robust yet sensitive flesh between her fingertips. 'This will sound mixed up. Irrational, maybe, but before I met you, I might have been able to establish the sort of one-on-one relationship that most people do. And now I don't think I can.' Still fondling him ever so lightly, she met his eyes, which were filled with lust, pleasure and, to her joy, the beginnings of understanding. 'Meeting you changed me. Revivified me. I woke up somehow and I realised that I need more now than I used to do. I'm sorry if this sounds like a no-win situation for you, but you set the spark to a very big fire in me and I have no intention of putting it out.' He was still with her, still understanding her, despite being so close to the point of no return. It clearly wasn't only in the realm of scholarship that his mind was awesome. 'I'm fond of Melody. Of Beatrice. Of Tristan, even. I have something with each of them.' She looked away a moment, aching with desire for him, and with the enormity of another realisation. 'Nothing to the degree I feel for you, I admit. But I can't declare any of them invalid in my life.'

It all sounded like nonsense and even more so for being quoted at such a time. Leaving it to be absorbed, she set about giving Paul exactly what he had come for.

Kissing the tip of his cock, she released him for a moment and quickly peeled off her jeans and her panties in a bundle. Then, bereft of all clothes, she stood before him and took hold of his thighs, manhandling him into the position she wanted. When he was placed thus, his legs a little splayed, his cock rising magnificent and starkly exposed at his groin, creating a perfect contrast with the rest of his fully clothed body, she climbed on top of him and sank down happily upon his flesh.

The power she experienced was astonishing; a match and an enhancement to the contentment and sweet sensation she experienced at having him inside her. She felt strong because she was naked. It was broad daylight and she was a woman in her forties, and yet her bare body was an instrument of subtle dominance. And not so subtle a one, perhaps, she thought, beginning to come and seeing the answering look of awe-struck climax in the eyes of the beautiful, beloved man whose vulnerability had somehow recreated her.

'I have to work, Claudia. There are things I must achieve that are important, for more than just my own satisfaction. But other than that, in every other area, whatever you want is what I want too,' he proclaimed quietly, much later, as she lay on him, sweating, sated and quiescent, her mind prepared to accept whatever might happen. She was enriched for having loved him, even if he went away a second time.

Whatever you want.

The significance of the words finally filtered through and she sat up to find him looking at her. She questioned him, silently, with her eyes.

'The times we had when I was here, without my memory, changed me too.' He nodded his head, as if he were working out the theory, then smiled as it obviously pleased him. 'I *like* your new world and I can cope with the . . . the variations. Just as long as you're here, at the hub of things, to be my centre.'

Claudia felt her sense of well-being double, treble, quadruple . . .

'Well, that's the first time I've been called a "hub",' she murmured, reaching down and taking him by the lapels of his elegant but now rumpled frock coat. 'Should I feel flattered?'

'Yes!' said Paul, rising up to her and pulling her against him; against velvet, against denim, against the droopy, sad-eyed face of brilliant Einstein. 'I *want* you to feel flattered. I want you to feel happy. Soundly fucked. Out of your head. Exhausted.' He paused to kiss her, then took her hands off him so he could shake himself free of the frock coat. 'Now, Mrs Marwood, can I get undressed so we can make a start on all that?'

'Gladly, Doctor Bowman. I can hardly wait,' she said, looking down into his blue eyes as she lifted up her body to free him.

He was the stranger and she knew he would always surprise her.

Want more sexy fiction?

September 2012 saw the re-launch of the iconic erotic fiction series *Black Lace* with a brand new look and even steamier fiction. We're also re-visiting some of our most popular titles in our *Black Lace Classics* series.

First launched in 1993, *Black Lace* was the first erotic fiction imprint written by women for women and quickly became the most popular erotica imprint in the world.

To find out more, visit us at:
www.blacklace.co.uk

And join the *Black Lace* community:

🐦 @blacklacebooks

f BlackLaceBooks

BLACK
LACE

The leading imprint of women's sexy fiction is
back – and it's better than ever!

And available digitally, a brand new collection in our best-selling **'Quickies'** series: short erotic fiction anthologies

QUICKIES: GIRLS ON TOP
Emma Hawthorne

This new collection of sensational, sexy stories will arouse and, occasionally, even shock you. This volume contains brand new stories from women who ignore the rules, unleash their sexual fantasies and find out just how wildly delicious sex can be when you take it to the limit – and, sometimes, beyond....

Includes:

Darkroom – Jen and her boyfriend explore group sex

Doctor in the house – Debbie's visit to A&E results in a romp with a doctor which gives a whole new meaning to the term 'bedside manner'....

Mistress Millie – when Millie meets fit farmhand Jake she knows exactly how to put him in his place...

Juicy – Samantha is about to discover her husband and his best friend are hiding a sexy secret...

Festival Fever – Leanna shares a tent with her friends Dee and Mar. And they get up close and very personal...

Top Brass – She's the boss's wife and Cindy knows she shouldn't say no to any of her demands...